BETRAYED

ANN El-NEMR

BETRAYED

ANN EL-NEMR

Published November 2013
Little Creek Books
Imprint of Jan-Carol Publishing, Inc.
All rights reserved

ISBN: 978-1-939289-30-8
Library of Congress Control Number: 2013956304

You may contact the publisher:
Jan-Carol Publishing, Inc.
PO Box 701 Johnson City, TN 37605
E-mail: publisher@jancarolpublishing.com
jancarolpublishing.com

Jan-Carol
Publishing, Inc
"every story needs a book"

To my children Fouad, Badih, and Amiranour—

You make my day when I see you smile.

You are the most precious and important people in my life.

I love you all.

LETTER TO THE READER

I hope your enjoyment from reading *Betrayed* reflects the joy I found in writing it! Despite many years of writing for pleasure, *Betrayed* is my first publication. Writing is my passion!

The plot of *Betrayed* centers on the town of Shediac, located on the east coast of New Brunswick, Canada. It is my hometown, where I was raised and began to write for fun. Even today, Shediac is a preferred vacation spot of my family. I urge you to visit this quaint, charming little town. Writing *Betrayed* has been a wonderful voyage for me, personally and professionally, and I have relished almost every minute of the challenge. All characters in this book are fictional, not representing anyone in particular. I want to personally thank you each of you for choosing *Betrayed*; I hope to meet many of my readers during my New England book-signing tour. Please introduce yourselves! I encourage you to make *Betrayed* part of your library, and look forward to the sequel to *Betrayed*, which will be called *Forgiven*.

Yours truly,

Ann El-Nemr

ACKNOWLEDGMENTS

To my good friends, Donna Kiritsy and Amore Zamarro-Beiter—thank you for all the times you made me laugh and told me to not to give up but to keep going.

To Patricia Peterleitner—a special 'thank you' for being my rock. You have been more supportive and helpful during my journey with *Betrayed* than anyone else I know. I'll never forget how—even when I was ready to throw in the towel—you were there to motivate me to go forward.

To my sisters, Pierrette Cormier and Jaqueline Cormier—thank you for listening to me and for not thinking I was crazy for sitting at my computer for long hours.

To my children, Fouad, Badih, and Amiranour—thank you for not letting me quit and for helping me to figure out things when I was in despair. Thank you for your words of encouragement, which continue to inspire me, and for believing in me. I love you all.

To my husband—thank you for your advice and guidance. Love you always!

INTRODUCTION

This novel is definitely a love story, whose many difficulties need to be surmounted for the survival of this bond. The story is also about the determination of an enforcer—hired by the young man's father—who goes rogue as he tries to break the relationship between the couple. Despite the enforcer's efforts to protect the name of his wealthy employer, his boss betrays him, and he seeks retaliation.

The events begin in a picturesque town in eastern Canada but end in the father's mansion in the Boston area, where the underlying treachery and deceit are revealed. I hope you enjoy the twists and turns of this book as much as I loved writing it!

CHAPTER 1

"Mon Dieu! It is much too hot. I can't stand it!"

Gabrielle stood up from her lounge chair and put her drink on the end table. Small beads of sweat dripped from her forehead as she walked to the steps of the pool and jumped into the water.

"That feels so much better. Why don't you come in the water? It's so refreshing," Gabrielle said. She could feel her body cooling down as the water engulfed her.

"I do not like the water, and besides, I am not that hot," Sophie said to her friend.

Gabrielle looked over at Sophie, who was taking a sip of her cocktail and smiling at her. It was a humid, sunny day at the beginning of May. The two friends in their thirties were lounging outside by an Olympic pool behind an enormous brick home in a small town called Newton.

Gabrielle swam to the edge of the pool, pushed herself up, and climbed out. She walked to her chair to grab her towel and wrapped it around her body.

Gabrielle could see Sophie's husband Mike walking toward them with a briefcase in his hand. He approached Sophie, kissed her softly on the lips, and then handed her a rose. Gabrielle turned her head and looked away. She felt a pain in the pit of her stomach. She wished she had someone like him for herself.

Sophie and Gabrielle were longtime girlfriends. They had met ten years ago on the first day of school at Boston College. Gabrielle had been wandering the corridors looking for a classroom when someone had tapped her on the shoulder. She had turned around to face Sophie.

"Excuse me, but would you know where Mr. Chung's room would be? I'm lost," Sophie had said while looking around at the numbers and names on the doors.

"Well, to tell you the truth, I'm new here, and I'm looking for the same classroom," Gabrielle had answered.

"Would you mind if we joined together to try to find it? My name is Sophie Smith," she'd said and had extended her hand toward Gabrielle.

"I'm Gabrielle Leger and that sounds like a great idea." She had shook Sophie's hand, and together they had walked down the hallway trying to find their classroom. They had been friends ever since that day in the Business Building.

***

"Good afternoon, gorgeous," Mike said to Sophie in a sexy voice. She smiled at him and touched his arm lightly.

"How was your day?" Sophie asked, smiling at him lovingly.

"Oh! The legal business is tiring. There are always contracts to go over and briefs to be read. Are you two enjoying your day?" he asked them.

They both nodded. Gabrielle was a dreamer at heart. She was always thinking about how she would like to meet someone special, somebody who would love her as much as Sophie's husband loved her.

"Have you told her yet?" Mike asked his wife while throwing a glance at Gabrielle.

"Tell me what?" Gabrielle asked, lifting her eyebrows in surprise. She then sat up straighter and looked at Sophie for an answer.

"Not yet," Sophie replied and motioned with her head for him to leave.

"Well, then I shall see you later." He said goodbye to them, silently walked away to the entrance of the house, and disappeared.

Gabrielle felt a bit out of place. She was visiting her friend Sophie from a small French town called Shediac, Canada. She had a habit of casting her head downward when people approached her. She felt a little nervous at her friend's house, and she didn't know Sophie's husband that well. Although she was not used to all the attention, she was trying to enjoy herself.

"Okay, I have a surprise for you. Tomorrow night we are invited to a surprise birthday dinner party at the Four Seasons Hotel for one of Mike's partners, and we are all going."

"Sophie!" said Gabrielle, her eyebrows frowning and her eyes widening. She really did not want to go to a formal affair. "I didn't bring anything fancy to wear to an event like that. I ... I don't think this is a good idea."

"Oh! Relax, I've got it covered," said Sophie.

Gabrielle got up from her chair and stood in front of her, looking at Sophie with concern.

"Yeah, I have heard that before! Every time we go someplace, you try to fix me up. I can find my own man. I am not ready to date yet," said Gabrielle, pointing her finger at Sophie. "Do not set me up!"

"Well, I haven't seen any romance or a man in your life for some time, missy ... so."

"I know, but ..." Gabrielle bent her head down to look at her hands and started biting her fingernail. She knew Sophie was right; she needed to go out more if she was to find this Prince Charming she wanted. Sitting at home was not going to make it happen.

"That's not true! I do not always set you up! All right, I promise I won't set you up. It will be fun. Come on, we'll go shopping tomorrow and get ourselves all prettied up."

There was not anything else Sophie loved more than when she was on a mission, and this one was huge. All she wanted was for Gabrielle to find a man.

"I promise," Sophie said, crossing her fingers over her heart. "I'll behave."

After some persuading, she had agreed to come for a visit for a few weeks before her work became too busy.

"Gabrielle, are you still with me or what?" Sophie asked her, as she applied a second coat of sunscreen on her legs. She had noticed how quiet and distant her friend had been during the last hour.

"I'm sorry, I was just daydreaming as usual." Gabrielle's thoughts always returned to that horrific evening, even though she was trying hard to forget and not go there.

"Well, snap out of it! What's your problem today? I know what you need: a tall, ripped, gorgeous, good-looking man." Both of them started to giggle. Sophie always knew how to make her laugh.

"Here we are enjoying a nice afternoon, and you're God only knows where."

"I'm sorry. I was just thinking about work." She did not dare mention the real reason, because tears would definitely start to flow. She felt vulnerable and lonely, like she was alone in this world with her broken heart.

Gabrielle had graduated from college a few years back. She had worked at a motel as a manager in the city until her grandmother had passed away. Gabrielle was her only grandchild; her grandmother had left her enough money to put a down payment on a business of her own. Gabrielle had decided to buy a small inn in her town. The only time her business was booming in this small community was during the summer months when the weather was warmer and the town was mobbed with tourists looking for a good time. The beaches in the area were the main attraction. They lined the coast for endless miles. The accommodations in the region were selective.

Gabrielle was determined to make her place a touristic attraction that was unforgettable and loved to cater to her guests by supplying information about the region, excellent food, and a comfortable bed to sleep on. She loved her work—meeting people and making their sojourn at her place pleasant and relaxing. She made sure there were fresh towels in every room, flowers on the table, and chocolates on the pillows at night. In her kitchen, she only used fresh herbs from her garden and locally grown produce.

Her inn was the only thing that had saved Gabrielle from total despair after her heartbreak. From that day on, she had put all her energy in her work so she would not have time to think about her sorrow. Gabrielle was a beautiful woman, a little shy at times, especially when it came to men, and she did not have much experience when it came to keeping a man. She was beginning to think there was not a man on this earth who could love her like she was the only one. She wanted a man who could touch her tenderly and hold her tight.

***

In a corner office on the 25th floor of the Prudential building in downtown Boston, Bernard Rian was seated at his desk, looking out the window as he debated whether he should attend the party at the Four Seasons that evening. His father wanted him to go with him, and Bernard really didn't like disappointing his father. He ran his fingers through his hair and sighed. He knew his father wanted to introduce him to another of his chosen women for him. Bernard had to play the role of the dashing single businessman for his father's benefit. He remembered the last party his father had taken him to. "Bernard, I would like you to meet Nancy Hunter. Her father owns Hunter Constructions," said his father, introducing them.

Bernard had extended his hand to hers, then brought it to his mouth and brushed his lips across the top of her hand.

"Nice to make your acquaintance. You look lovely tonight."

She had looked him straight in the eyes, smiled, and said, "The pleasure is all mine." She had stayed by his side the whole evening.

"So, tell me about your company. I heard you did well with your last hotel opening," Nancy said. She had pounded him about his work all evening. She would touch Bernard's arm or stand too close to him. Her perfume was too strong. She had overwhelmed him. *He thought how suffocating her attitude was toward others by ignoring them or remarking, "Well, look at this or that ..."* And she was only interested in his material things. She would follow him around, not letting other people come close to him.

"I like your blue eyes, I like your suit, I love your car, and I love your father's home ..." This was all that these women would talk about: what he had. They would compliment him all night long. Bernard would play their game for his father's sake, because he knew it was important to be gallant and receptive for his hotel company. He hated how they all looked at him and talked about him behind his back. "He's single. He would make a nice catch." He would overhear the guests talking about him, then look at him and give a fake smile. That was why when he attended these events, he would walk with long strides, without looking at anyone in particular, like he had a chip on his shoulder. He rarely smiled and ignored the sexual passes the women would offer, either by the way they touched him or the sweet things they would whisper in his ear. He knew most people wanted to know him because of his money. There always was a hidden agenda.

Bernard decided he would go to this event with his father, even though he knew his father would try to set him up again.

***

"Do not tell me it is not ready yet! Get it done in the next hour, or don't bother coming in tomorrow," Ron said, slamming the phone down. "Damn!" he said. He had been talking to one of his attorneys about a business contract.

Ron Rian, Bernard's father, was the sole heir to a Fortune 500 company. He lived on a grand estate outside of the city of Boston. He had inherited his fortune and his home from his family. Aggravated that his business deal was not ready to go, Ron walked to the bar area in his library, poured himself a single-malt whiskey, and swallowed it in one gulp. He returned and sat behind a huge mahogany desk, tapped his fingers on the desktop, and then grabbed the phone again. He dialed his son's number.

"Bernard, we will meet at the house before we go out this evening," Ron told him.

"Yes, Father. I suppose you've decided I will be joining you this evening? Or do I even have say?" Bernard did not like the way his father always told him what to do instead of asking.

"Sorry, Bernard, please join us. I am not having a great day, and seeing you would help cheer me up."

His son always came around when it came to pleasing him.

"Very well, Father. I'll be there around seven o'clock."

If only everything went that well, Ron thought. Ron was hosting a small, intimate party at his home before the grand party at the Four Seasons.

It was an older mansion that he had remodeled a few years back. He had spent millions spared no expense. Everything was restored to its original beauty. It was situated on top of a hill, behind large oak trees that lined the road to the front entrance. It could be seen from miles away. He had also bought hundreds of acres of land attached to the property.

Six-foot-tall cement walls were constructed all around the perimeter of the property, which gave him a lot of privacy and protected him from intruders. He also had a state-of-the-art alarm system that was backed up with armed men. These men were all ex-Army or ex-police officers who were well-trained in anti-terrorist tactics and security protocol for wealthy customers. They all lived on the premises when they were working. At the back of the property were green fields that extended for acres, acres of forest, and a few barns that housed some of the most beautiful horses in the world. A moderate guesthouse was wedged between the pool and the tennis courts. It had lodged some of the most prominent people in the world. Ron had many discreet security men at his disposal that would do inconceivable things for him—even murder for the right amount of cash. Ron was the worst adversary to have, because he would not hesitate to destroy his enemies and he always chose his battles carefully. The only person for whom Ron would make an exception was his only heir, his son, but he still he often interfered in his life without telling him. Bernard's mother had died in childbirth, so Ron had been the sole caregiver for his son. Bernard had been his whole world ever since that horrendous day.

Ron was determined to start executing some changes in Bernard's life. He wanted grandchildren before he died, and he was not in the mood to wait much longer. His son was going to marry before the end of this year and he was going to help him. Ron had already taken care of one of Bernard's love interests a few years back, a girl he believed was not suitable for his son. It had cost him dearly, but in the end, it had been the best thing for him.

This weekend was going to be different, because he had invited a special lady for his son. Ron had plans to introduce Bernard to Isabelle Richard. She was the daughter of an old friend and associate from Chicago. They were visiting the Boston area, and Ron had made it a point that they stay at his home for the weekend. They also had been invited to the exclusive party for one of his attorneys. Ron had discussed a union with Isabelle and his son with her father. They had agreed that it would be a great way to merge the two families. Ron had asked that it be kept between them because he knew his son would not approve.

Isabelle had been educated at private boarding schools in Switzerland, first in her teens at a school called The American School of Switzerland,

and then at the Geneva Business School. Her background was impeccable. Ron had seen pictures of her, and she was truly stunning. She also was in her early thirties, of childbearing age, and willing to start a family. In Ron's opinion, Isabelle was the perfect match for Bernard. She was the chairwoman of numerous charitable organizations that helped the needy around the world. She was articulate and was admired by many of her peers. Ron hoped that Bernard and Isabelle hit it off, or else he would be very disappointed. He was going to focus all his energy on this unification.

***

Gabrielle and Sophie came out of the boutique with two divine gowns and shoes that matched. Gabrielle was not so sure about her dress because it revealed a little too much of her breasts, but Sophie would not take no for an answer. Gabrielle had finally given in after useless protests, and she hoped for the best.

"Let's walk down to Boylston Street. I am sure we can find a restaurant over there," Sophie said. She noticed her friend was not paying attention to her.

"Gabrielle, are you listening?"

Gabrielle had stopped walking. She stood in the middle of the sidewalk. She was admiring this gorgeous man coming out of a white Range Rover about fifty feet away from her. She was so stunned that she could not move. She just stood there, staring at him like she had never seen a man before. She could not take her eyes from this delectable specimen of human perfection. He was tall and dark, his torso looked hard, and his biceps bulged out of his short-sleeve t-shirt. *Mon Dieu! How beautiful and exquisite was this man?* Gabrielle thought to herself. His beauty hypnotized her. He must have half a dozen girls running after him daily, with those looks. She observed him, mesmerized like she was watching a movie unfold in front of her and he was the star. In her mind, it seems his moves were in slow motion, although they were not.

Suddenly, she was sexually aroused just looking at him. It was something that rarely happened to her. A feeling was growing between her legs, an electrifying sensation that had not happened in a long time. She could not see his eyes, as he was wearing dark shades. She always said when you look at someone's eyes, you can tell a lot about a person, because all expression originated in the eyes. She wondered what color his eyes were behind those sunglasses.

All of a sudden, her lips parted a bit, and her tongue licked her lips. She wanted to go up to him and feel his mouth on hers. She wanted to press her body against that muscular body of his, and she had this desire to touch him. For just a brief moment, there was no one else around her—only the two of them. She could already taste him. She brushed her tongue against her lips like she wanted to savor and lick him, like a delectable dessert.

"Oh! *Mon Dieu,* have you ever seen such a perfect man?" said Gabrielle, her eyes glued to him.

Sophie looked at her friend, who was immobilized in the middle of the pathway, people passing without concern. Sophie had to haul her away.

"For God's sake, Gabrielle, stop it. You're drooling," Sophie said, laughing.

By this time, Bernard had gotten a warm feeling, as if he was being watched. He gazed around and noticed the two women looking his way. He did not know who they were, but he turned and gave them a wicked grin, as he usually did when women glanced his way. For some unknown reason, he couldn't take his eyes off the brunette. Her beauty enthralled him. She looked unsure of herself. Something about that woman brought the animal instinct in him to life. He thought she was sexy and seductive. The need to meet her overwhelmed him. He loved the way she just stood there with her mouth open, the way the wind made her hair move around her shoulders.

A split second later, before he had time to compose himself and approach her, she had disappeared around the corner. He hurried toward their destination, but he was unlucky. He had lost them. *They must have gone into one of the stores, but which one?* A shiver passed through his body, as if he had lost something very valuable, but he did not know where to find it. He just stood there, defeated. He bowed his head for a minute and ran his hand through his hair. After a few seconds, he proceeded to slowly walk back in the opposite direction, toward where he had been in the first place. He walked with an empty feeling that needed to be nurtured back to life.

"Damn, I must be crazy, chasing a woman I don't even know in the streets," he said to himself. But that was what he really wanted to do. *If only he could find her.*

***

Sophie had grabbed Gabrielle by the arm and had started walking—or rather dragging—her away toward the bistro. Gabrielle could not tear her sight from him until they were around the corner, and he had disappeared like a mirage.

"Did you see him? I wonder who he was. You wouldn't know him, would you, Sophie? You usually know everyone in this town. Oh! *Mon Dieu.* Wow!"

Gabrielle was making a fool out of herself. She was babbling, and she knew it but could not stop herself. Sophie started laughing at her aloud. Gabrielle had not felt that strange feeling of lust in a long time, not since the day she had met her last lover.

"Settle down there, girl. You look like you've never seem a man before."

"Not like him, I haven't."

Ready or not here I come, Gabrielle thought to herself, smiling about the upcoming evening.

CHAPTER 2

Meanwhile, Isabelle and her father had arrived at Ron's home for the weekend festivities. She had heard such glowing reports about Bernard from her father—that he was a very wealthy bachelor, at the top of his game in business, and he needed to get married as soon as possible, by his father account. Actually, Isabelle was a little nervous to even meet him. She could not sit still for long, and she kept looking toward the entrance. She reapplied lipstick and touched her hair to make sure it was okay. She had plans to entice him with her education and her sexual abilities. Isabelle was not shy. She loved to talk and had a tendency to touch people when she spoke. She was going to try to make sure Bernard remembered her after this evening.

She had to make an unforgettable first impression if she was going to catch Boston's most eligible bachelor! She needed him. He was crucial for her family's survival. His money and his position would help maintain her lifestyle. She also knew how important it was to her father's company that she hit it off with Bernard. They needed Ron's approval and his financial support for a new business venture. This gave her the incentive she needed to capture his heart. The stakes were enormous, and Isabelle was on high alert. She wanted to win him over. She was beautiful, with the features of a model, and her body had been enhanced in the right places over the years, especially her breast area. *Whatever it took, she was ready!*

Bernard arrived at his father's estate for drinks around seven o'clock. When Isabelle saw him, he reminded her of a magazine model that was advertising a product. He looked dashing, with his dark hair slicked back with gel, and he smelled like the fresh scent of musk. He was dressed in a black Armani tuxedo with a bow tie. He strode slowly into the room with his head held high, his arms by his side, and his eyes looking straight ahead.

Bernard really was not in the mood for this evening, but his father had insisted, and Bernard did not feel like arguing with him. He did not like to disappoint his father. After all, he was his only son, and he didn't want to disrespect him by not showing up. Bernard knew if he did not come, Ron would be mad. Anyway, it would have been fruitless to have an argument, as his father usually won. He knew about his father's scheming ways of trying to set him up with potential women. Bernard was not interested because he would decide who he wanted to be with when the time came.

Bernard walked toward the library section of the house. He passed a servant without acknowledging him. He knew his father would be impatiently waiting for his arrival and that he would keep looking out the window or glancing toward the doors of the library, as he did on nights like this evening. Ron liked to show his son off like one of his prize stallions, and that was when Bernard really felt like a prostitute ready to be sold to his prospective buyers.

The library was the meeting room in the house, the place where Ron's guests were always introduced to each other before an evening out. This room had two walls of handmade mahogany bookshelves that were filled from top to bottom with rare books. The room had an ornate ceiling and a huge crystal chandelier in the middle. In the back portion of the library, near the patio doors that opened out to the garden portion on the estate, there was a huge marble fireplace that contained a roaring fire. A large Iranian carpet covered the marble floor. This room had a comfortable feel. It was his father's favorite room for relaxation because the leather chairs in which he had rocked and held Bernard as a sleepy infant were still there. Family pictures were on his desk and end tables. Ron felt at home in this room and that was why he greeted new people there.

Bernard had been in this situation with his father many times before, and he did not like it, but he took a long sigh and moved forward. Ron's guests were anxiously waiting for his arrival while they sipped their single-malt whiskey. Bernard first noticed the blonde woman smiling at him. Her eyes were locked on him, ready to jump him as if he was her next meal, when she saw him approaching. She straightened her stance and brought her chest out. How he hated women that looked at him that way. She was wearing a black tight-fitting gown that was low-cut in the front. She sure had the figure to wear it, Bernard told himself. Her eyes never wandered from him for one second.

"Good evening, Bernard. We have been waiting for you."

Ron was annoyed that Bernard was late again, and he kept rubbing his hands together as he was eyeing him. Bernard just nodded. He did not care at all what his father thought.

"I'd like you to meet John Richard and his lovely daughter Isabelle. They are visiting from Chicago, and they will be staying with me for a while."

"Nice to make your acquaintance," said Bernard. He shook both their hands, but Isabelle held on to Bernard's hand for an extra moment, and she gave it a soft squeeze. Bernard made eye contact with her, and she gave him an alluring smile. Bernard looked at her and grinned. He noticed that she was examining his body from head to toe, but he ignored her and cast his eyes away. He was already despising this woman just by the way she was scrutinizing all his moves.

"They will be attending the event at the Four Seasons this evening with us. I thought it would be nice if you escorted Isabelle and introduced her around since she doesn't know too many people," his father said. He was up to his old tricks again. He was setting him up to date this woman.

"It would be my pleasure," Bernard said, looking at Isabelle with a fake smile on his face. It was what was expected of him. He knew exactly how this went. This was another one of his father's ideas—trying to set him up, trying to find him the perfect wife. He would go along for the ride for a bit and then disappear as he often did or just enjoy her pleasures for the evening. His father would be furious. He would slam doors and swear, but eventually he would calm down.

Bernard walked to the bar and leaned his elbow on the edge of the bar, leaving Isabelle standing by herself. He turned toward the guests.

"Can I get any one a refill while I pour myself a drink?"

Isabelle immediately approached him, and she gave him one of her best smiles, "That would be lovely." She handed her glass to him and, at the same time, brushed her arm against his.

"I hope it's not too much of an inconvenience—this evening, I mean," Isabelle said, still staring at him.

"Not at all." He filled her glass and gave it back to her. By now the older gentlemen had discreetly wandered outside. Bernard and Isabelle were left alone to get to know each other better. She was not Bernard's type of woman. She wore too much make-up and was too privileged for his taste.

"So tell me, Bernard, what do you do for entertainment around here?" He saw her approaching him again, like a cougar about to attack its prey. One of her hands was sliding up and down her hip. She reached over and touched his arm lightly. *She was ready for the hunt.* He could see it in her eyes by the way she moved her hips seductively from side to side towards him, how she tilted her head toward him without moving her eyes away from him. *This one is like all the others,* he told himself. *He might as well play the game for a bit.*

"I wouldn't know. Most of the time I'm working. I am sure you will definitely find something to do. You could always go shopping." He was not receptive to her. She smiled at him, then nodded.

Bernard did not intend to sugar-coat this encounter, but he would be polite. He started walking away toward the front entrance. He stopped midway and then turned his head slightly toward her, and she followed. It was getting time to leave for the reception. The older gents had already come in and were lingering at the entry.

"Shall we?" Bernard extended his hand to her and grinned. She nodded and gave him an enticing smile, but instead of taking his hand, she slid her arm into his. She squeezed it faintly, and her hips touched his as they walked. *This was going to be the last time he would put up with his father's match-making!*

Isabelle was making small talk, and Bernard was not really hearing her, as he was trying to ignore her. He was not answering her questions right away. He was pretending he did not hear her and would wait for her to ask him again. The older gentlemen joined them outside after a few minutes.

"Is everyone ready to go?" Ron asked, then glanced at the younger ones and eyed Bernard. "Bernard, I was thinking, why don't you take Isabelle with you? That way, if you decide to stay longer than we old folks, we will not inconvenience you. As you know, we get tired a lot earlier that you," his father said.

Bernard did not care for the suggestion, but what choice did he have? At least he knew Isabelle was pleased by the look on her face as she nodded at Ron. Before Bernard could object, he heard her say, "That sounds like a great idea. You don't mind, do you Bernard?"

"Not at all. It would be my pleasure," Bernard replied sarcastically. He looked at his father with much dissatisfaction, but Ron just turned his back to his son. They were all standing at the entrance of the house where the automobiles were parked.

"I'll be right back. I need to use the powder room," Isabelle said, excusing herself for a moment. It gave Bernard the opportunity to pull his father by the arm to the side so he could give him a small piece of his mind. In a low, stern voice he said, "Father, this is the last time that I will be your escort service for your guests, and you know what I mean. Don't do it again. Understood?" He then smiled at his father so his visitor would not know he was angry and walked on.

Irritated, Bernard stayed by his car and drummed his fingers on the top of the car while he waited for Isabelle. He stood with the passenger door of his black Bentley open until Isabelle came out. Bernard could tell she was on the prowl and wanted him to notice her. Every step was calculated to the right pace, her chest was out, and her hips were moving from side to side. She was taking her time getting back.

Isabelle stopped in front of Bernard and said, "Thank you for waiting for me." She then proceeded to sit down in the car. He watched her as she pulled her dress up above her knees so he could notice her legs, but he ignored her by looking away and closed the door of the car.

He had no sexual interest in her because he figured there was always a price to pay when his father chose his escort to a function. His father always had an ulterior motive. Bernard knew this, but he would be courteous and would accompany her for the evening. But after tonight—well, that was another story. Isabelle was sitting next to him, and as soon as the car started moving, she slipped her hand on his knee to see if he would reject or accept it. He did not say anything, instead giving her a half smile.

"I really appreciate you taking the time to help me out this evening. I don't know too many people at this party," Isabelle said in a soft voice.

Her hand started sliding up his leg. He glanced at her hand briefly, cocked his head sideways, and gave her another smile. "I bet you'll do just fine," he said, and then he kept his eyes on the road. He did not speak to her unless she talked to him first for the rest of the way.

This was going to be an intriguing evening—he could feel it in his gut. He might as well make the best of a bad evening. Maybe he needed a vacation to clear his mind. Always this rushing around. City life was taking a toll on him. He was tired, and he had recently been getting headaches from all the stress from work. A vacation would be a nice break from his father. He wanted go where the ocean was blue, where he could feel the breeze upon his face, where the people were friendly, and where he could lay on the beach with the hot rays warming his body. He could put all his worries aside and concentrate on peace and quiet. He wondered if such a place really existed. It had been years since his last vacation. It was something to think about tomorrow.

***

Gabrielle, Sophie, and her husband arrived at the Four Seasons Hotel on time. It was seven o'clock. There were many valets running around, picking up the keys of the expensive Bentleys and Mercedes so they could be parked. So many beautiful, rich, influential people all dressed up in tuxedos and long gowns and decked out in jewels. They had gathered for an evening out. The lobby was busy with people arriving and being directed to the Grand Ballroom, where the festivities had already begun a half hour earlier.

They walked to where they could hear music and many loud voices. There were a quartet of violins and a lady playing classical music on a baby grand piano. It was the cocktail hour, and the waiters were dressed in black tuxedos with white gloves. They were offering the guests wine and champagne in crystal flutes. The servers mingled with silver trays of delicious hors d'oeuvres, serving appetizers of all kinds ranging from lobster tails and caviar on toast to delicious lamb kabobs. One corner of the room contained an ice sculpture of a ship, with raw oysters and crab legs. An assortment of vegetables, cheeses, and crackers was laid on another table for the invitees. Everything was so elegant that Gabrielle wondered how in the world she had gotten here from a small town in Canada.

The room was decorated in gold and white. Small but tall tables with gold tablecloths were positioned all around the perimeter so people could talk and have a bite to eat. The paisley carpet was of red and gold, and it blended beautifully with the gold in the wallpaper. Large windows in the back of the room were crafted with stained glass that reflected the lights of the magnificent crystal chandeliers. What a place! It was breathtaking!

Gabrielle and Sophie watched and listened to people.

"I just love the way your hair looks." "I heard you just bought a new boat." "You should join us at the country club for dinner." "Did you see that the mayor is here?" They were mingling and rubbing elbows, trying to impress each other. They complimented each other on their attire or the food just to make conversation. It was a night of who's who in the city of Boston and a chance to be seen at this affair. This was the kind of social affair featured in the Boston Globe or another magazine.

Sophie looked at Gabrielle and winked as she pulled her among the large crowd that was gathered in the room.

In a hushed voice she said, "Darling, shall we go to the bar for refreshments?" They both giggled discreetly and tried to hide their playfulness by putting a hand in front of their mouths.

"Of course, *ma chere*, lead the way," Gabrielle said with a hint of humor. They had both been somewhat of a bad girl in their younger days, but tonight they were ladies, so alcohol was being drunk in moderation—only one or two drinks. They held hands as they went to get a cocktail to quench their thirst.

Sophie's husband Mike had already wandered away and was talking business with other men, but that was just fine with the girls. They had each other's company, and it felt like old times. Sophie introduced Gabrielle to many prestigious people during the evening. They would smile, chat with them, and then continue on their way. Gabrielle hadn't had so much fun in a long time. Her worries had vanished, and for the time being, she felt a hint of joy in her life. She felt beautiful in her red gown, and once or twice, men gave her compliments that made her blush. It was nice to be able to laugh aloud without any torments about anything. They conversed with socialites, investors, judges, and all kinds of people.

All of sudden, the large mahogany doors opened at the other end of the room. The staff started telling guests that dinner would be served shortly and advised them to enter and find their seats in the Grand Ballroom. Everyone slowly moved toward his or her destination. Gabrielle, Sophie, and Mike found their seats at a table situated on the right side of the ballroom. They sat down and waited for the room to fill up as the crowd filed in one by one.

This room was even more exquisite that the other. The crystal and the fine china on the tables were plated in 18K gold. Four humongous chandeliers hung overhead, and an orchestra of fifteen musicians, all dressed in gold tuxedos, were playing 1950s music. There were gold and white decorations everywhere you looked, just like the other room. You could smell the flowers arrangements of white orchids and yellow roses the minute you entered the room. A large parquet wood floor was in the front of the room for an evening of dancing and laughter. Gabrielle hoped someone would ask her to dance tonight. She really wanted to dance. She did not want to be a wallflower.

***

Bernard and Isabelle finally arrived at the hotel. They were a little late, but there still were some people who were having cocktails outside the Ballroom. He did not care. He was just biding his time until he could escape. His father arrived shortly after him with John. Numerous business associates came by to greet them. Bernard introduced them to Isabelle. She was charming to everyone, but she kept an eye on her prize. She kept sliding her arm in his. Bernard noticed how closely his father was watching him. Ron would glance at them from time to time, and then smile at them. This was odd for his father, but he just brushed it off. Bernard would do as he pleased at the end of the evening.

"I do believe we should head to our table before they close the doors," Bernard announced to his father and his guests.

Bernard started walking toward the door. Isabelle gladly took his arm again as if he belonged to her. It irritated Bernard, and he did not acknowledge her advances, but kept on looking straight ahead. Therefore, his father gave him a friendly nudge forward toward the ballroom. They proceeded to find their table. The crowd was a bit noisy. You could hear people talking and laughing loudly. *There has to be five hundred people at this event*, Bernard thought as he looked around the room. It was giving Bernard a mild headache, and Isabelle was not helping the situation. "I'll sit beside you. I'd love to dance with you later." Isabelle was pawing him all through dinner, touching him lightly on the arm or his knee every time she spoke to him. He'd had about enough of it. Bernard was courteous and pleasant to the people sitting at his table. He would smile and make small talk with them. A senator gave a champagne toast. Bernard could not have cared less. The birthday boy thanked everyone for attending the evening. The celebration was progressing slowly, and Bernard just wanted to go home. The band started playing music, and a number of people got up to dance the night away.

On the other side of the ballroom, Gabrielle had just finished eating her meal, and she was beginning to feel tipsy. It was a good, happy feeling. She had not felt happy in a long time, and she kept laughing with the people at her table. She told herself it had to be from all the wine that she had been drinking during dinner. Suddenly, there was a young gentleman in his thirties standing beside her. He tapped her on shoulder and said, "Sorry to interrupt, but would you like to dance?" She looked up at him. He was standing beside her; he was tall and attractive. Sophie touched her hand gently and gave her a sly smile.

"Gabrielle, this is Jean-Luc, a friend of Mike's from work."

Gabrielle nodded. She knew instantly this was her friend's doing.

"Nice to meet you. My name is Gabrielle, and it would be my pleasure to dance with you," she said, as she took Jean-Luc's hand and stood up from the table. He guided her toward the dance area. She did not care who this man was—all she wanted to do was dance and have fun.

Bernard was watching the people dancing when he froze. For a brief moment, he could not breathe. *It was her!* She was dancing so gracefully with another man. Her arms were up in the air moving to the beat. Her hips swung from side to side, slowly with the rhythm of the music, her leg showing through the slit in her dress. Bernard's eyes were glued to her, and a twinge of jealousy went through him. *She was not alone.* He could sense his face getting hot, even though he did not know with whom she was dancing. It was too much to take in. He wanted to meet her at that moment. This was the woman he had seen this afternoon and had intrigued him so much. He could not his believe his luck. *God must have sent her to him.* He watched and smiled in amazement every movement she made. She would giggle and giggle, then would look downwards and blush as if she was embarrassed. She reminded him of a kid just having fun. She would say sorry to the other dancers when she bumped into them, and then put her hand on her mouth. He needed to meet her.

He had to do something, but he could not move. He felt like he was in a trance. What was the matter with him? He did not want to budge, but he was afraid she might disappear. He had not wanted to meet someone so strongly since he had lost his beloved Danielle years ago. He had to speak to the woman. He needed to find out who she was. The music stopped for a brief instant as the dance ended. He followed her every step with his eyes. She was heading outside of the room. He got up from his chair when he felt a hand on his arm and he heard, "Where are you going?" His father looked at him with a puzzled look. "I'll be right back." Bernard walked away and disappeared behind the huge doors. When he arrived in the hallway, she had vanished. He concluded she must have gone to the ladies room at the other end of the room. He was nervous, his palms were sweaty, and his heartbeat accelerated, but he had to meet her, so he decided to wait outside the entryway of the restrooms. He leaned against the wall nonchalantly, his eyes not leaving the entryway. He waited impatiently and kept fidgeting with the greatest anticipation

Suddenly Bernard saw her come out. She was looking for something in her handbag. He approached her cautiously and stood in her path. To his surprise, she bumped right into him. The slight contact of her skin touching him made him want to caress her. She dropped her bag on the floor, and everything flew out and fell onto the carpet. Bernard bent down to pick it up. His fingers touched her hand briefly while he was giving her stuff back to her. Bernard felt an undeniable need to enfold her in his arms.

"I'm so sorry! I didn't see you!" Gabrielle exclaimed, and then she lifted her head and looked at him.

"It's you ... from today."

He could not stop gazing in her brown eyes. It was as if time had stood still for a moment.

"You," she said, finally finishing her sentence. He noticed an accent in her voice right way. He wanted to hear more of her unique voice.

"It was my entire fault. My apologies," he said and gave her the rest of her belongings. He just watched her. They stood there looking at each other for another moment. Finally, Bernard said, "Can I get you a drink for the inconvenience?"

Gabrielle just nodded and gave him a smile.

"My name is Bernard Rian. And you are ... ?" he continued.

"Oh! My name is Gabrielle Leger."

They started walking toward the bar area. His arm brushed hers lightly. It sent a chill down his back.

"I hear a slight accent in your voice. I gather you're not from around here."

"No, I'm actually French-Canadian. I'm here visiting a friend of mine for a few weeks. And you?" she asked, as they arrived at the bar.

"Born and raised in the Boston area. What can I get you?"

"Water, please."

He ordered the drink plus a whiskey for himself. He gave her the glass, and his fingers accidentally touched against her. Goosebumps ran across his skin at that moment.

"Thank you," Gabrielle said. Then she turned and nodded to thank the server.

"So, what have you been doing with your time?" he asked.

"Not too much. Relaxing and doing a little shopping."

"Have you been to dinner in Boston yet? There are a lot of very good restaurants."

"Not yet. I've only been here a few days," she answered shyly. He dug in his pocket, and he took his business card out and extended it to her.

"Well, let me give you my card. I'd be happy to show you around town. Please give me a call tomorrow. My private number is on the back, okay?" He wanted to embrace her and taste her mouth until he couldn't stand it anymore.

"It really would be my pleasure if you called me," he repeated, still looking into her eyes.

"Very well then, I'll call."

"Don't lose it. Call me," he said and hoped he was not being too forward.

"There you are. We were wondering where you had disappeared."

Bernard heard a familiar voice behind him. He turned around and saw his father eyeing Gabrielle as if she were some high-end escort. Bernard noticed how he looked at her from head to toe with a suspicious, menacing look. Bernard saw he made her a bit nervous, as she was now looking at the floor, so he turned toward the voice.

"I'll be right there. I was just heading back." Bernard took one last look at her and winked, as he was about to depart. "It was nice chatting with you, Gabrielle—hope to hear from you soon." He took one last look at her as if he were photographing her image in his mind. He wanted her picture to stay in his mind forever. He took her hand, and he brought it to his mouth and gently kissed it.

"Thank you. Hope to see you soon," she whispered. Bernard had not even introduced her to his father.

"Who was that woman?" Ron asked his son.

"No one of importance. I just met her now," Bernard answered nonchalantly. He knew his father too well, and he was not about to let him spoil this for him. He would not let him hurt her like he had done to so many others. Bernard observed her as she strolled back into the ballroom. He had a feeling that they would see each other again soon. Otherwise, he would have a hard time forgetting her.

CHAPTER 3

Gabrielle and Sophie were having coffee with jelly croissants on the terrace. It was such a gorgeous day. The sun was warming their backs with its rays. A perfect day for a new escapade, thought Gabrielle.

"He was so handsome in his tuxedo with his dark hair slicked back. I thought about him all night. I could not go to sleep," Gabrielle told Sophie.

"Are you seriously thinking about calling this guy?" Sophie asked. "You are delusional. You know nothing about this man. He could be a rapist or worse. God knows!"

"I doubt that. Plus if I don't take a chance, I'll never have a date," Gabrielle told her.

"I'm afraid you might get hurt."

"Sophie, I want to go out with him. I have a good feeling about this man. Don't worry. I'll be careful."

Everywhere Gabrielle looked, she would see reminders of what had perished on that night in her hometown. Gabrielle had arrived home earlier than expected one evening from work. She had walked to the door of her boyfriend's apartment and heard voices talking and laughing. She had quietly opened the door and walked in. Her head began to spin and she could not breathe. It felt like someone had punched her in the stomach. She saw her man making love to another woman. She had stood there in shock. Her heart had shattered. All she had said was, "How could you do this to me?"

She had turned around and run out, tears pooling in her eyes, falling down her cheeks. She never spoke to that man again. She held her head high the following weeks strolling down the streets, but she still remembered overhearing two people whisper, "sleeping with someone else." She would turn away, embarrassed, tears stinging her eyes. His betrayal was unforgivable. She had called Sophie to talk. She had needed a sympathetic ear.

"Hi Sophie, it's me. I … I caught my boyfriend with another woman." Gabrielle could not speak because she was sobbing so much on the other end of the phone.

"I'm so sorry. What happened?" Sophie had asked. Gabrielle had told her the whole story. Sophie had listened quietly while she unloaded her pain.

"Stop. Don't cry. It's going be all right. Come visit me for a while it will make you feel better. It will be a change of scenery. We will relax, go shopping, and you can clear your mind," Sophie had said, trying to encourage her.

This conversation had been going on back and forth ever since Gabrielle had told her about her encounter with Bernard the night before at the Four Seasons. Sophie was worried, but deep down Gabrielle knew it was a risk she had to take. Otherwise, she might regret it for the rest of her life. She was not afraid. She had seen goodness in his blue eyes. He made her heart beat faster and faster, her palms sweat. Something had awakened in her. She had not felt lust in a long while, but she felt it now. She did not want to think any further about this situation. She was ready for whatever the future brought her way. She only hoped for love.

***

Bernard had not been able concentrate all day. He kept looking out the window of his office and moving his contracts around his desk without really reading them. He was waiting by the phone for Gabrielle's call. He should have taken her number. What if she did not call? Then what? Every time the phone rang, he would jump out of his chair to grab and answer the telephone, hoping it was her. It was late afternoon, and he was losing hope that she would call. He kept watching the clock on the wall as the minutes went by. The phone rang again. He answered it quickly.

"Bernard Rian, can I help you?"

"Allo, this is Gabrielle, Gabrielle Leger from last night. How are you?" she asked.

"Well, hello there, I'm glad you called." he said. Bernard was aroused by her soft voice. Just thinking about her brought a smile to his face. He felt relieved she had finally called. He passed his hand through his hair. He could not wait to see her again.

"How are you today?" he said, trying to make small talk.

"I'm just fine. Just a little nervous I'm not used to calling men. How about you?"

"Great, now that you called."

He smiled to himself again. *Luck had finally arrived on his doorstep.* He remembered the small, shy smile she had given to the bartender to thank him for her drink.

"I hope I am not disturbing you at work."

"No, no. Work can wait," he told her. *How considerate to think she was disturbing him.* The line was quiet for a moment. He held the phone tighter. He held his breath. "How about I take you out on the town tonight? We could go to dinner?" He thought maybe he was being too forward, but he did not care. He really wanted to see her again.

"I'd love that, if it's not too much trouble," she said cheerfully.

"No problem at all. That would be great. How about seven o'clock?" He was ecstatic. His heart was pounding in his chest ,and he started pacing around his office.

"That's perfect."

She gave him her address. He wrote it down immediately with a shaky hand. He could not wait to see her again.

"See you later then. Bye," Bernard said.

He hung up the phone. He had not been so excited about a date in a long time. What was she going to wear? Where was he going to take her? He did not care. All he wanted was to be next to her. He started to blush and jump up and down in his seat. He was acting like a teenager on his first date.

***

Bernard decided to make a reservation at Mamma Maria, an Italian restaurant in the North End of Boston. The restaurant was located in an old brownstone house in North Square Street and was known to serve authentic Northern Italian cuisine. He decided to rent a whole room so there would not be any distractions. It would be a very intimate dinner, as he did not want to share her with anyone. He wanted her all to himself. It was a romantic thing to do on the first date. The owner was a friend of Bernard's, and he could afford anything he wanted.

Bernard took his time showering and shaving. He could not decide what to wear. He tried on blue pants and gray shirt, then a suit, but finally he decided on a tight black pair of jeans and a white shirt with loafers. He looked at himself in the mirror, grabbed a bottle of his favorite cologne, Blue de Chanel, sprayed it on his shirt, and he was on his way to find her. He finally arrived at her house around seven, and he knocked at the door. The door opened.

"Hi, how are you?" she said. He stood there admiring her. He saw her blush as she looked down a bit.

"Great. These are for you. Hope you like roses." He grinned again as he passed her the roses. He could not keep his eyes off her. She started to blush a little again, and he loved it even more.

"How thoughtful. Thank you. They are beautiful," she said as she brought the roses to her nose and inhaled the fragrance.

"Are you ready to go?" He asked.

"Sure, just let me get my purse."

He watched her walk away. The movements of her hips were so smooth, and he had to look away. She returned a minute later. He had to touch her, so he took her arm and placed it into his so he could walk her to his Range Rover. He opened the door for her but before she could sit down, he looked into her eyes, and then his arms wrapped around her waist. He brought his head down, and he kissed her so ever gently on the lips. He was amazed how good it felt to hold her close.

"I have wanted to kiss you since I met you last night," he whispered.

They arrived at the restaurant, and they were sitting in the back of the room by themselves at a table by the window. Candles had been lit on the mantel of the fireplace and at their table. The lights had been dimmed, and soft music was playing in the background. It was a romantic room.

"I hope you like Italian food," Bernard said, after they had been given their menus.

"Oh! Yes," she said, and then she kept looking at her menu, unsure. Bernard could see she was trying to understand the menu.

"But I … don't know any of these dishes and …" she said, looking at him confused and biting her lower lip. Bernard reached over across the table and gently took her hand in his. She glanced up at him.

"Don't worry. Would you like me to order?" he asked and smiled at her.

"Chicken would be great," she said and smiled back. The waiter came to take their order, Bernard ordered for both of them, also ordering a bottle of white wine.

"All right then—tell me about yourself. What brought you here?" he asked quietly.

"Well, my parents died when I was a small child. A drunk driver killed them when I was ten years old. My grandmother raised me. She was my best friend, and we kind of took care of each other. She always encouraged and supported me. We did not have much, but we made do." Bernard felt pain way down in his gut, as it brought back memories of his lost love, Danielle.

"How did you end up in Boston?"

"I was very lucky. I came to Boston College on scholarship. The town I come from had a fundraiser for me to help raise money. I'll never forget how they believed in me," she said, then cast her eyes downward.

"You were very fortunate to have all this help from a community." Bernard wished he had so many people believing in him. "What kind of scholarship?" Bernard asked, intrigued and impressed that she had made it by herself.

"Soccer. I used to be pretty good at it," she said, then giggled shyly.

"Used too?" he teased her and laughed.

"I still have some moves. I'll take you on any day. I still play sometimes," she answered. The waiter brought their food, but it was too much food for Gabrielle. She looked at her plate.

"Wow! That's a lot of food. I cannot eat it all."

Bernard laughed at her outburst. He looked at her, and she blushed. He liked how she was so spontaneous.

"Sorry," she replied. "You can have half if you would like." She began eating while Bernard enjoyed her company.

"So what exactly do you do for work that you can afford to get this whole room just for us?" she inquired.

"I'm CEO of my own company. I buy and operate hotels around the United States. My father helped me get started a few years back."

"What about your mother?"

"She died when I was born. I never knew her, except what people have told me about her," he answered without thinking. He rarely talked about his mother.

"I'm so sorry."

Gabrielle reached over and squeezed his arm. Bernard lifted his eyes to look at her. Her eyes were filled with tears. She turned her head away from him, but Bernard could see she kept blinking, trying not to let a tear fall.

"I know how hard it is not to have your mother near you when you are growing up. I really missed mine," she whispered, while her voice cracked. No one had ever talked so sincerely with him about his mother. It warmed his heart that she understood. Most of his dates did not care about his family—only his money.

"How about something sweet for dessert?" he asked, and then called the waiter over.

"Only if you split one with me. I do not think I can eat a whole one. Anything with chocolate is fine. I'm trying to watch my weight," she said and giggled. He loved how direct and carefree she was about it. Most of the women he knew would not have desserts.

"Okay."

He ordered chocolate mousse with two spoons. She picked one spoon up and started to feed him. He loved how playful she was with him.

They were walking to his Range Rover outside the restaurant, and he did not want the evening to end, so he invited her for a nightcap at his apartment.

"I'd like that," she answered. He leaned forward, then took and gently cupped her face in his hands. He then kissed her passionately before they took off for his condominium.

Bernard and Gabrielle arrived at his home, a penthouse in the historical Beacon Hill area. Bernard glanced at her standing at his door. She looked so inviting. He softly touched her cheek with the back of his hand, then he smiled and kissed her gently on the mouth. He watched Gabrielle walk to the large windows facing the park.

"You have the best view of the park. Don't you love the trees when they are in bloom? It's so pretty. And the skyscrapers in back, wow! It's so beautiful." She kept looking out the window.

"It is nice. What would you like to drink?" Bernard asked. He was standing at the bar area with a bottle of liqueur in his hand.

"I'll have coffee with cream. I think I had enough to drink tonight." She turned and looked at him standing at the bar. Bernard was surprised she did not want any, so he headed for the kitchen. She followed him.

"I will make it," said Gabrielle. "Have a seat on the couch. It's the least I can do for the expensive dinner you paid for tonight."

Bernard was stunned she was trying to repay him for the dinner. He sat down as directed and watched as she opened the cupboards looking for coffee. She seemed right at home, and a few minutes later she had made a pot of coffee.

"There we go. How would you like your coffee?" she asked, carrying a tray to the living room and smiling at him. They drank, and he listened to her talk about her hometown, and he admired her honesty. How her eyes glowed. How excited she was when she talked about her inn. She mesmerized him. He listened to her every word and encouraged her to tell him more about herself. He was very comfortable with her. He could be himself. She was so beautiful and interesting. He had not felt this happy in a long time, and he held her close against him. He listened to her every word and encouraged her to tell him more about herself. Bernard liked how easygoing she was. They talked for the longest time about their lives, interest, values, and more. He especially loved her laugh and the way she blushed at unimportant things, especially when he gave her compliments about her appearance. Bernard could see she was getting tired, but he did not want her to leave his side. She was leaning against him. She closed her eyes and fell asleep, and he did not move. Bernard just watched her until the sun came up over the city and then fell asleep himself, with her in his arms.

***

By the time Ron arrived at the country club that evening, he was fuming. He was not smiling, and he was snapping at the staff serving him. His brows were furrowed, and his mouth curved down. His assistant Tom had not been able to

29

contact Bernard all night. He had called repeatedly, but still no response. *Why did he not answer his phone? Where could he be? Maybe something bad happened to him.* Ron had made his guest wait a while at the house, hoping Bernard would show up late, but he had not come at all, so they had gone ahead without him. Ron had excused himself to another room when he arrived at the club. He tried to think of a solution for Bernard's absence. He was embarrassed. His hands were shaking, and he was getting a pounding headache, thinking that Bernard was not going to be coming for dinner. He had told him of his plans last night not once, but twice. Bernard knew how important it was that he be here for Isabelle.

Ron walked back to the bar area of the club where his guests were waiting and told them, "Bernard was pulled away unexpectedly at work at the last minute. It happens all the time. My apologies."

Isabelle would have to understand. He knew they both had the same goal in mind. Well, that was that, Ron thought. She would have to wait to see him later, but tomorrow Bernard was going to hear an earful from him, that was for sure. Right now he had to calm himself. He ordered a double whiskey, gulped it down, and sighed. He then smiled and introduced them around. He had to entertain his guests tonight; he would deal with his son later for not showing up.

CHAPTER 4

Bernard awoke to the sun's rays streaming through the windows of his living room. He could hear Gabrielle's shallow breathing beside him, and he could feel her warm breath on the side of his neck. His arm was wrapped around her. It felt good to be so near to someone. He loved the feeling of waking up next to this woman. He had the most wonderful night just talking and snuggling with her. Bernard did not want it to end. He placed his lips next to her ear, kissed it gently, and then whispered in a low voice, "Hey there, sleepyhead," gently waking her up by pulling her closer to him. He could feel her against him. He watched her stretch her arms. Bernard smiled and kissed her cheek.

"How about I cook dinner for you tonight?" Bernard asked.

Gabrielle turned toward him. Her hair was messy, and he took his hand and moved it out of her face.

"Depends," Gabrielle replied, while her fingers teased his ear.

"Depends on what?" He was surprised she might not want to come.

"How good of a cook you are!" She chuckled and hid her face in his chest. "Will I survive if I eat it?"

He playfully poked her in the arm then kissed her.

"I would love to have dinner with you again."

Bernard was thrilled she wanted to see him again.

"Meet me here at six o'clock," he said. "You'll be amazed and what I can put together." They both laughed. He called a car service to drive her back home to Sophie. He kissed her goodbye once more, and she was on her way.

***

Ron was sitting outside on the patio with Isabelle and John. They were having a leisurely breakfast. It was a beautiful morning. The sun was bright, and there was just a slight breeze.

"I have to apologize again for Bernard not coming to dinner last night. I hope you enjoy your day shopping in Boston today. I will have my chauffeur accompany you," Ron said, trying to make amends with Isabelle.

"Thank you it is kind of you. I understand that Bernard had to work last night. I surely hope we will see him this evening," Isabelle said, looking directly at Ron.

"Yes, yes. I shall call him today, and we will get together. Your father and I have business to discuss and contracts to go over, but we will be back for dinner." Ron felt confident everything would be fine this evening.

"Have a great day. We will see you later on." Ron said. Ron and her father, John, stood up and left to attend to business. They had made plans to meet a few of their advisors of different companies to exchange their point of views, and then they were going to have lunch at Grill 23 on Berkley Street in the Back Bay area of Boston. It was well known for its delicious steaks.

Ron was still trying to reach his son in the late hours of the morning. Bernard was not answering his cell phone. He had tried his office many times, but his secretary had not been helpful. He still had not come in yet, and he had not called. He did not have anything on his calendar until later in the afternoon. His cell phone was on, but it kept going to voicemail. Ron was really getting frustrated and extremely annoyed with Bernard. Ron had left numerous messages on his cell phone's voicemail but to no avail. He knew that Bernard had received them, but he still had not succeeded in getting back in touch with him. Ron also knew when his son wanted to hide and escape from him, he could, but sooner or later he would have to resurface. Ron was going to chastise his son for his behavior. *It was not acceptable for him to leave his guest without an escort.* It was an awkward situation for Ron and a real shame to leave a woman as intelligent as Isabelle

32

waiting on the sidelines. Tonight it would be an entertaining evening, he thought. Bernard would show for dinner and maybe they would hit it off. *Where the hell was he?*

***

Bernard had a lot to do if he was going to impress this woman with his culinary skills. He went grocery shopping for his gourmet meal—something he had not done often since Danielle had passed away. He usually just ate out because it was faster and more convenient since he was alone. He had loved to cook for Danielle, and he could still hear her laughter on those special evenings. He walked the aisles of the store and looked for an answer on what to buy, finally deciding on steaks and lobsters. He picked up fresh bread and greens for a salad. *How easy was that?*

He also picked up a couple of fine bottles of red and white wine. He was not sure which one Gabrielle preferred, so he bought both, and then he headed back to his condominium to start preparing dinner.

When his phone rang, he somehow knew it was his father again. He figured he would call him back later. He really did not feel like dealing with him at this time. He still had to go by the office for a few hours of work, and he would call him then.

By the end of the day, Bernard decided that he would eventually have to face the music and call his father, so it might as well be now before he started to prepare dinner for Gabrielle. He dialed the all too familiar numbers of his father's private telephone. It rang twice, and then he heard an annoyed voice.

"Good afternoon, Bernard."

Bernard could hear the discontent in his father's voice.

"Good afternoon, Father. I saw that you called several times. What can I do for you?" he asked, trying to sound casual.

"Where were you last night? I had made reservations for dinner at the country club with John and Isabelle. I was expecting you to be there. You know how important these people are to us." Ron said.

"I had another engagement, and these people are important to you, not me," Bernard replied quietly.

"What do you mean another engagement? We were expecting you. You didn't even call to let me know, and I was embarrassed you stood us up."

"I never told you I'd be there. You assumed I'd be there. Plus you know I really don't like to be told what to do." Bernard had decided he had had enough of his father giving him orders.

"Bernard?" He could tell that Ron was trying to control his anger. "This is important ... let's start over. I invited a few people for dinner this evening at the house around seven. I'll expect you to be there."

"Father, stop it. I will not be there tonight. I already have other plans for this evening." Bernard was not going to be intimidated by him. All his life, his father had manipulated him so he could win his way, but not this time. He really wanted to be with Gabrielle tonight.

"Well, change your plans! I have worked hard to get you where you are, and I will not tolerate this bullshit from you. Do you hear me?" Ron said.

"I'm sorry, but you have got to stop trying to tell me what to do. I'm a grown man with my own decisions to make. Not this time, Father. I will not be there, so call me later when you are reasonable about things."

Bernard hung up the phone before Ron could say anything else. Bernard was so mad he was shaking. But he also felt relieved, like a large load had been lifted off from his shoulders. He needed to sit down in a peaceful place for a few minutes so he could regain his composure. He took long, deep breaths and sat down, trying to relax. He had finally stood up to his father. He should have done it a long time ago. *Enough was enough. He was a man not a boy.* His father had to cease trying to control his life. He poured himself a glass of vodka on the rocks. He needed to settle his nerves and get his father out of his mind. *His father was not going to ruin his evening with Gabrielle.*

***

Ron just stood with the phone in his hand. He noticed his hands were trembling from anger. He kept looking at the phone. He could not believe his son had hung up on him. He took the phone and threw it against the wall. He grabbed another phone and called Tom, his head of security. Ron told him to come to his office immediately. Ron informed him he had a new confidential assignment for him. Ron knew it would be a delicate task, but he also knew Tom was the man for the job. Ron trusted him and Tom knew how to keep his mouth shut. They had worked together a long time and he was being handsomely paid to do so.

Tom Smith was an ex-army sergeant from the special ops department. He had served two tours in the Middle East and was a veteran of the Iraq war. He had gotten a dishonorable discharge for disobeying orders several times, but that did not bother Ron. He was a good man, and he definitely was not afraid of getting his hands dirty. Tom had never failed him in all the years of service with him. He had connection with other veterans all around the country and abroad. He was a tough, dangerous man to cross. Tom had always followed his orders, so Ron was satisfied with him. Tom was his right-hand man when he needed things done. Tom had many men at his disposal if he needed them. He was a specialist in demolition, but guns were his passion. He had a collection of firearms at his home that he only showed to a handful of friends—mainly because most of them were not legal. The only problem that Ron had had with him was that he occasionally took things into his own hands when they could be somehow averted. He had been with Ron for over ten long years and sometimes they knew each other too well ... all too well.

Now Ron was pacing back and forth in his office waiting for Tom to arrive. Ron had a job for him.

CHAPTER 5

Fifteen minutes later, Tom arrived at Ron's office. Ron was looking out his large windows behind his huge desk in the library. He was just standing there, staring at nothing in particular. After a minute, he turned around to face Tom. Ron greeted him in the usual manner, with a strong handshake, and then he told him to have seat. Tom declined, telling Ron he preferred the military stand. Ron was always controlled when he was facing a crisis.

"Tom," Ron started, "I have a fragile matter. I would like you and only you to take care of it."

Tom listened attentively without speaking.

"It concerns my son Bernard," Ron said painfully. He paused and he cast his eyes toward a picture of Bernard that was on his desk. Ron hated to do this to his son again, but he needed to know everything that was going on in his life, especially when he wanted to try to arrange his future.

"I want you to follow him, find out where he goes and especially whom he spends his time with. I want names, places, anything you can find. Be discreet, and do not let him know you are there. At this moment in time, I just want information. Do you understand?" Ron asked.

"Yes, sir," Tom replied. "When did you want me to start surveillance, sir?"

"Right away. You know where he lives, so start from there. Give me a call when you know something."

"Right away, sir. I just need to pick up a few things from home, and then I'll be on my way. Anything else, sir?" the ex-Sergeant said, happy to have another operation to handle.

"No, that will be all Tom. Oh! And Tom, thank you for coming so fast."

Ron felt relieved that he was going to find the underlying cause of this bad situation. He knew if anyone could find information, it was Tom. He trusted him implicitly.

"No problem, sir. I'll be in touch."

Tom turned around and left without another word. Ron watched him walk away. He hoped he was making the right decision. He needed answers and there was not any other way. He just hoped he would not regret it one day.

***

Tom went home to pick up what he needed for the next few days of surveillance. One look at his boss, and Tom knew someone had made him mad or hurt him. He could not tell which one it was, but he knew it was serious. Ron had looked preoccupied. Tom could tell he was agitated, and the only person who could do that had to be his son. He knew one thing: never double cross Ron, because he would stab you in the back when you were not looking. He was a powerful man with the means to bring you down faster than you could blink. Tom had seen how Ron had destroyed people. One time he had hated the way the landscaper had planted the flowers. Ron had fired him and then made sure most of his contracts were terminated. All that over silly flowers.

Tom was an extremely patient man. The Army had taught him skills with explosives and he was an expert in firearms. He also had been raised in the streets of Boston, so he had very good connections in the city and around the world. He was what one called a mercenary, and he was quite good and proud of his work. He hurried home to pick up his camera and its long lens, his binoculars, his night-vision goggles, and his hat. He put everything in a duffle bag and threw it in the back seat of his blue 2007 Ford truck. He waited until it was dusk, and then he drove into the city to Bernard's home. He got lucky and found a parking spot for his truck about half a block away from Bernard's condominium. He could see the entrance perfectly and had a view of certain windows facing the park across the street. Tom quickly spotted Bernard inside. *He was home.* He took his camera and attached one of his lenses so he could have a better view. It definitely was a waiting game. Nightfall was approaching. There was no moon tonight, and he would have much more cover now that it was dark. An hour passed without anyone coming or going into the building. Everything was quiet. Suddenly, he noticed a cab slowing down. The cab door opened, and out came a lady. She went directly to Bernard's door. It gave him a chance to snap a few pictures of her. Tom had to be careful not to be spotted because it would mean trouble with his boss. Bernard knew who he was. He had personally met him several times. Bernard knew he worked for his father.

Outside, Tom could see them laughing and chatting together. They were having a glass of wine. He watched them kissing. He had to find out who she was for Mr. Rian. He would have to follow her home tonight so he could at least have an address of a residence. He grabbed his phone and dialed one of his best friends, Al O'Connor. He was a big guy, with a head of reddish hair and a face only his mother could love. He was tough and a straight-shooter. He was always available to assist him. Tom had saved his life one night while they were patrolling in Baghdad. Rebels had ambushed them and Al had been shot in the leg. Tom had dragged him out of harm's way and he had stayed with him until the medics had arrived to airlift him to safety. Because of this, Al had always been grateful and loyal to him.

Al now worked for Boston Police Department, District A-1 located on Sudbury Street in Boston. He worked the downtown and in the Beacon Hill area. Al was born and raised in the South End of Boston. He had made it to the detective division a few years back, and he was a whiz at finding people's identities. He also had many resources at his disposal that Tom did not have, like the Department of Motor Vehicles agency and other sources that dealt with finding missing people. He also had a few friends at the Federal Bureau of Investigation who owed him favors from previous dealings, so Tom was confident Al could help him. Al answered on the second ring.

"Hi Al. How are ya? How's the wife?" Tom asked him.

"Hey, buddy. How's everything? Celia is fine, thanks," Al replied in thick Bostonian accent.

"Ah! Same old, same old. Still on the job. I was wondering if you could do me a favor?"

Tom asked.

"Sure what do you need?"

"I have a picture. I need an ID."

"I'll do what I can. Send it over. Give me a day or two, okay?"

Tom e-mailed him a picture of Gabrielle. Al would find out who she was. Tom would follow her back in his truck to her home later on and get her address. He made himself comfortable in his truck. He put a pillow at the back of his head and took his shoes off. Tom unwrapped a power bar and took a bite. He had a feeling it was going to be a long, sleepless night ahead.

***

Bernard heard the door ring and he hurried to open it. The vision he encountered was the same one that he remembered from the previous evening. He wrapped his arms around Gabrielle's waist and brought his lips down on hers.

"Hi there. Welcome back."

"Hi, I brought you a present. I baked you a chocolate cake this afternoon," she said and gave him the box she was carrying.

"You made it?" Bernard was surprised that she had made him a cake. *How thoughtful!*

"Yes, I did. It was the least I could do since you were cooking dinner," Gabrielle replied, and then looked away. Bernard appreciated her gesture of kindness.

"Thank you. I bet you it's good. Come make yourself at home. I have some cooking to do."

"Let me help you. I like to be productive."

She started to walk toward the kitchen. Bernard followed her, smiling. He gave her a knife so she could finish cutting the lettuce and tomatoes for the salad. He watched as she began to chop as if she had been doing it all her life. He really liked that she did not mind getting her hands dirty and helping.

"Do you want a glass of wine?" He asked and showed her a bottle of white and red.

"I'd love one. I'll have white, please."

Bernard opened the bottle and poured her a glass. When he passed it to her, their fingers touched. He felt a shiver run down his back. He glanced at her, and she was smiling at him. Everything was ready except the steaks. He grabbed himself a cold beer from the refrigerator.

"Now, come sit next to me."

She did as he asked, and he then put his arm around her shoulder and kissed her on the lips.

"Don't move. I'll be right back," Bernard said. He went to the counter and took the bottle of wine. He walked back quickly. He took his seat next to her. He refilled her glass.

"So, tell me what's for dinner. I'm starving," said Gabrielle.

"Surf and Turf. I only have to cook the steaks—the lobsters are all ready to go."

"Wow! I'm impressed." She took a sip of her wine.

"So, if you'll follow me this way."

They got up after a minute and headed to the kitchen to finish preparing dinner. She was surprised and amazed by all the effort he had put into this supper. He grilled the steaks to a perfect medium rare while Gabrielle watched from her seat at the counter. He tossed and then passed her the salad. They ate and laughed all through dinner. He glanced at her from time to time, and she smiled at him.

"You did a great job. I'm stuffed!" she said. She had been hungry, and now most of her meal was gone. She got up and walked around the counter. "I'll clean up since you prepared such a delicious meal." She started to pick up the dishes. "My compliments to the chef. I have to say, nicely done. I didn't think you could cook," Gabrielle said enthusiastically.

He walked over, stood next to her, and touched her arm lightly. She turned around, and he kissed her passionately. He then kissed her neck. He could smell lavender on her skin. He unbuttoned the first few buttons of her shirt, and he could see her round breasts. He reached up and cupped them in his hands. He heard her moan softly. He looked her in the eyes and whispered in her ear, "Come to bed with me so I can make love to you."

She smiled then nodded at him. He took her by the hand and led her to his bedroom. She followed him without hesitation.

A few hours later, they were still in bed relaxing and enjoying each other company. He was looking at her as if he wanted to ask her something but was hesitating.

"Let me asked you something: I know we haven't know each other very long, but ... do you have plans for this weekend?"

"Why? What did you have in mind?" she asked while playing with his hair.

"Well, I was wondering if you would like to go away for the weekend."

She did not answer, but she seemed to be seriously thinking about it. She raised her index finger to her mouth and tapped it while pondering the question.

Bernard was worried he might be moving too fast for her when he didn't get the response he was hoping for, so he said, "I'm sorry."

"No, no. That's not it. I'd love to spend more time with you but ..." She paused for a moment. "It's just I feel I've neglected Sophie the past few days, and I kind of feel guilty. I did come to see her. What did you have in mind?"

His face lit up immediately, and then he grinned at her. "Well, we could drive down to Newport, Rhode Island. I own a small house on the beach. It might be nice to spend some time there, just to relax. We could go swimming or just hang out for a bit." He was getting excited at the prospect of spending a whole weekend with her.

"That sounds like a lot of fun. I haven't been to Newport since my college days. Let me talk to Sophie tomorrow. I'm sure it will be fine, and I'll get back to you."

"All right then, it's settled. I'll arrange to have the house ready for us," Bernard said. He was dumbfounded that she thought about her friend's feelings before accepting his invitation. He thought it was considerate of her. Most women he knew would never have hesitated for a second to come with him.

The last time he had been there was when Danielle had crashed her car and died. He had not had the heart to return until now. He really wanted to bring Gabrielle to Newport, to try and erase the bad luck he felt when he was there. Gabrielle was his good-luck charm now. He had not been this happy in a long time.

They spent the rest of the evening snuggled together on the bed, talking about their pasts, their hopes, and their accomplishments. It felt like they had known each other a very long time even though it only had been a few days. She told him about her work.

"I bought this old estate a few years back. I always had loved this house—it was grand, but it needed some repairs. My grandmother had left me enough money for a down payment, and the bank loaned me the rest."

He could see how excited and passionate she was. Her smile and her eyes were alive. He loved to hear her talk.

"I had to knock down walls, replace the main kitchen, fix some of the plumbing, and paint—on my budget—but I had lots of help from friends. And guess what?" she said enthusiastically.

He just loved how she talked with her hands. Her wrists would twist so gracefully, and her fingers would jump in the air. She was so bubbly. She could not sit still.

"What? I cannot imagine. Tell me!" He loved to tease her, but at the same time, she was astonishing.

"I opened a week in advance. I was so pleased with myself," she said, looking at him, so proud of herself. She would kiss him in between stories.

"You should come visit my town. The people are so friendly, and there are no major crimes. Most of the folks do not lock their doors during the day. It is not like the city where you always have to look over your shoulder ... and the beaches are not crowded and the water is so cold."

He listened and listened with fascination.

"I am going to come visit you so you can show me everything you are telling me about," he told her, and a wide smiled crossed her lips.

"Really, I would love for you to come visit. I'm talking too much. Now tell me about your company."

"Well, my life is different from yours. I was fortunate. My father already had made it in the business world, so he took me under his wing and taught me all I needed to know. Then I branched out by myself and bought my first hotel. From that day forward, I kept working and it kind of fell into place." He usually did not talk about himself. He wanted her to keep telling him stories.

After two bottles of wine, she said, "It's getting late. I have to get going."

"No, don't leave. Stay for a while longer," he said and pulled her close to him, wrapped his arms around her, and kissed her playfully on the neck.

"It's three o'clock in the morning already, and I do not want Sophie to worry."

"Stay the night with me."

He wanted her to stay by his side, but Gabrielle decided to return home. He watched her put her dress back on, pick up her heels, and prepare to go. He made a sad face. He did not like that idea of her leaving, but he knew he would have her for two whole days this weekend. He called her a car to drive her home. He kissed her goodbye, and he accompanied her to the front door. Bernard walked with her to the town car and opened her door. He kissed her one more time, and then closed the door. He watched the car drive down the street and disappear around the corner. When he turned to return inside, he noticed a blue truck parked down the block. Someone was sitting in it. It kind of looked familiar, but he could not place it. He shook it off, returned inside, and locked the door.

***

Sitting outside in his truck, Tom observed the whole interaction between Bernard and this woman he had seen earlier arrive at his residence. When Bernard had reentered his home, Tom turned the key to start his truck and followed the town car to its destination at a safe distance so he would not be detected. Half an hour later, the car pulled into a beautiful estate. Tom slowed down in front and casually looked around, and then wrote the address down on a piece of paper. He would check to find out whom this property belonged to. There was not much more he could do tonight, so he decided to head home. He could use some shut-eye. He probably would start surveillance again in the morning at this address. He hoped that Al would have some news about this woman by tomorrow morning.

***

Isabelle knew something was up when Bernard had not shown for dinner for the second time in a row. Ron had been distant and in a foul mood. He

43

was not talking much, but you could tell his frame of mind by his expressions. All Ron had said was that Bernard had been called away on business for a few days and that he would not be able to attend dinner.

Isabelle had noticed that Ron was drinking heavily, more than the previous evening, and he had not touched his food. He kept looking at and playing with his food. There was not too much she could do concerning this, so she just had to make the best of a bad situation and appreciate the company at hand. She was meeting other people and enjoying herself, regardless. It just was not meant to be. She would have to find another available prospect. She was a smart woman, and she knew Bernard was not interested. She would return to Chicago tomorrow and continue her hunt.

***

Gabrielle had arrived late, and the house was quiet. She wanted to talk to Sophie, but she was asleep, so she went to bed. She must have woken up three or four times before the sun came up. Finally, Gabrielle sprang out of bed in the morning hours and she went looking for her friend. She found Sophie sitting in her lingerie at the counter in the kitchen, sipping a cup of coffee. She walked over to Sophie and gave her a big hug.

"Well, well. Tell me, how did I come to deserve this big hug?" Sophie said, laughing. "I can see someone had a good evening."

Gabrielle went to the counter and poured herself a cup of coffee. She turned to face Sophie while sipping her hot cup of coffee.

"Okay, I know you're dying to tell me something, so dish it out."

"Oh! Mon Dieu, Sophie, this man is unbelievable. He asked me to go away this weekend to Newport, Rhode Island. What do you think?" Gabrielle said, practically jumping for joy. Sophie just sighed and rolled her eyes.

"Gabrielle, what are you doing? You know I'm happy for you, but let's talk about this. Let's be realistic, please. Be careful. You know you have to return home in the next few days, and then what? I do not think this is a good idea at all. First of all, you did come to visit me, not take off with God's knows who on a romantic fling." Sophie did not look pleased at all. She turned her head away. Gabrielle sensed a bit of bitterness in her voice.

"I know. It's just that I haven't ... really liked anyone since that bastard cheated on me. You know who I mean. I'm just having a good time for once. That's all."

Sophie looked at her friend with concern on her face.

"What are you doing this weekend?" Gabrielle wanted to change the subject, but it did not work.

"Well, Mike is working on a case, and I am going to be alone. I had thought we could go into Boston and have a good time, but now I can see it is not going to happen," Sophie said. She crossed her arms over her chest and looked away from Gabrielle.

"I am sorry, Sophie," Gabrielle said in a quiet voice.

"I thought you came to visit me. Why can't you just tell him you have other plans?" Sophie was pouting. She had her sulky face on. Gabrielle knew this look. She had seen it many times over the years when Sophie did not get her way.

"What if I spend the whole day and evening with you today? We could go shopping. I need to pick up a few things. We could have a late lunch, whatever you want. Are you game?" Gabrielle was hoping it would smooth things over a bit. She walked up to Sophie and gently poked her arm with her finger, then tilted her head and gave Sophie a sad smile with her lower lip sticking out. Sophie looked at her and could not help but laugh.

"I still do not want you to go," Sophie said again, serious.

Gabrielle really felt guilty. She walked to the window with her cup of coffee and glanced outside. What was she going to do? She was going to try once more. She did not want to have to make her decision without Sophie's approval, but if it came down to it, she would. She was going to Newport.

"Sophie, I am truly sorry. Let's try and make it work for both of us. We will have fun ... come on."

"All right, but I still do not like it. You know you will be going home soon."

"I'm truly just having fun ... really. I know. I'll think about going home after the weekend." Gabrielle did not want to think that far out.

"All right, then. I'm just looking out for you. I don't want you getting hurt, that's all," Sophie replied.

"I'm fine, really," Gabrielle answered; relieved she was going to go.

"I'm all yours," Sophie said.

"I just have to make a few calls this morning, and then I'll get ready and we can go. But I want to hear more about this Mr. Rian, especially the juicy stuff."

They looked at each other and started to laugh aloud.

Gabrielle gave her another hug, and she disappeared to her bedroom to get ready for a day of shopping. She was excited at the prospect of spending a whole weekend with Bernard, but one thing was still ringing in her ears: *Remember you have to return home in the next few days.*

Sophie had uttered those words just before Gabrielle had left her. Now these words were haunting her. She dismissed them, and she continued on her way. She would deal with it later.

CHAPTER 6

Al got ahold of Tom on his cell phone, just as he was about to go out the door from his home to resume following the girls. Al wanted to tell him the information he had discovered. Some of it was good, but some of it was not so good.

"Hey! This is what I received on that address you gave me. A certain Mark Smith and his wife Sophie live there, and they have owned the house for the last five years. He is a corporate attorney downtown Boston, and she does not work. There's a lot of money."

Tom listened attentively at Al's report.

"Now concerning the picture, since you only have that, I'm going to put it through a face recognition program that will take at least a day, maybe longer. I did not get any hits from the motor vehicle or criminal records departments that looked close to this picture. My friend at FBI has nothing. He doesn't think she's American," Al said.

"We are waiting for Homeland Security to try and find out her identity through passport identification. Immigration said she never applied for a work visa, so that's all I have at the moment."

"Thanks for all your help. I know it took many favors. I appreciate it. Keep in touch. Let me know as soon as you get a hit."

"You got it, buddy," Al said, and then hung up the phone. Tom had parked his truck down the street from the house, so he'd see when the girls came out of their driveway. Tom had arrived just before dawn. He was observing the comings and goings of this household. He had not gotten much sleep last night. He'd had a long night of tossing and turning. He never slept much when he was on the job, but his body had adapted over the years. He could easily see the front entrance. He was waiting for the woman he had followed home the night before. He saw two women come out of the garage in a Mercedes. One of them was definitely the one he needed to watch. He started his truck and followed them, but kept his distance until they arrived at the mall.

Every time they took a turn, he did too. He was right behind them. He hid in the shadows of the entryways when they would go into stores to browse. He would be one step behind them at all times, as he was trying not to be spotted. He wanted to pick up incriminating evidence against her to relay to his boss. The only way to do this was by standing close to them so he could overhear their conversations. Tom found out the girl names by listening to them say each other's names. They were Gabrielle and Sophie. It was better than nothing. He would have to relay this information to his friend Al. Tom would have to report to his boss soon, and he would not be happy if he did not get the identity of this girl.

"Christ, how difficult can it be?" Tom thought aloud. Tom figured she was a girlfriend of Sophie's—a foreigner, probably from Canada or France. He had detected a heavy French accent when she spoke. He would find out if she had gone to school here in Boston years ago, where Sophie had gotten her education. He would look into that area if he did not hear from Al in the next few hours. Tom focused on the girls again.

***

Sophie and Gabrielle had been shopping for two hours when Gabrielle noticed a man dressed in jeans, a black t-shirt, and a baseball hat, lurking around the stores that they visited. She also noticed every time she would look his way, he would look away, pretending he was looking at something. He would leave the store, but she would see him again later on. She was getting a bit nervous. She thought he was creepy, and he kept watching them, so she decided to tell Sophie about him. She was starting to be afraid that he might be following them.

"Sophie, come here. Follow me." Gabrielle said in a hushed voice. She grabbed a random dress off the nearest rack. "I want to try this on."

Sophie looked at her puzzled. Gabrielle was motioning her with her head to follow her. She was headed toward the ladies dressing room.

"Come with me," Gabrielle whispered to her friend. Sophie looked confused, but followed her.

As soon as they were inside the women's area, Sophie looked at her and said, "What's the matter with you?"

"Shhh! I think there's a man out there following us," Gabrielle whispered in a low voice.

"Where? Are you crazy? You are imagining things," Sophie chuckled.

"No, I'm not. I noticed him when we were at Macy's, then when we stopped at the book store, then now."

"Are you serious? You're being paranoid," Sophie said.

"He's wearing jeans, a black tee, and a Red Sox cap," Gabrielle answered.

"Maybe he's just shopping, like us. You are exaggerating." Sophie poked her head out the door. Gabrielle yanked her back inside.

"Okay then do me a favor and keep an eye out for him, and then you'll see I'm not crazy."

"Fine, I will. Now let's get out of this dressing room," Sophie said, not taking her seriously.

They decided to change stores to see if he really was following them.

"Do you see him?" Gabrielle whispered, pretending to be going through the rack of clothes, not wanting to look up.

"Yes, I do. Let's change stores," Sophie said, playing her game and smirking.

They calmly left the store, and they walked to the next one a few doors down. He was still lurking around outside the store. They stayed for a while to see if he would be on his way, and then proceeded to the next store. He was still there, waiting and watching. The girls were getting anxious.

"See, I told you he is following us," Gabrielle said nervously.

"We don't know that for sure. Let's get out of the mall. We'll go to a nice restaurant and get a bite to eat. He will not follow us there. You will see," Sophie said, and then continued talking.

"I still think you are paranoid. Be optimistic about the situation. It is going to be just fine. Now pick up your bags and start walking to the parking area of the mall."

"I think we should call the police," Gabrielle said.

"And tell them what? That we think this man is following us, but we are not sure. That's crazy," Sophie replied.

"Okay, but if I see him near the restaurant, I am calling," Gabrielle whispered to her.

They were walking at a normal pace back to where they had parked Sophie's car. Gabrielle kept turning around looking for the man, but she did not see him anymore. They got in their car, and Gabrielle locked the doors. She sighed with relief then they drove off. Sophie was laughing at her.

"I told you, he wasn't following us. It was your imagination, you idiot," Sophie said in good humor. They drove away. They did not have a worry in the world.

***

Tom had noticed the girls were more jumpy than usual. They were not laughing, and Gabrielle kept looking around. He thought maybe he had been spotted, but he was not sure. He decided it was better to pull back and track them down later than to raise suspicion. He watched them leave the mall from the other end of the parking lot. He let them go because he knew they had to return home at one point during the day. He could resume his surveillance at that time. Tom decided to go see Mr. Rian and report on what he knew, but first he needed to call Al again to see if he had any news. This time around, Al had great news for Tom. Tom listened intently to every word Al said to him.

"I found her name, Gabrielle Leger. She is Canadian. She came to Boston in the late nineties to go to college. She graduated from Boston College the same year as her friend Sophie. She has been residing with Sophie for the past week at that address. She has no prior arrests. She does not live in the United States, so probably she is visiting her friend, as you had deduced."

"Thanks a lot, buddy. I owe you one. Talk to you later," Tom said and hung up the phone. Al had never disappointed him. He had always come through with the information.

Tom arrived at Ron's house in the late afternoon. His boss was at his usual place in library.

"Good afternoon, Mr. Rian. I hope I'm not disturbing you. Could I have a moment of your time, sir?" Tom was always polite to his employer.

"Yes, Tom. Please sit down, and tell me you have good news for me."

Tom never sat. Instead he stood by the desk, his arms folded on his chest, his legs slightly parted. He was at ease, military style.

"Last evening, I went to Bernard's residence where I observed a young woman meet Bernard. She was in her late twenties, early thirties. I found out her name is Gabrielle Leger—she is from Canada. She is here visiting her friend Sophie Smith from Newton. As far as I can tell she and Bernard are intimate, sir." At that instance, Tom handed him the photos he had taken the previous night of Gabrielle and Bernard. Ron looked at them attentively. He was not pleased. He crushed one of the pictures between his fingers and threw it into the garbage pail next to his desk. He stood up from his desk turned around to look out the window. Tom heard him swear.

"God damn it, boy!"

"What would you like me to do next? Shall I continue to follow them? Sir?"

"Do you know when she is planning on returning home?" Ron asked him as calmly as he could. Tom noticed a small tremble in his voice, and he knew his boss was mad.

"No, sir. She's probably going to return soon."

"I am a patient man, Tom. Bernard will return to me in a week or so. I know it. I have seen her before ... I remember at the Four Seasons last weekend. He did not introduce her to me ... hmmm! Now, I wonder why? What is so special about her?" Ron was talking aloud like he did sometimes. Tom just stood there and listened to him until he was done, not saying a word.

"Well, keep tracking them and watching. Let me know when you know more. Good job, Tom. Keep in touch, and make sure Bernard doesn't spot you."

"Yes, sir." Tom turned around and headed out the door to continue his assignment.

***

Gabrielle must have been seeing things. She truly thought they were being followed. They went to have lunch at Legal Seafood. They had a delicious meal of seafood with a nice bottle of white wine. She looked around, but she had not seen the man again. Now she felt foolish. At least she and Sophie had had a good laugh afterwards.

She had bought a sexy, sheer nightgown for that special evening in Newport. She was excited at the idea of spending more time with Bernard. She also realized that this was her last weekend in the Boston area. She had to return home before the end of May. Tourist season would start soon. She would be going home the day after she and Bernard returned home. She was not going to think about that day now. She would deal with it when it happened. Right now, she was happy.

She could not wait to spend more time with him. The girls had decided spend the rest of the evening at home. Sophie told Gabrielle that her husband was working late on a new case.

"Oh! Come on, let's watch a romantic movie," Gabrielle pleaded.

"Let's watch an action movie," Sophie said.

"No way."

They finally compromised with a comedy called, "Night at the Museum," starring Ben Stiller.

"Do you want to order pizza now?" Gabrielle asked.

"Sure. I know this guy down the street that delivers. I order from him a lot," Sophie answered.

"Okay, you call it in, and I'll open the wine," Gabrielle said to Sophie. She passed a glass to Sophie.

After a few drinks, the girls were just talking while waiting for the pizza.

"I think he is going to break your heart, and you are going to cry all the way home, you know. He does not care. All he wants is sex," Sophie blurted out.

"How can you say such a thing?" Gabrielle was appalled at her.

"Because you are going away with him, and you are going to like him a lot, then you are leaving. That's why you should not go," Sophie exclaimed.

"Sophie, I know what you are trying to do, but stop. I'm a big girl, and I can make my own decisions. Now, watch the movie and be quiet."

Gabrielle was fed up with her being so negative. She turned the movie on and did not say anything else about Bernard.

"Fine. I warned you," Sophie answered.

Gabrielle was watching her, and finally Sophie sat down and started watching the show. Around midnight, they called it a night and they went to bed. Gabrielle wanted take a break from Sophie to call Bernard to tell him she could not wait to see him this weekend. The girls were tired. She did not want to spoil their special time together since she was not going to be here the next few days.

Gabrielle slid under the covers of the huge bed she was sleeping in. She pulled the cover up to her chin. Why was it she had not known him that long and yet she had feelings for him? She fell asleep with the image of him.

Gabrielle woke up to the birds singing outside. She'd had a good night's sleep. The sun was shining and the only thing missing was her man. She closed her eyes and, for the first time, she had a bad feeling of dread. She would have to leave him in a few days, and then what? She knew she could not stay. Her life was in Canada. She had worked too hard to achieve her successful business. She loved her inn and it had taken her a long time to fix all the rooms of the dilapidated, broken down estate to its original beauty. She was so proud of it.

She had finally found a great chef who could whip up the most amazing meals. The clientele was beginning to be a steady stream during the summer months. She was not going to think about this now. She had too many things to do before she met Bernard. If only he lived in Canada, closer to her, she would be the happiest person. But sometimes you cannot have everything. She was fortunate that she had this time with him now. She would think about talking to him about a long distance relationship.

First thing, she got up. She grabbed her phone out of her purse, and she dialed those precious numbers. Her heart began to pound. She could not wait to hear his voice.

"Hello there!" Bernard answered, and her heart jumped a beat and goosebumps went down her back all the way down to her toes. She could get used to him very fast.

"Hi, I just wanted to let you know I'd love to go away with you this weekend."

"I'm happy to hear that. How about I pick you up around one o'clock? I can't wait to see you," Bernard said.

"I'll be ready and waiting. See you then," she responded in a soft voice.

"I can't wait. See you then. Bye."

***

She was anxious. She could not wait to see him. She put her mind to the task. She had to finish packing a small bag for the weekend. She wondered what his house looked like and if it was on the beach. She hoped it was nice and in a private area. It really did not matter. As long as he was there, she knew she would enjoy herself. When she had finished packing, she jumped in the shower and washed her body and her hair with a new lavender soap she had bought the previous day. She put on a pair of white shorts and a pink t-shirt and sandals. She tied her hair up in a ponytail. She looked in the mirror and smiled. She was delighted at the upcoming weekend. She went downstairs to the back of the house, where she laid down on one of lounge chairs by the pool. She closed her eyes again to suck in the rays and waited patiently for her knight to come pick her up.

He arrived on time. *Bernard looked good in his khaki shorts and striped polo shirt*, she thought. He leaned forward and kissed her gently on the lips. He then proceeded to go into the house. He picked up her small bag and was ready to leave instantly.

***

Tom noticed Bernard's Range Rover coming toward him. He watched him turn into the driveway. He ducked down just in time so he would not be seen, and then he sat back up to observe him go to the door. A few minutes later, he came out carrying a flowered duffle bag that he put into the back of his truck. The woman got into his vehicle. She waved good-bye to her friend, and they took off. Tom knew they were going away for the weekend, but the question was where? He loved it when his job took him to new discoveries.

He would have to call Ron and tell him about this new development, but first he decided to follow them at a discreet distance. He did not want to be spotted, especially by Bernard. Ten minutes later, they were headed south on highway 128, so he continued following them. He decided to only call Mr. Rian when he knew what their destination would be. He also needed Mr. Rian to give him further instructions on what he wanted him to do.

CHAPTER 7

It was a warm day, and Gabrielle could feel the air against her skin as they drove down to Newport, Rhode Island. The traffic got busier as they got closer to Newport. Gabrielle loved the huge bridges and the sights of the white sand beaches wherever she looked. Bernard and Gabrielle were enjoying each other's company. She chattered, and he listened attentively.

She needed to talk to him about her feelings and where their relationship was going.

"Bernard ...," She could feel her heart throbbing hard against her chest, but at the same time she hoped she was doing the right thing. "As you know, I'm going to leave the day after I return home from Newport and ..." She decided to give him the floor and see what he said.

"You are wondering if we are going to see each other after this weekend?" Bernard turned toward her and looked at her. He then reached over and took her hand in his. "We can make it work. Long-distance relationships can be fun. I could come surprise you. You would love it."

His voice brought a smile to Gabrielle's face. Now she could relax.

"I never really told you why I came to Boston," she said.

Gabrielle gazed at him and wondered if he was going to break her heart like all the others. Maybe Sophie had been right. He was watching the road, hands on the wheel.

"I came here because a man had hurt me badly, and I needed a break. I did not intend to meet anyone. I do not want to get hurt again." Gabrielle was waiting for his response, but it was slow in coming. Finally, after a minute of dead silence, he spoke.

"I have no plans to hurt you. And to the man who caused you pain, he was a fool to let you go. I am getting over someone else, too. I understand. We will figure something out so we can see each other. You don't live that far away. You're only in Canada."

They rode in silence for a few minutes.

"You should come see my town. The French people are the friendliest, and I would definitely show you around town," she said and started to laugh.

"Oh! Ho! Now I know why you like me. It must be my good looks," he said, cracking up. She leaned over and kissed his cheek.

"Gabrielle, I truly respect the struggles you faced and how you surmounted them. I personally know sometimes it is not easy. You have, from what I hear from you, a beautiful inn and you should be proud."

She felt a warm feeling go through her. She was going to really have fun with him this weekend. She talked to him about where she came from, her French culture, and her values.

It took them about two hours to reach the island. He took her on a drive to Orchard Point Avenue by the famous mansions of Newport. They saw The Vanderbilt and the Cliff Walk and where the waves were pounding away on the cliffs. She had never seen such humongous homes. He told her they could visit some of them later on if she desired. They also passed in front the campus of Salve Regina University. He continued to drive around the winding roads on the other side of the island that led to his summer home.

It was a modest home located on the edge of a cliff overlooking the ocean. The house had been built about six years ago. It was made of shingles that were painted white, and the roof was a dark blue color. It had large windows in the front facing the water and a porch that wrapped around on three sides. A swing was balancing to one side of the porch. It astounded her. It was so inviting and secluded from other neighbors. Gabrielle thought this place must have cost him a bundle of dough. She absolutely loved it.

"So what do you think? Do you like it?" Bernard asked casually.

"Oh! *Mon Dieu!* Who wouldn't like this place?" she said, staring at the place with excitement. "It's perfect. Do you come here often?" she asked, and then she noticed a dark cloud roll over his expression. She looked at him, and she saw his eyes tear up.

"Bernard, are you alright?"

She did not know what was happening. She was scared, so she placed her hand over his and waited for a response. It took him a minute to compose himself.

"I'm okay."

She could see he was trying to put up a front. He smiled, but Gabrielle knew something was not right.

"I wanted to bring you here to try and bring joy again to this house and to me," he said and turned away. Her heart went out to him. Someone had destroyed him. He was hiding his hurt, but Gabrielle saw a small piece of hope slowly emerging.

"Let's go in. We'll talk later." He got out of the truck and went to the trunk to get their bags. "Come on. Let's go in." He motioned her to follow him. She did so with enthusiasm.

He had lost his only love Danielle years ago, and now he had a barrier no woman had been able to tear down because he could not bear the pain again that had followed this tragedy. She had been driving to his Newport home alone. She had lost control of her car and gone down a cliff. He still could feel the emotion upon receiving that phone call from the police department.

* * *

"Good evening, Mr. Rian. My name is Officer Carter from the Newport Police department. Do you own a red 2007 Jaguar, license plate BRR?"

A chill had gone through his body at that instant. His legs had gone weak. He tightened his grip on the receiver.

"Yes, has something happened? My girlfriend Danielle has the car," he had said. He held his breath and waited.

"I am sorry to inform you there was an accident," the policeman said calmly.

"Is Danielle okay? Is she in the hospital?"

"Could you come to the station, sir?"

"No. Please tell me, is she hurt? Where is she?" Bernard was beside himself, and his body shook uncontrollably.

"*Sir, I am sorry, but she died. Now if you could come ...*" Bernard had not heard the rest of the conversation. He fell to his knees and tears fell down his face. His hands pulled at his hair.

"No ..." He still felt pain in his heart when he thought about that evening. He would always bring his hand over his heart when he thought about her.

Only one person had ever had his love in his lifetime: his precious Danielle. His heart had been broken to a million pieces when she had died. He had always blamed himself for not being with her in the car instead of working that night. It had taken years for him to be able to return to a semi-normal life. Bernard missed how she used to smell of roses when she was near him. *The way she would touch him so tenderly with her fingers.* It would send electrical jolts of pleasure through his body. How he loved to just look into her eyes as a desire for her would overcome him between his legs. Her soft cries and moans when they made love. How her velvety breasts would brush against his body. How thoughtful she was to everyone around her. There would never be another like Danielle. She was dearly missed. His eyes watered at the thought of her. They both had been on an equal level emotionally and sexually. He wished he could turn back the passage of time and undo the events of that unfortunate night.

***

Bernard went up to the front door and put the key in the keyhole. He turned the knob, and he swung the door open so Gabrielle could enter. He turned toward her and said, "Welcome." He walked in, and he went to the bedroom to drop the bags on the bed.

The house was splendid. The kitchen was in the rear of the house, and it was all done in white, from the cupboard to the tiles on the wall. In the middle was an island with a granite counter top and red stools. The kitchen opened to a big living room with red leather couches facing the view of the ocean. The dining room consisted only of a long wood table with matching chairs with red cushions. There were oil paintings of beaches and boats on the walls. They looked amateurish, but extremely nice. She also noticed a pair of wood rocking chairs next to the stone fireplace that had been painted white, next to a bookshelf was full of old novels, and it gave the room a cozy atmosphere. It was a place where you could really relax and be at peace.

When he came out of the bedroom, he looked at her with that devilish grin she loved and walked right up to her. He put his hands on her hips and he pulled her right against him. He held her tight and tilted his head, and laid his lips upon hers. She loved to taste him. She pulled back from him, and she was breathless.

She gazed at him then said, "Now, that's a welcome kiss." She started to giggle.

"I'm all yours. What would you like to do first?" The sun was still bright and warm in the sky. There was a slight sea breeze, but it was perfect weather for the beach.

"I know exactly what you want to do first," she said and pulled away. She started to tickle him and then ran away. "I'm going for a swim. Are you coming?" she yelled.

He was laughing, trying to get to her, but she was determined to go to the beach. She kept squirming out of his grip when he would grab her playfully, so he finally gave in to her demand.

"All right, all right, I give up," Bernard answered.

Gabrielle ran in the direction of the bedroom. She entered and was amazed. She had to stop to admire the artwork; it looked like a big cloud. The walls were light blue, and huge puffy clouds were painted on the bedroom ceiling, like the sky on a baby blue background. On the bed was a big, white down comforter that was full of feathers. The white net surrounded the four posts of the bed and were tied to the posts with white ribbons. The bed faced the windows that overlooked the ocean on three sides, with white sheers that seemed to float with the breeze and the sunlight.

"Do you like it?" she heard him whisper behind her, as he wrapped his arms around her waist, and then kissed her neck softly.

"It's stunning. Yes, I do like it," she said, and he smiled.

"Did you paint those pictures and the mural up above?" she asked, but suddenly his expression changed again from happiness to sadness. He became very quiet.

"Was this the person you mentioned who hurt you before?" she asked quietly.

"No, I didn't paint it. My fiancée Danielle did. She died in a car accident a few years ago. I did not have the heart to change it. I have not been here since she passed away. She was the artist, not me. She loved it here. One of the reasons I brought you here was because I like you, and I was hoping to instill new memories in this house." She could see the hurt in his eyes. Her heart broke for his pain.

"I'm so sorry. The paintings are beautiful." She turned around and she gave him a big, huge hug. He bent down and kissed her gently on the cheek. They did not move for a minute, they stood for a moment just holding each other. Gabrielle pondered if she could live up to his fiancée or if she would always be second best in his mind. *Would he break her heart and leave her like Sophie had said?* This notion was beginning to haunt her.

"Do you still want to go swimming?" he asked, interrupting her thought.

"Sure. Last one on the porch is a rotten egg!"

Gabrielle took off running to find her suit in her duffle bag. She knew how to make him laugh with her funny sayings, and she watched him trying to hurry up, but she was gaining ground. He grabbed her on her way out the door. He spun her around, and then wrapped his hands around her. He started kissing her playfully.

She finally managed to get away from him. She was breathless, and she yelled to him, "You are cheating."

He was laughing again. He grabbed his trunks, took her hand, and together they ran down to the beach for a swim.

***

Tom was hiding in the tall grass not too far from the house. He was observing everything unfold. He saw them run down to the beach, and he knew they were going to be occupied for a while, so he decided it would be a good time to update his boss about their activities. The last time he had been in Newport was when he had confronted Bernard's fiancée Danielle a few years back. It had not ended well. Tom had tried to explain to Danielle that she was not right for Bernard, because she was only an artist and she could not marry him because she did not fit in his world of highly influential people. She had nothing to bring to his family but embarrassment. She had to leave him and never see him again, but she would not listen to reason.

61

Tom had told her, "I do not want to hurt you. Take the money and disappear, or you will regret it."

"I do not want his father's money. I love Bernard, and he loves me. We are getting married. Leave us alone!" Danielle had shouted.

He had orders that needed to be followed to the letter, but her dying was not one of them. Ron had never found out the facts. He had explained that he did not have anything to do with it. It was a car accident, and it ended up for the good of the family. He had to be more careful this time. He wanted to stay in Ron's good graces.

A struggle had taken place and, unfortunately, Danielle had lost. During the encounter, he had grabbed her arm and twisted her around, wrapping his arm around her neck to stop her from straying. He had accidentally broken her neck. Well, not really an accident, but it turned out for the best. He had to make it look like a car mishap, so he had carried her body to her car, and he drove it to a secluded area. He then rolled her car off the cliff into the water. There had been an investigation or autopsy. It was ruled as a tragic car accident at the time. Only he knew the truth. He had been paid generously for his work and his silence. It had been an interesting mission.

He discreetly slipped back into his truck, being careful so no one would notice him. Only a few passing tourists had gone by to go to the beach. He found his cell phone and dialed from memory the number that he knew so well. It rang once, and then a familiar voice answered.

"Yes," Ron answered quietly.

"I followed them to Newport. He brought her to his summer home. They are probably staying for the weekend. They both had luggage. What would you like me to do, sir?"

Ron thought about it for a moment. "Good work. Did they see you?"

"No, sir." Tom said.

"Good. Then that will be all for now. Come home. They are not going anywhere."

"Yes, sir. I'll be back in a few hours," Tom said and hung up his cell phone.

***

Ron was sitting in the library behind his mahogany desk. He stood up and went to the bar area. He rubbed his temples. He had hoped his headache would disappear, but no such luck. He poured himself a stiff scotch and gulped it down. He felt a burning sensation as the drink went all the way down. He knew that Bernard had not been back to Newport since Danielle's death, so he must care for this woman. Ron also knew she had a business back home in Canada, so she would have to return eventually. What if Bernard did not let her return or she decided to stay? Questions needed to be answered and soon, but sometimes things had a way of working themselves out.

His mind went back to a few years ago when Bernard thought he was in love with this artist called Danielle. Ron had sent Tom to try to reason with her, pay her off, but a car accident had occurred before Tom had had time to offer her money to leave. It was unfortunate because Bernard had suffered greatly, but he had gotten over it. *She probably would have taken the money he had offered. If she had, she might have still been alive today, living well somewhere else.* Ron would not be humiliated again and have his name associated with this second-class girl from Canada. He wondered what his son saw in this woman. She had very little money, just her inn in Canada. She was pretty, but that was it. She would never fit in with his class of people. She had no understanding of the rich and what it took to be one of them.

Ron decided he was going to bide his time for now. He would reevaluate the situation after the weekend when he knew they were back in town. His son's future was his first priority ,and he would do what he needed to ensure that Bernard married a suitable woman. It might be easy or it might be a difficult task. It did not matter to him. *What needed to be done would happen.* He poured himself another drink and went to sit back down to try to concentrate on some work.

***

Bernard and Gabrielle spent the afternoon on the beach. They walked down beach while Gabrielle picked up seashells. They watched the kids playing in the water, and they made a giant sand castle with some of the children. She noticed how Bernard would show the younger ones how to build it. It was a special moment, this powerful wealthy man kneeling in the sand enjoying the pleasure of nothing but the sand. He took his time and joked with the children. Bernard and Gabrielle swam and sunbathed by the water.

"It was a fun afternoon. I have not laughed so much in a long time," Bernard told her.

Around five o'clock, they decided to head back to the house to get ready to go out to dinner. It had been an incredible afternoon, and they had behaved just like children, splashing each other in the water and diving for crabs. They really did not want to go home, but the sun was going down, and they both needed to get out of the sun before they burned. They walked back to the house, hand in hand. They were still covered in sand when they arrived at the beach house, and they both needed a shower.

It was such a hot day when Gabrielle got to the house. She did not want to go inside. Instead they decided to sit on the porch and enjoy a cool beer. Bernard went inside to get the beers, and she went to sit on the swing. She sat down and thought how fortunate she was to have met such an exceptional and loving man. She was going to have a hard time leaving him in a few days. The sun was setting over the ocean. She watched the blue heron birds flying low in the sky occasionally diving for fish. The vibrant colors of orange, red, and yellow over the lower sky were amazing. It was so peaceful. Gabrielle closed her eyes, and she could smell the ocean in the air. She truly loved this place. It reminded her of home.

He came out with the beverages. Gabrielle opened her eyes and saw him standing there with two cold beers.

"What's the matter? Come sit next to me," she said.

He sat beside her, and he gave her a gentle kiss on the lips. "You are so beautiful. When I saw you sitting there it reminded me how much I missed being here. Danielle used to love sitting here, and now I have you here. It is perfect. I am going to have to come here more often," he said, and Gabrielle felt a trace of jealousy come over her, but she shook it off.

"So did you enjoy your day?" she asked. She just wanted to make him happy.

"I did. It's so tranquil. I really like it here."

They just sat in each other arms and drank their beers quietly.

"I have to tell you, something really weird happened yesterday when Sophie and I went shopping. I thought someone was following us. I kept seeing this man. I saw him three, four times at the same stores we were in."

Bernard was quiet for a moment. "So what happened?" he asked.

"Well, we left the mall, and we went to lunch but we didn't see him after that. For some reason I thought it was strange, but he just disappeared."

"It was probably nothing. You worry too much. I will not let anyone hurt you. I will protect you," he said, and then kissed the top of her head. He then wrapped his arm around her shoulder. She felt a safe.

"So tell me, what did he look like?"

"He was tall, muscular, and he always had a hat and sunglasses on. I really couldn't see his face."

"Maybe you were wrong. We will have to be more vigilant from now on and keep our eyes open for anything suspicious. If you see him again, tell me and we will call the police, okay?" he said

"You're probably right."

She continued drinking her beer and really did not think about it anymore. Bernard kept on talking. They sat on the swing for another twenty minutes until the sun was no longer visible. Gabrielle was the first to get up from her seat and stroll inside.

"I'm going to take a shower. Would you like to join me?"

She loved to tease him. She started to walk away and gently brushed her leg against his leg. He followed her inside the house. She turned her head and saw him watching her go into the bathroom and take off her suit. She turned the knob of the shower on, and she turned around to face him. She smiled. Gabrielle stepped into the shower. The hot water was gliding freely between her firm breasts all the way down to her legs. A soothing, calm feeling came upon her. He opened the door of the shower and stepped in.

***

Gabrielle was falling in love with him. She never thought she would have love again. She was still uncertain about what would happen when she had to leave to go home. How were they going to see each other? How did long-distance relationships work and did they last? Would her heart be heavy or would she just walk away? He was such a generous and kind man. How was she going to leave? Did he feel the same way she did? She did not dare ask. Not yet. She decided not to worry about it today because she still had tomorrow. She had so many questions with no answers. She would cross that bridge at that time. She told herself to enjoy today and take advantage of what she had now.

CHAPTER 8

Ron was having coffee alone on the terrace, admiring his landscaping and thinking about Bernard. What should he do? He believed he could be forbearing, but he was not as patient as he thought. He was debating what to do again. He had pulled Tom away, but now Ron was rethinking the events of the past few days in his head. He also knew his son would be furious if he interfered with him. He looked at his phone, and then put it in his hand. He played with it for a few minutes and then, unable to help himself, dialed that familiar number.

"Good morning, Tom."

"Good morning, sir."

"I would like you to try to find out a little more about this woman Gabrielle who Bernard's with in Newport, especially when she's leaving to go home, if you can."

"Yes, sir. Do you need anything else, sir?"

"That will be all for now, thank you."

He had hung up the phone before Tom could say another word. Ron was anxious, as he hated waiting for answers. He was rubbing the back of his neck, hoping he was making the right decision. What bothered him was that Bernard had brought her to Newport. *All the other women he had dated had never come close to this place, so he must see something special in this one, but what?* Ron could not see what she could offer Bernard. She had nothing to her name except beauty, from what he saw of her.

Tom was always ready to go. He got into his truck and drove toward Newport again to see what he could find out about this woman. He arrived in Newport in record time—less than two hours. He parked his vehicle not too far from the house, but far enough they could not see his truck. He began hiking toward the woods behind the house with all his gear. He would camouflage himself easily so he would be undetectable. Since it was still early in the morning, he was hoping they had not left the house yet. He quickly set up his things and grabbed his binoculars, and spotted them right away. They were talking while drinking coffee on the front steps, looking at the small fishing boats out on the ocean.

***

Gabrielle and Bernard had had a good night's sleep. They were refreshed and ready for an adventure. They were trying to decide what to do on their last day. Gabrielle had to return to Sophie's home in the evening to pack. She was flying out first thing in the morning on the 6:00 a.m. Air Canada flight out of Logan Airport. This was her last day, and she wanted it to be memorable.

"What would you like to do today?" Gabrielle asked him.

"Well, we could stay in bed," he said to her. She poked him playfully in the ribs. He laughed, then kissed her on the neck and inhaled her scent.

"Please, please, please?" He was joking.

"Seriously!" she teased, and her laugh made his heart melt at the thought of never hearing it again after today.

"We could go visit one of the mansions that we saw yesterday, and then we could go to Thames Street to get something to eat. There are lots of small boutiques on that street. How about that?" he said.

"That sounds like a plan. I've never been there," she said excitedly.

He wanted to do something eventful that he could look back on and reminisce after she left for Canada.

"All right, then let me get ready and we'll go." She started to get up, but Bernard stopped her. He grabbed her by the waist and whispered in her ear.

"Are you sure we can't stay here instead?" he asked while kissing and tickling her.

She was laughing like a schoolgirl. "If you continue, we won't be going anywhere. Now stop it and let me go get ready," she said, but not before she kissed him hard on the lips.

"That's not fair."

She twisted herself away from him. She laughed, and then ran inside to get dressed. He followed after her a second later. She put on a white button-down shirt, khaki shorts, and sandals in record time. As usual, he looked nice even in casual clothes. She grabbed her hat on the way out the door, and she went to wait for him on the porch while he locked the house up.

Tom could see they were leaving. He packed up all his possessions and ran to his truck. He barely made it. He had to scoot down in the seat so Bernard would not see him. After they drove by, he waited a minute before he came back up to start the engine and proceeded to follow them at a safe distance. He started to pursue them again. When he saw they were going to The Breakers Mansion, Tom turned his truck around and headed back to Bernard's house. He parked nearby and walked up to the back door. He opened the back door with two metal hooks with no problem. He closed the door behind him and started toward the bedroom.

He was looking for Gabrielle's bag. When he found it, he searched it carefully. He was hoping to find her plane tickets. He found them in the side zipper pocket. He examined and memorized the time and date, then placed the tickets back where he had found them. He turned, but something caught his eye. It was a small safe like those in hotel rooms, probably Bernard's, in the closet. He decided to try to open it, but it had a four-digit password. He knew people usually used a familiar number, so he first put Bernard's birthday. It did not open. He tried his mother's birthday. Nothing. Tom kept thinking *which four digits would he use?* He had one final thought: *Danielle's birthday. She had lived here, so it would have been something both of them knew.* Tom heard a click, and the door opened. There were a few legal papers and a small black box in it. He opened it. This was interesting. He would have to call his boss right away.

"Mr. Rian, I found the information you wanted. She is leaving tomorrow morning on a 6:00 a.m. flight," Tom told him.

"That is excellent news. Anything else?" Ron asked.

"I went to the beach house and searched it to find the information and I also found something else. I'm not sure what it means."

69

Ron cut Tom short. "What the hell did you find?"

"I found a small box with an engagement ring in it, sir."

After he said it, there was silence at the other end of the line.

"Just keep following them and try to find out more information," Ron answered.

"Yes, sir." Tom hung up and was on his way again.

***

The two lovers were driving slowly, savoring the views of the island. They were headed downtown. The sun was bright and there was a soft wind coming from the ocean. Bernard had noticed a blue truck parked on the side of the road again when they left the beach house, but there was no one in it. *The truck looked similar to the one he had seen outside his house in Boston, but then many people owned blue trucks.* He shook it off and continued toward Ochre Point Avenue.

They decided to visit one of the Newport mansions. Gabrielle had never seen any of them, so Bernard chose The Breakers, the Vanderbilt's summer home. It had been built in 1893. It used to belong to Cornelius Vanderbilt, but now it belonged to The Preservation Society of Newport County. The property was a grand mansion with seventy rooms in sixty thousand square feet of living space that spanned across thirteen acres of land. Gabrielle was anxious to visit it. Bernard hired a private guide for their tour so that Gabrielle could know everything about the mansion and have all her questions answered. She was excited and astonished by the estate.

They finally arrived and parked across the street from the mansion. They walked toward the estate hand in hand. Gabrielle was amazed at how majestic the mansion looked, and she thought it was spectacular. The tour guide was a young woman who was very meticulous about explaining the history of each room. She was charming and articulate. Gabrielle was in awe at the beauty of this mansion and at how people used to live in the 1800s. The guide even told them that Anderson Cooper, the journalist for CNN, was Gloria Vanderbilt's son. It took most of the morning or them to see all the unique rooms. The history of the grand parties and the way that they lived in the 1800s was fascinating. The long stairways, the woodwork on the ceiling, and walls were expertly craved with beautiful designs. Afterwards they went downstairs to the gift shop. Bernard saw a hardcover book of the life and times of the Vanderbilt family. So while Gabrielle was busy browsing around, he purchased the book for her as a reminder of The Breakers and their day there together.

Their next stop was lunch and a bit of shopping on Thames Street, the center of all activity in Newport. This street was located downtown near the waterfront area. On the way out of the parking lot, Bernard noticed the same blue truck. He saw no one was in it. He did not want to worry Gabrielle so he memorized the plate number and decided he would try to find out who owned it later today. He hoped it was not one of his father's employees, because he was going to be furious at him. He planned to call someone once they arrived at the restaurant, and he was going to keep an eye out for that truck. He parked the Range Rover once again near Thames Street and they decided to walk for a while.

"Where are we going to eat?" Gabrielle asked.

They were walking down the street, which was packed with tourists walking along on both sides of the street.

"I thought we could walk further down here. There's a restaurant called Brick Alley Pub. They are famous for their burgers. They make the best burgers in town. What do you think? Does that sound okay?" Bernard asked.

"That sounds perfect," Gabrielle replied.

They continued walking, looking at different storefront windows along the way. The street had small distinctive stores, most of which were privately owned. The stores had something for everyone, from ice cream shops to clothing stores, to places that carried ship parts. She stopped him midway down the street and pulled him aside, out of the people's way. She turned towards Bernard took his hands in hers. She looked him straight in the eyes and said to him. "I'm happy I came. Thanks for inviting me. This town is great. I just love it and being with you."

He did not say anything, he just bent his head down and kissed her passionately right in front of everyone on the street. He was not concerned who saw them. After their kiss, he smiled at her and said, "You are most welcome. I'm happy you came."

For the first time in a long time, he was enjoying his time with a woman. They continued down the street to the pub. The Brick Alley Pub was an old, three-story building with a unique decor. The original woodwork of the house had been kept and the plank wood floors were authentic. A bar was in the middle of one of the main rooms with all kinds of stools that wrapped around it. The service was always great, and the food unquestionably good. Bernard had made reservations for a quiet table. When they got there, it was ready, so they were seated outside in the back under an oak tree. They both ordered a beer and examined the variety of dishes from the menu. They finally decided on the burgers because it was the pub's specialty.

"Gabrielle, I wanted to talk to you about us," Bernard started the conversation. "I want to ask you a question."

Gabrielle lifted her head to look at him.

"Can't you stay here with me in Boston a while longer?" asked Bernard.

Gabrielle was stunned. She could not speak. "I wish I could, but I'm so sorry, I really have to return home. I have my inn, and they will need me. I also wish we had more time. Maybe you could come visit me in Canada? You could stay with me for the summer." She took his hand in hers and she squeezed it. She glanced at him. Bernard did not know how to answer her. He could not leave his work for that long, either.

"I ... I want to see you again, but I don't know if I can be absent for that long. I am in the process of signing one of the biggest business deals of my life. I have to be here for the final contracts and negotiations, but I want to come see you afterwards. I will find a way." He was trying to be positive. "I will call you, and we can keep in touch," he said.

"That sounds good." She looked away.

She had to return to her business and her life up in Canada. He knew this from the first day he met her, but now he felt differently. His life was here, and that was how it was. He did not want to accept it, but there was nothing either one of them could do.

Bernard excused himself, telling her he was going to the men's room, but actually he was going to call a friend on his father's compound that he could trust for information. He dialed the number, and he waited for someone to answer. He had helped this man's family few years ago when he was losing his home to a mortgage company. Bernard had lent him money so he could keep his home. He had always kept his ears and eyes open for information on his father for him. Bernard knew if his father ever found out, he would fire him instantly, so they were always discreet about their relationship. Bernard knew his father was probably mad at him for not showing up for the dinners with Isabelle. If he understood him well, he probably had him followed to see whom he was with. Bernard had caught him twice before when he was dating Danielle. Bernard hated it when his father would try to control his life, which was why he would always look around his surroundings.

"Good afternoon, Ramos. This is Bernard."

"Good afternoon, Mr. Rian. How are you?"

"I'm fine, Ramos. I'll make this quick. I just need you to find out if there is anyone on my father's compound you know who owns a blue pickup truck with license plate MBL 278."

"Yes, yes, Mister Rian. That is Mr. Tom's truck. He has a blue truck," he replied in broken English. "But he not here today. He been gone a lot last few days."

"Thank you, Ramos. That is all," Bernard said and shut the phone. He was getting mad. Bernard was trying to stay calm and not raise his voice. He was upset, but he had to stay tranquil.

***

"Hello, Bernard. How are you?" Ron answered.

"You better call your fucking dog off my trail, the one with the blue truck. You are up to your old tricks again. I will call the police. Do you understand?" Ron could sense Bernard was really trying hard not to yell at him.

"Bernard, I don't know what you're talking about," his father replied.

"There is a blue truck following me. It belongs to your personal assistant. You had him follow me."

"Now, I would not do that. Why would I do that? It's ridiculous," Ron replied calmly.

"I do not believe you," Bernard said. "To find out whom I'm spending my time with. I've got to go."

Ron heard the click of the phone Bernard had hung up on.

***

Tom's phone rang. He knew it could only be one person, so he answered it immediately.

"Tom, come home now. I have to rethink this situation," was all Ron could say.

"Are you sure, sir?"

"Yes, I'm sure."

Ron was not pleased. He figured he had enough information for the moment. Ron would have to find another way or just wait and see what happened with this girl. He did not even say goodbye, he just hung up the phone. He was frustrated with Bernard's choice of woman right now, but he would have to wait. He did not want to alienate his son from him anymore than he already had.

***

Bernard would not let his father ruin his day with Gabrielle. He went to the washroom and washed his face with cold water. He looked in the mirror and tried to calm himself down. He then wiped his face with paper towel and walked out of the bathroom. He went back into the restaurant area to find Gabrielle.

He walked to the table and kissed her on the cheek before he sat down. He opened the bag that was beside his chair, and then he presented her a box that was gift-wrapped in beautiful, flowered paper with a big purple bow.

"This is for you," he said.

"What is it? It's for me?" she asked and blushed a little as she reached for it.

"Open it!" Bernard could see the surprise on her face. She kept looking at the box. She started slowly and carefully unwrapping the paper and then opened the box. Inside was a book about The Breakers. She touched the cover ever so lightly; as if she was reliving the morning they had just spent together.

"I love it," she said in a hushed voice. "Thank you. I'll treasure it." She leaned over and took his hand, bringing it to her mouth and kissing the tips of his fingers. She opened the book to take a quick peek at it. She felt warm all inside, thinking of how thoughtful he was.

The waiter came by with their burgers. They looked delicious with all the trimmings. There was bacon, cheese, lettuce, tomato, and mayo on top. They each ordered another beer and then took a bite of their burgers. Suddenly they were very hungry.

"That had to be the best burger I ever ate," said Gabrielle on the way out of the restaurant.

"What do you want to do now?" Bernard asked her.

"Let's just walk for a while. I'm so stuffed I can't do anything else."

"Do you want bet? I bet if we went home ..."

She started laughing. She took his arm and started walking down the street. Bernard kept checking to see if they were being tailed, but he did not see anyone. He did not want to alarm Gabrielle by telling her about the situation. He hoped his father would listen to him.

"Look over there!" she said excitedly.

Gabrielle was pointing at the small store across the street. When he saw what she was pointing at, he just started to laugh. She was pulling him towards the entryway of the shop. It was called, "Miss Mimi's Tarot Card Readings."

"You can't be serious. It's all but a scam," Bernard said to her.

"Oh, come on. It will be fun!" Gabrielle answered.

Bernard finally agreed to go in with her, but she could have her cards read, not him. He was a skeptic when it came to these kinds of things, but he would be a good sport about it.

A bell rang as they opened the door and entered the business. A couple of empty chairs were leaning against the wall and there was a door nearby that was closed. A sign said, "Have a seat. I will be with you in a moment." Gabrielle pointed to the chairs, and she moved Bernard toward them. He rolled his eyes at her and proceeded to sit down. She smiled at him.

"Not one word, you hear me?" she warned him in a hushed voice.

"Cross my heart or hope to die." He was playing along. He did not believe in card readings, but she liked it, so he sat quietly. Suddenly the door opened and a woman came out. She was in her forties, a little plump, and was nicely put together in a beige dress. Her hair was in a bun on top of her head. She looked at both of them and greeted them with a bright smile.

"Welcome. Can I help you?"

Gabrielle stood up immediately. "We would like our cards read."

"Not we. She wants her cards read," Bernard uttered, and Gabrielle just laughed at him and discreetly poked him.

"I see we have a non-believer, but that's okay. Follow me, please."

She directed them to the next room that consisted of what looked like a card table with a red tablecloth and three chairs.

A few pictures of stars with a moon and different scenes of beaches with large waves hung on the walls. A long white candle was lit next to the table.

"My name is Mimi. I will be reading for you today. The fee is thirty dollars for a spread."

Gabrielle took out money from her pocket and paid her. Mimi passed her a deck and told her to shuffle it. She then cut the cards; all the while Bernard smiled at them. Mimi laid the cards down and started to read them to Gabrielle.

"There will be sadness in the near future, travel, and a battle. You must stop worrying about things you cannot change." The reading went on for about fifteen minutes. When they were finished, Bernard and Gabrielle got up and proceeded to the exit, but Mimi was not finished with her reading. She had one more thing to say, "Be very careful. Someone does not like you. He will bring you harm. Be very careful."

The warning came as a surprise to both of them, but especially to Bernard because he did not know what his father was up too. The premonition was directed at Gabrielle. They both chuckled and continued on their way.

After they were back on the street, Bernard rolled his eyes again and said to her, "I hope you don't believe what she says. It's all fake, you know."

"I hope she wasn't right, but I do think it is funny," she answered.

They decided to head back to the house because Gabrielle still had to get home early so she could finish her packing and get ready to go back to Canada. He scanned the area again to see if he would spot the blue truck anywhere, but as far he could see, it was nowhere in sight. They drove back to the beach house quietly. He watched Gabrielle gather her things together, but what he really wanted to do was make love to her one more time and not let her leave. He sadly helped her put her bag back in his vehicle, locked the door of the house, and walked away. He would not come back here, because every woman he had brought here had left him one way or another.

They drove away in silence. She reached over and lightly placed her hand over his while he drove. He could feel her pain. It was written all over her face, but he had no words to comfort her. His heart was also aching, but he did not know what to say. So instead, he turned his face toward her. He could see tears starting to fill her eyes. It finally hit him that she was leaving him in the morning.

"I really enjoyed our time together. It was special. I'll never forget it," said Gabrielle. She started to choke up.

"Gabrielle, I haven't had so much fun in a long time. I truly hope we see each other again someday."

"I hope so, too."

Tears were trickling down her face. He gently rubbed her hand and told her not to cry, it was going to be okay. They finally arrived back at Sophie's house. Gabrielle had calmed down and had apologized for her behavior, and he told her not to worry about it; he understood. He took her bag out from the trunk and he walked her to the front door. He stood in front of her, just staring at her.

"Don't move just for one minute." He wanted to paint her face in his memory. She was so gorgeous. They just stood there gazing at each other, and then he reached for her hands. They were so soft to hold. He bent his head down and he kissed her. Her lips touched his, and he put his strong arms around her. He held her so tenderly. He wanted to remember her taste, her lavender scent. One last tear fell from Gabrielle's eye, and she wiped it away. She leaned forward again and kissed him one more time.

"I'll call you soon, okay?" he said to her.

"You know where to find me. Au revoir!"

She took her keys out of her pocketbook, put the key in, and unlocked the door. Bernard watched every little movement she made. His eyes were glued to her. The door opened, and he savored a last glimpse of her as she closed it behind her. He stood on the other side of the door for a few seconds. He could not move. He was hoping she would open the door again, but alas, it did not happen.

She heard the Range Rover drive away. Her heart was breaking in her chest. She wanted to open the door and run after him, but she knew he was gone. Sophie appeared at that instant. She approached Gabrielle, and she gave her a big hug.

"I told you not to go, that he would break your heart. You should have listened to me," Sophie said to Gabrielle. Tears started falling down her cheeks there was nothing either one could do or say. Gabrielle told Sophie she was going to be fine and that she just needed to be alone for a bit. She picked up her bag, she climbed the stairs, and she went to her bedroom to pack for her departure in the morning.

CHAPTER 9

Bernard drove home slowly, his heart aching. He could still hear her laugh in his head, and her scent was still on him. He was going to miss this woman tremendously. He was not sure why, but she had left an impression. She was stuck in his mind; he could not forget her. He returned home in no time and jumped into the shower. He closed his eyes, but not even the hot water could make him forget. It only brought back memories of his time with her in the shower. He turned the water off and stood there, not able to move. He held on to the shower walls for a moment, then a tear escaped from his eyes. It took all his energy to get out and towel dry himself. As he looked at himself in the mirror, he remembered the pleasure she brought to him.

"Stop!" he heard himself say aloud. He had to forget her for the moment. He had to concentrate on his work now. He picked up the comb to style his hair and went to his closet. He grabbed a pair of casual black pants and a matching black shirt.

He had to get out of the house. He needed to keep his mind busy, so he decided he would go for a ride. He drove around the north end of Boston, past the restaurant where they had had their first date. He was going crazy. He needed to get rid of some energy so he could focus on something else other than Gabrielle. Therefore, he drove in the direction of his father's home.

"Good afternoon, father," he said as calmly as he could. Ron raised his head from the contracts he was reading and put them down on his desk.

"Well, nice to see you. Have a seat," said Ron as he came around the desk and motioned toward the large chairs by the fireplace. "Would you care for a drink? I was just about to have one. Please join me."

Ron walked to the bar area, and he poured himself a scotch. He started to pour one for his son, but Bernard declined. Ron went to sit next to him.

"So, tell me about your lady friend," Ron said.

"You'll be glad to know she is returning back to Canada tomorrow morning, first flight out, and I really didn't appreciate you sending one of your men to spy on us."

"I'm sorry. I was worried about you." Ron took a sip of his drink nonchalantly and then put it beside him on the end table.

"If you wanted to know something about Gabrielle, you should have asked me," Bernard replied before Ron could say anything else. His anger flared up. His eyebrows frowned and his eyes squinted. Ron looked at him nervously.

"Next time I'll ..."

Bernard did not let him finish his sentence. He approached his father. He put his hands on both sides of his father's armchair. He stared at him with disbelief, and through clenched teeth said, "There will not be a next time, so help me God. I will leave, and you will never see me again. Do we understand each other, Father?" Bernard was inches from his father's face.

"I understand. My apologies. It won't happen again," Ron said. "Now, please sit down and have a drink with your father."

Bernard was still looking at him. His eyes were slanted he was so mad at him. He was trying to calm himself before he hit his father. He backed away, straightened up, and walked to the bar, and poured himself a straight shot of whiskey in a glass, and he downed it. He could feel it burn all the way down. He inhaled deeply then let it out. Finally, Bernard's anger diminished a little. He turned to face his father and spoke as calmly as he could manage at the time.

"You cannot run my life. One day I will find a wife without you trying to set me up or trying to move things along. When I am ready, I and I alone will decide whom I marry. Do you understand?" he said, looking straight at his father. Ron stood up, went to his son, and he offered him his hand.

"I understand. I'm really sorry."

Bernard shook his father's hand reluctantly, and then his father gave him a hug.

"Just so you know, I am going to go see her again, so do not even think of stopping me," Bernard told his father. Ron just nodded.

Ron invited Bernard to stay for dinner. He accepted because he really did not want to be alone tonight. At least his mind would be occupied with things other than his memories of Gabrielle.

***

Tears had fallen most of the night as Gabrielle had finished packing her suitcase the night before. Her eyes were red and swollen from crying. Her heart broke every time she looked back at her sojourn with Bernard. She had not slept much and had kept tossing and turning. Her mind was restless. All she could think about was the past week she had spent with Bernard. By morning, she was resolved that she had to return home because she had lots of work. She would see him again. She would not forget him. She had said her good-byes for now. A car picked her up to take her to Logan Airport. She felt numb the entire way there. She went through the motions, but her mind was elsewhere. She was now sitting on an Air Canada flight home. When the plane took off, one last tear fell from her eyes. She wiped it away and she tried not to look back. A few hours later, she landed home. She picked up her luggage, and she walked slowly to the parking lot where her car was parked. She decided she still had lots of work to do at the inn to keep her busy.

It was a short drive back to her town, and she was happy to be home. It was still spring, but summer would be here soon and she had many last minute things to do to make sure everything was in place and ready for the tourist season.

The next few weeks passed like lightning. It was like a blur. There were renovations to be done, things to pick up, reservations to make, and she was back on a regular schedule. She was working fifteen hours or more a day. She had tried to call Bernard numerous times, but he was always in a meeting or not available when she called. Only a few times during the whole summer had they been able to talk. *Maybe he does not care about me as much as I had thought. Maybe the relationship was finished,* she thought to herself.

The sun was bright outside, and the town was bustling with newcomers, yet there was not a day that she did not think of those days in Newport with Bernard. She could still hear him laugh.

Her heart would always be his and the hurt for him would diminish in time. The last conversation was still fresh in her mind.

"Gabrielle, I am so sorry, but I cannot come to visit because I am having major problems with the contracts, and I have to be here for the negotiations."

"I know how it is. I barely have any free time either. I am swamped with work, too." Gabrielle had tried to understand, but she was having doubts. *Maybe he did not want to come and see her.*

"I really miss you," he had said.

How she missed him too. She had only heard from him a few times. She wondered often if he had moved on and forgotten about her. She would never know, but her door would always be open to him. Sophie had called many times to see how she was doing, and it was good to hear her news. She was always busy, running around from one thing to another. Sophie had invited her to come visit her for a few days in the fall, but Gabrielle did not have the heart to return to Boston yet. There were too many memories, and she knew she would not be able to surmount them being so close to Bernard. She told Sophie she could not give her an answer until business slowed down and she had more time to think. Gabrielle was really kind of telling the truth. She was extremely busy.

The summer days were hot, and she occupied herself with chores of the inn. One day during the third week of July, she was in the backyard of the inn, weeding her herb garden. The temperatures had been hotter than usual. She was tired, but the cook needed fresh mint and basil for lunch dishes, so she had offered to go pick some. All of sudden she felt dizzy. Her head started spinning, she could not get her footing, and she fell to her knees. She closed her eyes and slowly tried to concentrate on getting up. She was so hot, and then a cold sweat fell upon her. She felt weak, and then everything went black. She fainted.

"Mademoiselle Gabrielle!" the pastry chef was screaming frantically, coming toward where Gabrielle was laying on the ground. She had seen her collapse.

"Are you all right? Wake up, mademoiselle. Help! Someone help!" she yelled. Suzanne was her friend and in her mid-fifties. She had been working at the inn for the last five years. She loved her employer, and over the years she had become her confidante. She would do anything for her. Gabrielle was the closest she would ever come to having a daughter.

A tall, lean man came running out the door of the kitchen. It was Suzanne's husband, Norman, who was a chef at the inn. He knelt down beside her, and he gently touched her face with a cold cloth. He bent down and placed it on her forehead.

"Mademoiselle Gabrielle, please wake up."

Gabrielle started to stir. Slowly she opened her eyes. She looked confused.

"What happened?" she asked in a frail voice.

"You must have fainted," Suzanne replied.

Norman and Suzanne helped her up. They put their arms around her and they guided her inside through the back entrance. They sat her down on the first chair they saw near the kitchen door. Gabrielle was pale, and she was trying to figure out what had just happened.

"I'll get her a glass of water. You stay with her," Suzanne told her husband. He knelt next to her. He was fanning her with a magazine he had found next to the chair. Suzanne returned quickly with cold water and another wet towel that she placed on Gabrielle's neck.

"Have a little bit of water. It will make you feel better," Suzanne said and helped her take a few sips. "How do you feel? You scared me half to death," she said with concern as she looked at her.

"It must have been the heat. I was picking herbs. I got dizzy, and then I don't remember," Gabrielle said slowly. She kept rubbing her hands on her face. She was feeling cooler now that she was inside the kitchen. "I feel much better now that I'm out of the sun."

"Can you stand?" Suzanne asked. She took her under the arms to help her stand. "You should lay down for a bit. Did you eat today?" she asked.

"I feel much better, thank you. Can you manage without me for a bit? I'm going to go upstairs and rest for an hour," Gabrielle said, feeling her strength return.

"Come on, I'll help you to your room, and later I'll bring you some soup," Suzanne said, still concerned.

Gabrielle agreed to rest for a while. They went up the stairs slowly, holding onto the bannister. She was trying to shake it off, but she was still feeling weak in the legs, and her head still felt like it weighed ten pounds too much.

She lay down on top of her bed, still feeling a little light-headed. Suzanne covered her with a light blanket and left her alone. This heat wave was great for the business, but not so great for her. It really was exhausting for her, and she was working longer hours every day. She closed her eyes and tried to relax, but all she could think about was all the work she had to do. This was her busy season, and she could not afford to be sick now. A half hour later, she heard a light knock at the door. She did not bother getting up, as she knew it was Suzanne.

"Come in. The door's open."

"You look a lot better. You are still pale, but some color has returned to your cheeks," Suzanne said.

"I am really baffled. I do not know what overcame me," Gabrielle said.

Suzanne was holding a tray with a bowl of chicken soup and some crackers with an ice tea. She approached the bed and Gabrielle sat up and leaned her back against the headboard. Suzanne placed the tray down on her lap.

"Thank you again. All this isn't necessary. I'll be just fine, and I feel much better now." Gabrielle felt a little stupid with all the attention Suzanne was giving her, but she had decided to please her. She just had to hydrate more from now on in this heat.

"Hush! Now eat and rest for a few hours, then you may come down to work, not before. Did you hear me? Not before," Suzanne said.

"I suppose arguing wouldn't do any good, now would it?" Gabrielle replied with a smile.

"No, it wouldn't, and you better call your doctor to get checked out tomorrow. I like my job and don't plan on having a new boss, mademoiselle Gabrielle."

Suzanne was smiling at her, but Gabrielle could see the worry on her face, so she agreed. Suzanne made her a promise that if something important came up, she would come to get her. Suzanne stopped at the door and took one last look at her, then closed the door. She left her alone so she could rest. Gabrielle felt fine, but to appease Suzanne's fears, she ate the soup and lay down for an hour or so.

***

Three months had gone by, and Bernard had tried everything to keep busy and forget Gabrielle. He had tried to go see her, but it was too hard to schedule time. Maybe it was best that he move on, but he could not concentrate on much. She was always on his mind. Not even his work had helped him. All he could think of was Gabrielle and how he really missed her. He had dated other women during these summer months, but he kept coming back to the memories he had of Gabrielle. He could not get her out of his mind and he did not understand why. He had never felt pain like he had the day she had left to go back to her hometown, except when his Danielle had passed away.

His father had been very kind to him. Ron had been keeping his distance and he had not fixed him up with any more women to marry, and that was a relief. *How could a woman he had only known for such a short time have had such a profound effect on him?* He was confused. He could not take it any longer. He decided he was going to go on a well-deserved vacation. A few weeks away from everything would clear his head or maybe give him answers. *Where could he go?* He sat at his desk in his office, looking out the window with the same relentless question: *Where could he go? He wanted to go someplace where he could spend time relaxing without any interruption from work or his father.* He wanted Gabrielle. He had thought about doing this for the last month or so, but he really had too much work to just leave. *He could drive to northern Canada where he was told life was simple and the folks were inviting ... where Gabrielle was.* He might be crazy, but he had to see her again. He got up from his desk and told his secretary to cancel his entire calendar until further notice. She did not object, but she thought he was losing his mind. She had watched him pace the floor and daydream for hours, sitting at his desk, getting no work done. *Who was she to question it?* She would do as he asked. Maybe some time away would get him back on track.

He picked up his phone. He played with it for a moment, and then he decided to call his father to tell him.

"Good afternoon, Father."

"Bernard, I was just going to call you to see if you wanted to come for dinner tonight," Ron said.

"No, thank you. I was just calling to let you know I was going on a well-deserved vacation for a few weeks."

"That's unexpected. So where are you going? Europe?" Ron asked curiously.

"I decided to take a drive up the coast. I need some relaxation, maybe a little white water rafting in Maine. I am not sure yet. I'm going to play it by ear, just drive until I feel like stopping somewhere." Bernard did not dare tell him his real destination.

"That's sounds great. Would you like company? We could have a father-and-son vacation." Ron said.

"Father, it's not I don't want to spend time with you, but I need some time alone to clear my head. I'm tired of all the running around with work and all." He knew his father would not like his answer.

"Well, then give me a call to let me know how you are doing in a few days or so, okay?" Ron answered.

"I will. Take care. Bye," said Bernard. He knew his father was hurt, but he had questions that needed answers about his feelings for Gabrielle, and he had to do this alone.

Ron had a feeling Bernard was lying to him. He had a weird feeling in his gut. Ron was afraid he was going after that woman from Canada. He had seen sadness in Bernard's eyes since she had left and knew he was still hurting from her leaving. He could not concentrate on work and he was distant. How he despised her for causing him pain. She would be his son's downfall and would ruin his whole future. Ron would not let that happen. She was not the right woman for his son in his eyes. He needed to know exactly where Bernard was going on vacation. He hoped he was wrong, but he still made the decision to call Tom, and, within minutes, Tom was standing in front of him.

"Morning, sir," Tom said cheerfully, but Ron had no time for small talk.

"I have a new job for you. I want you to go to Bernard's house and bring me back his passport if you can. Now, do not wait. If you can't get it, follow him."

"Yes, sir," Tom replied.

"I am pretty sure he's planning on going to see that woman in Canada. I am trying to delay his trip as long as I can. She is becoming a real pain," Ron thought aloud.

"Yes, sir."

"This time don't get caught. It was a mess last time. Here, take this. You might need money," said Ron, handing him a briefcase.

Tom took it and opened it. He looked inside, never flinched, just nodded. It was full of cash—fifty thousand dollars. Tom closed it and left. This time he changed his truck to an old, gold Toyota Corolla car. He figured it would be less obvious and less detectable. Many people had this very popular car. He picked up his usual gear, packed a duffle bag, and brought a disguise with him just in case he needed it. He arrived at Bernard's place, but he was already too late. Bernard was home and he could not enter the house while he was there. Tom decided he would follow Bernard on his own and report to Mr. Rian later. He would not fail this time. If he had to, he would get rid of this girl. *She was a problem to the Rian family.*

***

Bernard was excited at the prospect of seeing Gabrielle again. *He thought he might surprise her.* He packed his bags; it did not take him much time. He decided he would call her when he was on his way. *It was now or never.* He packed up the Range Rover and he started driving up 95 North toward the Canadian border. It was going to be a long drive. He had figured about fifteen hours, but it would give him time to think of what he wanted to tell Gabrielle. He was not sure how he was going to be received. *Maybe she had moved on.* They had not been in contact that much due to their busy schedules. He hoped that was not the case, otherwise it was going to crush him to pieces. Maybe it was only an affair, sex, a fling people have when they go on vacation. He should have called her more after she left, maybe then he could have communicated with her. He could have found the answers to the questions that haunted him, but now he was uncertain about what he was going to tell her. He did not want to give her empty promises over the phone. He knew which town she lived in. He would find her. He had to know how she felt about him and if she still had feelings for him or not.

He drove for hours before he finally stopped to refuel and to get a bite to eat. There were not too many places to stop unless you got off the highway. He drove until he was almost to the border. It was nightfall, and he had to find a place to sleep. He was tired and his legs were cramping. He needed to shower and sleep would help him think straight for the final leg of the journey.

It had been a very long day. Right off the highway, before the last exit to the border, he found a small motel that still had a few rooms available. It was not what he was used to, but it was clean. There was no room service, nothing luxurious about the place, but all Bernard needed was a hot shower and a bed to sleep on. The amenities he could do without. He paid the clerk and booked into a room for one night only. When he received his key, he walked down the hall to find his room. He swiped his card key and entered the room. The first thing he did was call Gabrielle to let her know he was coming to see her, but she did not answer and his call went to voicemail. He just told her he missed her and was thinking of her. He went to take a hot shower. He was trying to take the fatigue of his body away, but it did not work. He was not hungry, so he lay in bed, exhausted from driving for so long. He closed his eyes and told himself tomorrow was another day; he would fight his demons later. In no time, he was sound asleep.

CHAPTER 10

Tom woke up early. The sun was not up yet. He took a quick shower, repacked his gear, and he left the motel. He wanted to cross the border before Bernard woke up. He would wait for him on the other side.

He only had a small problem: his gun. He would have to leave it behind. He did not want to take the chance of a customs officer finding it. He did not have an international permit to carry a firearm across the border into another country. He figured he could always buy another one later if he needed too, so he hid it in the tall grass by the roadside. It did not have a serial number on it anymore. He had erased it so it was untraceable. He taped all the $50,000 on his body, just in case they searched his car. He knew you were only allowed to take $10,000 across the border in currency, but if they did not look, he was fine. He drove up to the border crossing. He waited in line patiently. Tom looked around. It was quiet, only one car in front of him. A camera took his picture when he advanced to the customs and immigration booth.

"Good morning," Tom said as he passed his passport, and swiped it in a machine. The officer looked at him.

"Where are you from?" the guard asked.

"Boston, Massachusetts," Tom answered.

"Where are you going?" he asked.

"I am going fishing in northern New Brunswick."

The guard eyed him then asked again, "What town?"

"Lameque," Tom said, smiling, but the guard just looked at him.

"How long are you staying?"

"One week."

"Do you have anything staying in Canada, like gifts?"

"No."

"Do you have mace or any other weapons?"

"No."

Tom was trying to stay calm, but then the guard looked in his back seat and said, "Open the trunk?"

Tom looked in his rear mirror. The guard came back to the car window looked at his passport picture and said, "Any alcohol or cigarettes?"

"No," Tom replied.

The guard gave him back his passport and said, "Have a nice day." Tom drove away, relieved.

He continued driving for about ten miles down the road, and then he pulled over on the side of the road. He pretended he was having car trouble. This way he could watch when Bernard passed by. The area only had one highway that went north to New Brunswick, so Tom knew Bernard had to go by him at one point or another. Tom decided he would get rid of his car if he thought Bernard recognized him when he got to his destination. He could always buy another car. He already thought he knew where Bernard was headed, but had to be positive, so if he lost him, he could easily find him. Tom knew he was going to the small town where Gabrielle lived.

About an hour later Tom spotted Bernard's Range Rover going past him, and he started his car to follow him. Tom decided it was time to update his boss.

"It's me. You were right about his destination. It looks like he's going straight to see her. What would you like me to do, sir?"

"Damn that boy! I was hoping he would not go find her," Ron said. "First watch them for a while to see if she accepts him. Then if she doesn't back down, give her a warning not to fuck with the Rian family, but not in those specific words. Understood?" Ron said.

"Yes, sir. I will let you know what happens. I know how to deal with gold diggers."

Ron just hung up. He did not even bother to say goodbye.

Tom looked at his phone in his hand. He knew his boss was extremely angry by the tone of his voice. *Well now*, Tom thought, *I have a real mission. It will be intriguing and exciting to see how it will play out between the Rians.* He liked the idea that there might be violence involving him in the future.

***

Gabrielle felt much better after she had eaten her soup and she had laid down for an hour. She had only meant to close her eyes for a few minutes, but she must have dozed off for a while. She woke up, checked her watch and saw it was already after lunch. She had slept right through the lunch rush. She got up slowly. She felt fine. Bernard had called and she had missed his call. She would try to get a hold of him later. She changed her clothes, washed her face, and headed downstairs to see how things were going at the reservation desk, and then on to the restaurant.

She made her rounds to see if they needed any help elsewhere, but to her surprise, the staff had everything under control. She was proud of them. Suzanne had made sure all sections of the inn were running smooth, and under no circumstance was anyone to disturb Gabrielle. Gabrielle went to find Suzanne. She was in the kitchen making coconut cream pies for the supper rush.

Gabrielle approached her and gave her a hug from behind, "Thank you so much for your concern. You're a true friend."

Suzanne turned around and faced her and smiled at her boss and said, "You are most welcome. How are you feeling?"

"I'm just fine. It was just the heat. Maybe I've been working too much. I'll be all right." Gabrielle was a little embarrassed about all the fuss. She blushed. She just had to hydrate more, that was all.

"So, how are the supper preparations going?" Gabrielle inquired while watching her roll out pie crust on a table.

"The only thing we need is more fruits, especially berries. We might run out."

"I'll take care of that. I'll run down to the supermarket and I'll get some more. Do we need anything else?" Gabrielle asked her while walking towards the back door of the kitchen to where her car was parked.

"No, that's it," Suzanne answered, trying to concentrate on her baking.

"I won't be long. See you in a bit. Call me on my cell if there is anything else. See you soon," Gabrielle said and grabbed her car keys as she went out the door.

The market was not far from the inn, just down the street. She drove slowly down the main street to the end and then turned right to a huge parking lot where the supermarket was located. For some unknown reason, after turning into the parking lot, she looked in her rearview mirror and she got a glimpse of a Range Rover going by on the street. She could not see the driver. She thought of Bernard, but she could only wish it was him. It was futile. The truck had gone by too fast for her to get a look at the driver. She was crazy to think it could be him. It was the same color truck as Bernard's, and there were not many luxury cars in the small town. *Probably some tourist visiting the area owned it.* It brought back memories of her time with him. How she missed him and just wanted to see his seductive face one more time, just once.

Stop it, Gabrielle, she told herself. *You'll lose your mind. Stop thinking so much.*

Gabrielle parked her car in front of the store. She walked out and entered the Sobeys's supermarket. She grabbed a basket on the way in and she went to the produce section of the store. She spotted the berries right away and took a few boxes each of strawberries, blackberries, and raspberries. She placed them in her basket and headed for the cashier at the register. There were not many people in the store, so she paid and was quickly out the door.

Gabrielle returned to her car and set out to take the fruit to Suzanne. She was on her way back to the inn, but when she got to the end of the parking lot, she saw that she was directly facing an ice cream parlor across the street. It was a tiny take-out store, but the ice cream was homemade, the best in town. They had all kinds of flavors all freshly made by hand. The wooden picnic tables painted in blue in the front of the store were always full with customers. They were all enjoying ice cream.

Yum! she thought. A chocolate or strawberry ice cream in a waffle cone sounded good right now. It had been a hot day and it would cool her down. She drove her car across the street and parked it. Gabrielle went to the window to order what would satisfy her craving: a strawberry ice cream cone. She did not give in often, but today was one of those days. She decided since it was such a nice day, she would sit outside and she would watch the people go by while she ate her ice cream. She rarely took the time to enjoy some of the summer's pleasure, but today the berries would have to wait. She was taking a well-deserved break from all the rushing around. Gabrielle felt guilty because she had eaten that whole ice cream cone, but it had been so good. That was going to be her one and only cone the entire summer, she decided. Now she really had to get back before they sent a rescue party for her.

***

Bernard had woken up refreshed from a good night's sleep. He had stopped at a local restaurant across the street from the motel. There was a small truck stop, so he went to eat a good, hearty breakfast that should last him until he got to the town where he would find his Gabrielle. His GPS had indicated that he had three hours and fifteen minutes before he could see her. Bernard was counting the minutes until he could be reunited with her. He had already passed the border without any problems and he had already been driving for an hour. He was getting anxious. His heart beat faster when he thought of finding his Gabrielle again.

The nearer he got to her, the more he wanted her. He thought about how much he admired her determination, how she made him laugh, and that she did not only care about his money. He had always thought that Danielle would be the only woman for him, but today he knew he was making the right decision for himself. *But would it be the right one for her?* He really hoped Gabrielle would accept him. He was trying to imagine her reaction, but he could not. All he desired was for her to embrace him and welcome him. He hoped that she would be happy to see him and not push him away because he had waited so long to come find her. He had too many unanswered questions. He was nervous.

Bernard arrived in town. He knew her inn was on Main Street, but did not know exactly where. He thought it really should not be that difficult to find it. He drove slowly until he saw it. He knew he had found it because Gabrielle had described it to him. A century old mansion had been reno-vated with fresh white paint, green shutters, and wine canvas awnings over the windows. A large porch had rocking chairs on both sides of the carved wood doors, and there was a stained glass window that wrapped around the door. It had multiple stained windows displayed in the front of the inn. Large windows were on all sides of the building. It was a splendid sight and he automatically knew it had to be hers. A huge sign with the letter G in neon lights illuminated the mansion. It had many flowerbeds in the front entrance that made the inn look homey, with a long circular driveway in the front. He turned in and he drove up to the front entrance. It was exactly as she had described it to him. It was a beautiful sight to see. He just stood there admiring her work. He was at the right place. He had found her.

His heart was beating hard against his chest. He was nervous. He should have called her at least to let her know he was coming. He felt like a teenager on his first date. He hoped she would be as happy to see him as he was to see her. He stepped out of his Rover slowly and took the long walk up to those big doors. He carefully put his hand on the knob of the door and turned it. *It was now or never.* His life would change the instant he went inside; it would never be the same again. Good or bad, he forged forward.

The beauty of the interior of the inn took Bernard aback. There was a wood-carved spiral staircase to his right. Light came through the stained glass, beaming down from the outside into the dining area. The high ceiling was adorned with two antique chandeliers that hung so gracefully in the middle of the room. There was a curved archway leading to what appeared to be a small restaurant with only eight tables, all dressed in lace with big colorful armchairs. The restaurant faced the main street so you could see the flowers blooming in the front and the flow of tourists driving by. The floors were made of a dark cedar wood that matched the staircase and the woodwork of the walls. A great stone fireplace was the focal point of the dining room. It was breathtaking and extremely charming.

Bernard thought, *What a very romantic and quaint place to have dinner!* It definitely was Gabrielle's taste. It exuded her style. He was standing in the middle of the entryway, just taking everything in. He could see why Gabrielle loved it here. He smiled because he could smell the lavender in the room. It was definitely her inn.

"Can I help you, sir?"

Bernard flinched when she spoke. He had not seen anyone when he came in. He was in his own world. He turned around to face a young blonde girl named Rita. She was sitting at a front desk on the other side of the room. Bernard approached the desk slowly and, for once in his life, he was speechless.

"Do you have or need a reservation?" she asked.

"No, no. I'm looking for a friend of mine. Her name is Gabrielle Leger. Is she here?" he asked. His voice was cracking, and he tried to give her a small smile.

"Let me check if she's here. I'll be right back."

She left the desk and she went through a door into the back area. Bernard started to pace. His palms were sweating, and his heart started to beat a bit faster. He waited patiently for what seemed an eternity, though in reality it was only a few minutes. He watched her come back to her desk. She gave him a flirty smile.

"I'm sorry, but Gabrielle is not here at the moment. If you want to leave your name or a message, I'll be glad to give it to her."

"No, thank you. I'll come back. When do you expect her?" He was taken aback by the smile she gave him.

"She should be back soon. She had an errand to run. Do you want to leave your name?" she asked again.

"No, thank you. I'll come back," he repeated. He did not know what else to say.

He turned around and strolled out the door. He was disappointed that he had missed her, but he should have called her earlier. He was so anxious to get here that he had totally forgotten. He would have to return a little later. He started his Rover and drove off. Now he had to find a place to stay. It was a very small town, so there were not many motels. Finally, he came upon what looked like a half decent one, so he decided to investigate. He pulled into the parking lot and he entered the reception area. He booked a room for the rest of the week. He wished he could stay with Gabrielle, but he did not know where he stood with her. He was tired from all the driving, so he decided to lie down. Maybe he could take a nap for half an hour before he returned to see her.

He closed his eyes, and good thoughts came to him about the last time he had been with Gabrielle her gentle touch and her laugh. He missed her giggling most of all. He needed to clear his mind and take a nap. He would feel rejuvenated when he got up. He had traveled this far, he could wait a few hours. He might not be so uptight if he rested.

***

Tom watched from afar. He saw Bernard leave, and Tom already knew Gabrielle was not at the inn. He had arrived at the inn before Bernard had even driven through town. He had parked his car down the street from the entrance of the estate. He had followed her briefly to the supermarket and he knew she would return soon. He pulled a hat down over his eyes and he put on a pair of sunglasses. He wrote a note, and then he put it in an envelope. He was going to deliver his warning. He entered the inn and saw the young girl at the front desk. He pretended he was looking at the menu until he saw the young lady go to the back area. He hurried and placed the envelope on the desk. It was addressed to Gabrielle. He then walked out as fast as he could without anyone seeing him.

Rita came back to the front desk after a few minutes, saw the envelope, picked it up, looked at it, and then put it in the drawer. When she looked up, the man had disappeared as fast as he had entered the place. Tom had positioned himself not too far from the inn where he could watch the comings and goings from his car.

***

Gabrielle returned to her inn and she went directly to the kitchen to deliver the berries to Suzanne that she was carrying. She then went out to the front desk to check on Rita.

"Hi Rita. How are you doing? Do you need any help?" Gabrielle inquired.

"Everything is in order, but let me tell you, this mysterious, tall, handsome man came by looking for you when you were gone, and wow!"

She made growling sound, and it made Gabrielle laugh at her.

"Oh! Ya? Who was he?"

"He wouldn't leave his name, but he said he'd return later," said Rita and shrugged. She put her hands up, "But he was fine, that I can tell you."

"Okay. Let me know when he returns."

Gabrielle was smiling and in a good mood. She wondered who he could be. She started to walk away, but Rita called after her.

"Another thing Gabrielle, I found this envelope on the desk. Your name is written on it," Rita reached into the drawer, and she handed her the envelope. Gabrielle took it from her, and then continued walking towards the kitchen. She opened it, and then suddenly she abruptly stopped. Gabrielle was staring at the note. She turned it over to see if anything else was written on the letter. Nothing.

She began to shake. Her eyes were fixed on the note. She was shocked, her heart was racing, and she was mystified by the piece of paper. She looked inside the envelope again. Nothing. There was no return address. She walked to the window and searched the front yard outside, her eyes darting from right to left. She turned and went to the dining area and looked at everyone. She retraced her steps to the front desk and asked Rita.

"Where did you get this envelope?" asked Gabrielle. Her hands were still trembling. She could not control them.

"I don't know. I turned around, and there it was. I did not see anyone."

Gabrielle walked away quietly. All she could think was who could have been that cruel to send such a message? It must be a bad joke. All the note had said was, "Beware, stay away from Bernard. Be very careful. You have been warned." It was written in bold letters. She put the letter in her pocket, and she pulled herself together. She had work to do and she went to help her staff. She could not think of anyone that would do this to her. *Stay away from Bernard?* How could she stay away from him when she had not seen him since the spring? Maybe he had a new girlfriend and she was warning her? She stopped worrying about it. She dismissed it as a bad prank. She had no time for this. There was work to be done.

***

Bernard woke up from his nap, and he had lots of energy. He felt regenerated. He took a shower and put on a pair of True Religion Jeans that fit his butt to perfection, a light-blue linen shirt, and a pair of loafers. He slicked his black hair back, and then he looked in the mirror. He sighed and thought to himself, *It's now or never.* He locked the door of the room and he retrieved his Range Rover. He drove down the Main Street. He was going back to the inn. He was more confident that Gabrielle would be pleased to see him.

It was dark outside. The night had fallen, but the stars were out. They illuminated his path. He walked up to the front doors one more time. This time he did not hesitate to open the door. He walked in like he had a vocation. *He would succeed, and she would be there !* He approached the young lady at the desk.

"Good evening. May I please speak to Gabrielle Leger?"

She looked at him and smiled. "I'll be right back. Please have a seat." She disappeared through a back door one last time. Bernard did not want to sit, so he just stood there looking out the window. It did not take long for Rita to find Gabrielle. She was helping Suzanne in the kitchen area. Rita was walking so fast she almost ran her over.

"Gabrielle! That handsome man is back—he wants to talk to you."

"Who is he?" Gabrielle asked nonchalantly.

"I don't know, but you better come see this man. He is hot."

Gabrielle took her apron off, kind of fixed her hair, and straightened her clothes.

"How do I look?" Gabrielle asked.

"You look great. Now come on," Rita said, pushing her toward the door. Gabrielle opened the door and casually walked out.

"Good evening. Can I help you?"

Bernard heard her. He turned toward Gabrielle and her mouth opened. The only thing that came out of her mouth was "Oh! Mon Dieu ... Bernard!"

He approached her, put his arms around her, and kissed her tenderly on the lips.

"What are you doing here?" she asked, looking at him with wide eyes.

She grabbed his hand and started pulling him toward the other side of the room. He could feel all eyes looking at him with her. He could see she was blushing.

"I was driving in the neighborhood, and I decided to come to see you. No, really ... I missed you. I called you earlier to tell you I was coming, but you did not answer," he whispered in her ear.

She gave him the most brilliant smile. She took his hand, and she guided him to a private room the other end of the inn.

Gabrielle softly touched his chest. She looked into his blue eyes, and then she put her arms around his neck.

"I guess you're happy to see me," he said.

"I'm not only happy—what a great surprise! You should have told me you were coming. I would have dressed up," she said, poking him and laughing at the same time.

"I tried to tell you. You look beautiful as always. Can you get away so we can talk ... alone?" He was dying to take her right there on the floor. He was caressing her back softly.

"Talk? Sure. Don't you move from here, okay"? Gabrielle got on her tippy toes and quickly kissed him again. "I'll be right back. Don't go anywhere."

"I'll be right here waiting."

***

Bernard and Gabrielle headed to his motel room. Her hand was on his thigh, and she kept stroking it. As they drove down the road, she kept looking at him and smiling.

"I can't believe you're here. I'm really happy you came. I thought a lot about you these past few months," she said.

"That's why I had to come and find you. I don't know why, but I couldn't get you out of my mind," he said to her.

"Well, you made the right decision. How was work? Did you close on the deal you were working on?" she asked.

"Yes, finally, but let's talk about you. How is the inn doing?" Bernard inquired.

"It's my busy time."

"I hope you can take some time off and spend it with me," he said.

"Absolutely. I will find a way. Do not worry."

They arrived at his motel, got out, and walked hand in hand to his room. He took his key out and opened the door. The instant the door closed, he pulled her against him so fast she was astonished, and a small cry came out of her mouth. He started kissing her fiercely. An hour later, after making love, they were just lying in bed talking.

***

Tom had succeeded in frightening Gabrielle. That he knew. From afar, he had observed the police cruiser pull up and the police survey the perimeter of the estate. He knew they would not find any trace of him because he had been extremely careful. Tom had been disappointed when Gabrielle had called Bernard. He had seen him arrive at the inn. He would have to call Mr. Rian soon. He needed to give him an update, and he knew his boss was not going to be happy about the situation. Tom also knew that Bernard had spent the night with her, because his truck was still parked in the parking lot the next morning.

He dialed the familiar number and waited. Ron answered after the second ring.

"Yes."

"I've given my warnings. I even tried to scare her, but nothing happened. She is still with him. What would you want me to do next, sir?" Tom waited in anticipation. The other end of the line was quiet.

"Do what you have to do, just take care of the problem. Scare the hell out of her. Don't call me until it's done," Ron said.

"Very well, sir."

Tom shut the phone off and he started formulating a plan to get rid of this girl. This was going to be an exciting scheme. He lived for this adrenaline rush. He was right in his environment. Tom was still hiding near the inn when Bernard arrived. He watched him go inside. He waited patiently and half an hour later he spotted Gabrielle and Bernard coming out of the front door. They both were getting into his Range Rover and then they took off. Tom had a feeling he knew where they were going, but he followed them anyway, just to confirm his suspicion. He let them take the lead, and then he stayed back so he would not be spotted.

He was right. They went to Bernard's motel room. Where else would they be going? He continued straight past them, and then turned around. It gave him some free time because he knew they would be busy for at least a few hours. He had some business in the nearest city, so he headed that way. He was going to meet a friend of a friend named Michel. He sold whatever you needed to buy but could not be bought in a regular store. Michel was a hoodlum from one of the major gangs from the east coast area, and he could find you any firearm you desired for the right price. It would cost him dearly, but what was money worth if you could not spend it?

Tom figured he should be back before midnight if there were no complications. He needed to have a clear head to be able to execute his plan, but first he needed weapons. It did not bother him that the stuff was illegal in his line of business. Many things were. Gabrielle had not listened to the warning, now he would have to talk to her directly and make her pay for going back to Bernard. She was not good for the Rian family reputation, and he owed Mr. Rian a lot. He had given him a home and had allowed him to work for him when he did not have a job. Ten long years he had been with him and he had never failed to protect them from anyone. He would take care of the problem tonight. It was the least he could do. Ron probably would not want this to happen, but that was why he hired him—to do things like this. Ron did not need to know all the details. He never asked, even after what happened to Danielle, so why should he ask now? Ron would thank him later. He was taking control of the situation. She had better listen this time, because he would not be so nice the next time around. A smile crossed his face and he went on to his destination.

***

"Why did you come back?" she asked. It had just come out of her mouth, but she really was just thinking about it. She had not meant to be so blunt, but now it was too late.

"Well, it's like this. Since you left, I couldn't get you out of my mind, so I decided to come find you to see if you felt the same as me."

"Bernard, I don't know how to tell you this, but I felt that way when I left Boston. I really didn't think you wanted a serious relationship, so I didn't mention anything."

"Boy! I have to admit, I am glad I decided I needed a vacation. I missed hearing you laugh and the way you poke me. I would have never known you felt this way about me," he teased her and then laughed.

She poked him playfully. Gabrielle was glowing with happiness. He drew her nearer and kissed her lightly on the lips

"I'm glad we got all that figured out. Now how are we going to do this? You live in Boston, and I live here," Gabrielle said. They lived hundreds of miles apart. It was an impossible relationship.

"We have to do a better job than we have been doing. Let us worry about it later. We will have time. We will make it work. Do not panic yet," he smiled at her and continued, "I'm starving. Do you know of anyone that delivers?"

She laughed aloud because she was almost nauseous from hunger. They settled on pizza from a local pizzeria that delivered. This way they did not have to leave the comfort of their bed. They were catching up on the last few months that they had not been together. It was as if they had never left each other. They were so thankful they had found each other again.

The pizza delivery guy arrived half an hour later with a large cheese and pepperoni pizza and two sodas. Bernard left the warmth of her body and threw on a pair of shorts. He answered the door while Gabrielle hid under the sheets. He quickly paid the guy and placed the food on the foot of the bed. He cleared his throat, and she reappeared from under the sheets.

"Don't worry, he didn't see you. Your reputation is still intact," Bernard said, laughing at her. Gabrielle picked up a slice of pizza and took the pepperoni off. She fed them to Bernard one at a time. She would place the pepperoni near his mouth, and he would snatch them from her hand with his lips. Bernard shared his crust with her.

"How long do you plan to stay?" She did not want to ask or hear the answer, but she had to know.

He stopped eating, and he put his slice of pizza down. His expression changed, and he became very serious. He took her hand in his and started caressing it as his eyes looked directly into hers. "I really don't know the answer to that question."

Gabrielle turned her head and her heart dropped to the bottom of her gut. She looked away from him.

He took her slice of pizza and laid it down. He took his hand and gently turned her face toward him, "I don't ever want to leave if you'll have me."

She was speechless. Large tears pooled her eyes, and she could not stop them.

"I thought you had just come for a few days and ..." She was trying to speak, but her voice was failing her.

"All these months away from you made me realize something," he said, hesitant to continue. He had stopped talking briefly, then continued, "I love you—I don't want us apart. We will find a way, so please stop these tears. I hate seeing you cry."

Her tears were still falling like a river, but they were tears of joy. She could not believe it. She jumped up and she wrapped her arms around him. She held him tight and into his ear she whispered the words that she had never told a man before, not even her ex-boyfriend. Bernard was her first—and hopefully her only—love.

"I love you, too. More than you'll ever know."

Bernard let out a sigh of relief, and he kissed her tears away. Gabrielle was so happy. There were no words to describe the sense of relief she felt knowing that he loved her.

"Why are you crying? Please stop. I cannot stand to see you cry."

She lifted her head to see his face. "I'm not sad at all. I'm elated and so fortunate that you feel the same."

"You have a funny way of showing it," he replied with a smile, and wiped her tears away with the back of his hand, then kissed her cheeks.

They both laughed together. They finished eating and she told him she had to return to the inn. It was important that she be there. It was her business. She still had a lot of paperwork that needed to be done. Summer was her busiest time of the year. She told him she would arrange to take a few days off when she finished work tonight. She truly wanted to spend some time with him. Nighttime had arrived, and time had passed them by without notice.

"Stay with me. I really do not want to sleep alone in this motel room," he pleaded playfully.

"Sorry, I have to return. Now, do not make me feel guilty," she told him back.

"Okay, I understand. I'll drive you back," he answered. She looked at him, and he reminded her of a child who had just been punished. She thought, *He is so amusing!*

She promised she would see him the next morning for breakfast. He watched as she got dressed. He tried desperately to bring her back to bed by holding her clothes hostage, but she was determined to go back to work. He pleaded all the way out the door. She knew his game, so she ignored him. He drove her back home. He kept kissing her goodbye until she had to pull herself away from him. She stood at the entrance of her inn, and she waved goodbye to him as he rode off into the darkness of night. She could not wait to see him tomorrow morning for breakfast.

Gabrielle was fumbling with her pocketbook for her keys when, out of the corner of her eye, she saw a shadow move. She turned around to see who it was and froze. There was a man beside her. He was all dressed in black. She could not even see his face, as he had some kind of black paint on his face. All she could see was two white eyeballs staring at her. He came running towards her, and he forcefully pushed her to the side. She tripped and fell hard on the ground, but he did not hit her. He just stood over her. She was horrified and just stared up at him.

"I don't have any money," she said, terrified. He never answered her.

He did not even bother to take her purse. He just stood over her, his feet on both sides of her body. It was only seconds, but it seemed like a longer time to her. She was so petrified, not a word would come out of her mouth. She could not even scream. She had lost her voice. All she could do was look at him.

He pointed his index finger at her and said in a low, hoarse voice, "No more warnings. Stay away from Bernard Rian." He finally stepped aside, and then he took one last look at her. He smiled, and he departed into the dark of night without another word.

Gabrielle lay there on the ground helplessly. She was in shock. Her whole body was trembling. Finally, after a few minutes, she found the strength she needed and she told herself to move. It was so quiet. There was not soul around. She looked around the floor for her pocketbook. It was lying next to her. She must have dropped it when she fell backwards. She reached for it with a shaking hand then quickly found her keys. Gabrielle inserted her key in the lock and opened the door. She walked into the entryway of the inn and shut the door. She turned around and she bolted the door shut. She leaned against the door for what seemed like hours, though it was only a few minutes.

She took out her cell phone from her purse and managed to find the energy to call the police. She told them she had been assaulted. She explained what had happened, and the police said they were sending a car over right away. She waited patiently by the door until the policemen arrived. She heard a hard knock on the door, and she abruptly took a step back from it.

"Police, open the door!"

She was relieved that the cops were there. She opened the door a crack to make sure it was them. Two uniformed officers were standing at her door.

"Good evening, Miss Leger. What seems to be the problem? You said on the phone you were attacked by an intruder?" questioned the older policeman in a concerned voice.

"Yes. Please come in," she said, barely able to talk, she was so shaken up.

"What happened?" he asked her again.

"I was on the porch outside. He came from nowhere. He threw me down on the ground when I went to open the door." Gabrielle was still distressed, but now that they were there, she felt a little better.

"Are you hurt?" the other officer asked her, but she shook her head. She was just sore everywhere, maybe a little black and blue from falling down.

"What did he look like? Did he say anything to you?" The older officer continued to question her. He was writing her statement down in his notebook.

"It was really weird. He was dressed all in black like the guys in the army, and even his face had some kind of paint on. He pushed me down and he said something like, 'No more warnings—stay away from Bernard Rian.' Something to that effect. I do not know what that means, but he really scared me," she said in a weak voice.

"Do you know who Bernard Rian is?" the police asked.

"Yes, he is my boyfriend," Gabrielle answered.

"Do you know of anyone who would not want you together?"

"No," she answered.

The officers told her they were going to look around the perimeter of her place to see if the perpetrator was still around. They called it in, and they went looking around. The officers said they would return in a little while. One of them suggested that she call a friend to stay with her this evening and advised her to stay inside until they returned. The officers came back about fifteen minutes later, but they had not seen or found any trace of the man. They told her whoever it was probably was long gone by now.

All of a sudden, it occurred to her that those words were the same as those in the letter she had received earlier in the day. She found the letter in her pocket, and she handed it to the officers. They examined it, and then put it in a small plastic bag.

"Do you know who delivered this letter?"

She told them she did not know, that someone had come into the inn and had disappeared right after he had placed it at the front desk.

"Do you know of anyone who would want to hurt you, Miss Leger?"

"I don't have any enemies." She was getting very nervous and agitated. Her hands were trembling, and she had weak legs. She was holding on to the bannister of the stairs.

"There's not much more we can do tonight. We'll write up a report, and we'll pass this letter to the detective department to investigate, but right now we suggest you have someone stay with you this evening. We will try to patrol the area a little more, but that's all we can do at this moment." The officers assured her once more the intruder was probably gone.

Gabrielle thanked them, and they left her. She locked her door behind them and she called Bernard's cell phone. He answered it on the first ring.

"Do you miss me already?" he said.

"Bernard, I need you. Could you come stay with me tonight? I just got attacked by an intruder after you left tonight." Her voice was still shaking, "I'm really afraid to stay alone."

"Are you all right? Did you call the police?" he asked her. She started to cry quietly.

"Yes, the police just left." She could not talk anymore. She was sobbing.

"I'll be right over. Do not open the door for anyone. I'm coming now."

He knocked loudly on the front door when he arrived. She opened the door, and when she saw him standing there, she broke down again. She started sobbing like a small child. He wrapped his strong arms around her, and he took her to the nearest couch to sit down.

"It's all right. I'm here," Bernard said. "I'm so sorry, Gabrielle. Don't cry. I'm here. No one is going to hurt you now." He tried to comfort her.

Gabrielle slowly stopped crying after a few minutes. She was holding on to him tightly.

"What happened?" he asked and wiped her tears away from her cheeks.

"I was so scared. This man comes out of nowhere and he threw me to the ground when I was opening the door. He did not hit me. He just wanted to scare me, and then he said something like, 'Stay away. No more warnings.' I don't know what it means." She was trying to stop sobbing now that Bernard was there. She felt much better, safer. She decided to tell him everything.

"This afternoon I received a letter from man basically saying the same thing. I don't understand."

Bernard held her close against him and told her he was not leaving her alone again. A few minutes later, they got up from the couch and they went upstairs to go to her bedroom. Gabrielle led the way to her small suite. He made her take a hot shower and told her to wear her pajamas and come lay down under the covers next to him.

"Try to sleep. I'll be right here." He lay next to her while he held her tight.

She was feeling much better. She felt secure with Bernard by her side. He would keep her safe from all harm because he loved her. *What if she had been injured? God!*

After half an hour, she dozed off.

***

Gabrielle woke up early the next morning, and she did not feel well. She had an upset stomach, so she decided to stay in bed for an extra half-hour, but still she was not feeling any better. Bernard was still fast asleep next to her. She slowly got up, and she went to the bathroom. She washed her face with cold water, but it did not seem to help. She looked in the mirror, and all a sudden a wave of nausea come over her. She ran to the toilet bowl and threw up.

This is all I need right now, she thought. It must've been the food she had eaten last night or maybe she had the flu. She returned to her bed, not feeling very well at all. She was a bit pale, and her stomach was still stirring around. Bernard had woken after he had heard her throwing up.

"Are you all right? I heard you throwing up."

"I think I might have gotten food poisoning from last night's pizza. I'm going to lie down a bit longer to see if it will pass," she told him.

"You should rest. I worry, you know," he said.

He got up and showered. He returned next to her afterward, and he told her he was going to get her some dry toast to try to settle her stomach. She told him to ask for Suzanne in the kitchen downstairs. She would gladly help him. He bent down, kissed her on the forehead, and then left her to go in search of Suzanne in the kitchen area.

CHAPTER 11

Bernard slowly went down the stairs in search of the kitchen. He was wandering around when someone spoke to him.

"Can I help you with something?"

He turned and there in front of him was a woman in a chef's uniform looking at him suspiciously.

"Hello, my name is Bernard. I'm a friend of Gabrielle's. I'm looking for Suzanne."

"Hi, I'm Suzanne. Nice to meet you. I've heard a lot about you. How might I help you?"

"Gabrielle is upstairs. She's sick. She does not feel good and is throwing up. I came to see if I could get her some dry toast and maybe some tea."

"Follow me," she said.

Bernard trailed behind her.

"When did she get sick? She was fine yesterday. Maybe she has the flu," Suzanne said.

"I don't know," Bernard replied. "She ate pizza last night. She thinks she might have food poisoning, but I ate it, too, and I'm fine."

"Probably a touch of the flu. I'll check on her later." She handed him a tray of dry toast, Gouda cheese, and tea. "Tell her not to worry. I'll take care of things down here. She should just rest, okay?" said Suzanne. She was always concerned about Gabrielle, but she would check on her later on.

Bernard took the tray, thanked her, and headed back upstairs to see his darling Gabrielle.

When he arrived back in the room, she was sleeping quietly. He put down the tray on a small table beside her bed. His heart warmed at the sight of her sleeping like a baby. He did not want to wake her, so quiet as a mouse, he found a piece of paper and a pen. He wrote her a note that he was going back to the motel to pack up his stuff, and he would come back to take care of her. He left the note on the tray. Bernard closed the door silently, and he went to find Suzanne to tell her that he was leaving the inn. He asked her to keep an eye on Gabrielle until he returned from the motel. He told her he would be back in about an hour or two, as he had a few errands to run.

Gabrielle woke up not too long after Bernard had left her room. She was touched that he had gone out of his way to get her food. He had tried to help her feel better, but the truth was she was still feeling sick to her stomach. She reached over when she saw the note and read it. He even had signed it "Love, Bernard." She knew she would be fine with a little rest. Gabrielle lay in bed thinking about what had happened the previous evening, about who would want to harm her. *Two warnings in one day. She had been warned, but about Bernard?* She could not fathom an answer to her question. She wondered if maybe someone was trying to tell her to say away from him because he was dangerous and he might harm her.

What had she done differently in the past few days to receive such a warning? She could not comprehend the situation. The only thing different was that Bernard had arrived to see her. Maybe she was being warned about him? She really did not know him that well, but what she knew was that he loved her, and he cared for her. She knew in her heart that he would never hurt her. It definitely had to be something else.

She closed her eyes, and she tried to wipe her thoughts clear. She wanted to start from the beginning to try to find out who would want to hurt her. She was running the events of her last few days over in her mind, but she was not having any success in finding the problem. It was getting close to afternoon. She had eaten the toast, but still she did not feel all that well yet. Suzanne had checked in on her twice.

"I want you to stay in bed and not to worry. I can handle it downstairs," she had said.

At least she was not throwing up anymore. She only had an upset stomach now and then. She pushed herself out of bed to shower. She decided to get ready for work, as it might make her feel better. She put on a blue summer cotton dress, but she did not feel any better, so she lay back down on top of the bed covers of her bed. She welcomed Bernard back a few hours later.

"Welcome back. You can hang your things next to mine in the closet," she told him.

"All right. How are you feeling?" He walked to the closet, grabbed some hangers, and started putting his clothes away. She observed every little movement he made.

"I am feeling much better. I think I'll go see how things are running downstairs."

She started to get up, but he lay down next to her.

"Why don't we stay a while longer? Let's talk," he said and patted the bed beside him. She lay down beside him on the bed and cuddled against him.

"I am worried about you. Are you sure you feel all right with everything that happened last night?" Bernard asked.

"I am fine, but do you have any idea who would do such a thing? I am afraid not only for me, but for you too. Someone does not want us together. They might try to harm you." She did not want to think that someone might be warning her about him being a danger to her.

"I will be fine, and no one is going to harm you if I can help it," Bernard answered her.

By late afternoon, she could not take it anymore. She had to get up despite all his protesting. She was feeling much better, so she went downstairs. Everything was running smoothly. She could always count on Suzanne. She was very efficient at making sure everyone performed his or her duties. Now Gabrielle could relax for a little bit, and she could spend some time with her love.

Gabrielle finished all her tasks and went to greet her prince to tell him that she had a few hours of free time, but he was gone. She could not find him anywhere, not in the kitchen or by the front entrance. She opened the front door thinking he might be outside, but to her surprise, he was nowhere in sight. She suddenly had a chill that went right down her spine, and she rubbed her arms with her hands. She remembered how terrified she had felt when that man had pushed her down. She hoped Bernard was all right.

She had just frozen last night. Her brain had gone to mush from fear. Nothing had ever happened to her like that before, and she would not forget it so soon. She figured Bernard had gone for a walk, because his truck was still parked out front. She was hungry, so she went back in to get a snack and wait until Bernard came back, when they could go to grab a bite in town. She was finally feeling back to normal.

***

Bernard swept the area with his eyes more attentively, but he did not see anyone. Bernard took it upon himself to casually go in the direction where a gold car was parked. He just wanted to make sure he was not letting his imagination go wild. There was absolutely no way his father could know his whereabouts, unless he had been followed. He slowed down his pace when he got nearer to the car. He was looking around for any signs of danger or evidence that could confirm his hidden suspicions. He arrived at the car and cupped his hands against the window so he could examine the contents of the car. Why? He was not sure.

There was nothing inside the car except food wrappers from fast food stores. A few maps and some clothes that were scattered in the back seat. It was not very clean at all. It looked like someone was living in his car, but he did not see anyone in the area. He tried to open the doors, but they were locked. He put his hand on the hood. It was cold, so that meant the car had been parked in the same spot for a while, but there were no houses nearby. Next, Bernard noticed something that made him very suspicious of the car; it had a Massachusetts license plate. He memorized the license plate so he could call a friend who would help identify the owner by its plates. He would have to watch to see if this car kept popping up around where he was. It was odd and questionable that this car came from the same state as him. He would have to keep his eyes open and be more vigilant concerning this vehicle.

Bernard wondered if his father had anything to do with the incident with Gabrielle. He did not want Gabrielle to worry and think his father was ruthless or didn't want her to be part of their family. He really could not accuse his father of wrong doing until he had proof. He hoped he was mistaken because he would never forgive him this time. He would sever all ties from him forever. Bernard would not live his life looking over his shoulder wondering if he was being followed around like a small child. He had the right to do as he pleased without his father's permission. He was a grown man. God help him if he was right.

After a few minutes, Bernard turned around walked back to the inn. Gabrielle must be done with her work by now. They might be able to spend some time together. He wanted to spend all his time with her. He also knew he had to eventually return to Boston. How was he going to be able to tell her? It was going to break her heart. But right now, he was here. He might as well take advantage of that and be with her as much as he could.

Gabrielle saw Bernard come through the front of the building. "Where have you been? I was looking for you." She came over to him, she put her arms around his neck, and leaned into him. She kissed him on the lips. He did not want to stop kissing her, but he knew her staff was watching them. He did not want to embarrass her in front of them. He was really trying to behave, so he pulled away from her.

"I went for a walk while you finished your work."

"Well, I'm free now for a few hours. What would you like to do?"

He looked at her seductively from head to toe and raised his eyebrows to give her that smile she liked so much. She shook her head at him.

"Ah, come on," he pleaded, half laughing.

"Come, I'll show you the town. We can get a bite to eat," she said, pulling him out the door by the arm.

"All right. Do you want to walk or drive? It's a nice day."

"Let's walk. You can build up an appetite. I'm going to take you to the most amazing bistro. They have the best seafood dishes in town."

She took his hand in hers, and they started walking down the main road that led to the center of the town. It was a nice day with an ocean breeze that kept them cool. You could smell the scent of the ocean. Their first stop was at a small park that had beautiful sculptures of dolphins and mermaids. There was also a famous sculpture of an old fisherman, which was a well-known one, as it was a fishing town. There were so many flowers that you could smell them just by walking by them. There was a small stage where local musicians played their music each night at dusk. Several benches lined the area near the stage, providing room for an audience. Each of the local merchants paid a small fee to make sure the flowers were planted and maintained every year. They stopped and sat on one of the many benches in the park and watched the passersby for a few minutes. It was one of the focal points of the town. There were many kids playing in the nearby playground, and the adults just walked around, leisurely enjoying the day.

They continued walking down the street, passing two women's clothing stores, a pharmacy, and a small hardware store. Straight ahead was a favorite local ice cream place. They kept on going until they saw the small bistro. An old Victorian house that had been restored to its original beauty; it was all painted in green with white trim all around. It was a great place to eat seafood. She asked for a table outside on the patio near the water. The chef was an old high-school friend of Gabrielle's, named Ben. He had opened and operated this small, intimate place for few years now. He was a very talented chef. This location was a popular restaurant for tourists, because it was right on Main Street and in the brouhaha of the area. There was always a person that played the guitar and sang love songs in his establishment. Ben knew she was coming, so he came out to greet them when he found out they had arrived. They were escorted to their table, and she introduced Bernard and they chatted for a few minutes.

"We are so hungry. Can you whip up something with seafood for us?" Gabrielle asked Ben.

"Coming right up! Why don't you get some wine? It won't be long," Ben answered, and then returned to the kitchen. Bernard ordered a nice bottle of white pinot wine that they enjoyed while waiting for their food.

"So tell me, how do you like my town compared to Boston?"

"I love it. It's so quiet, the people are friendly, and you are here. What else do I need?"

He leaned over, and he kissed her lightly on the cheek. She ducked her head down, and she blushed instantly.

Bernard thought she looked splendid when she blushed. It was a turn on for him. He took her hand and he caressed it, then he whispered to her, "You really do not like it when I kiss you in public, do you?"

She lifted her head and she smiled at him. "I am not used to it. Maybe it is because I know almost everyone in town, but I do like it," she answered. "So tell me, does your father know about of us? Our relationship, I mean. Did you tell him about us?"

Suddenly Bernard became extremely quiet and guarded. He kept moving in his seat and he avoided looking Gabrielle straight in the eyes.

When he spoke again, he looked her in the eyes and said, "Well, my father is a good man, but he can be domineering. He likes things done his way. He would like me to marry a woman that he picks. He wants a woman who has power and is groomed influentially. He also wants me to have children right away, and I am not sure if I want children, but I disagree with his theory of what a woman should be or when I should have children," he answered. "I will be with whomever I please, even if he doesn't approve, and so be it." He felt sad, so he put his head down and looked away from her.

"I'm sorry." She did not know what else she could say.

"Don't ever be sorry. It's not your fault. I love you just the way you are."

He truly meant it. He noticed tears forming in her eyes, and it broke his heart to think he was causing her pain. He took her hand in his and squeezed it softly, then he brought it to his mouth, and kissed her knuckles.

"I love you," he whispered to her.

The sun was going down and it reflected on the water behind them. It was a romantic scene. The waiter reappeared with the most delectable dish of mussels, lobster, and shrimp in a light wine sauce with pasta. They thanked him. It looked delicious. They both dug into it and ate most of it. When they finished the meal, they just sat there enjoying the view of the sunset and each other's company with a cup of coffee.

"I think I ate too much," Gabrielle said to him after the meal. "It was so good, but we definitely have to walk back now."

"I totally agree," Bernard answered.

They started walking back. They were strolling down the street when Bernard noticed the gold car again. It was parked on the side of the street, but no one was in it. *Strange,* Bernard thought, but he did not mention it to Gabrielle. He did not want to worry her. After what had happened the night before, he was on his guard. They finally arrived at the inn, and Bernard was relieved nothing had happened. Gabrielle was tired, so she decided to go to bed early. He told her he had a few calls to make and he would join her shortly. She kissed him goodnight, and she went upstairs to her bedroom.

He waited for her to vanish upstairs before he called his head of security at his company, an ex-cop named Paul Richards. He had been a good friend of his for many years. Bernard knew he would be discreet. and he could find information without attracting attention.

"Good evening, Paul," Bernard said.

"Hi Bernard. How is your vacation?" Paul asked.

"Good, good. I need you to check something out for me. To make a long story short, my girlfriend was assaulted last night. She is fine, but the cops have not captured the intruder. I have noticed this gold car everywhere we go. Maybe it is nothing, but could you check it out?"

"Sure. What do you want me to do?" Paul asked.

"Find out who it belongs to and get back to me. It has Massachusetts plate 667K98," Bernard answered.

"I will get back to you as soon as I know something," Paul said.

Bernard thanked him then hung up the phone. He wondered again if his father had something to do with this situation, but then dismissed the idea. His father did not know exactly where he was anyway. Bernard started to go up the stairs when he had a curious thought. He turned around and he went back down the stairs to look outside the window. He shut off the main light and he carefully pulled the curtains back. He wanted to see if the gold car was still parked on the street near the inn. Maybe he was being paranoid, but he had to check. There was no car.

He quietly went to join Gabrielle. Bernard could not wait to be near her. He opened the door of the bedroom and silently took his clothes off. He noticed Gabrielle's eyes were closed, so he slipped in bed next to her. She was sound asleep. He put his arms around her torso and she stirred a bit, but she did not wake up. He could smell the lavender from her long, luscious hair on her pillow. He put his face near her hair and spooned her. He knew she had been sick today, so he would let her sleep. He could not wait until Paul called him back tomorrow and appeased his fears that his father was up to his old tricks again. He loved his father, but if he had anything to do with this, he might not be able to forgive him. It would be a very difficult situation. He truly loved this woman. He was not going to let her go without a battle and Bernard was sure he would win.

***

Tom was still lurking around. He had followed them to the bistro. This time he knew he had not been detected. He had been disguised as an old man, and it had worked perfectly. They had not even glanced at him twice when he had walked by them in the small park. Tom was determined to take care of

Gabrielle as soon as he could, but he had to make sure Bernard was nowhere around. He also knew he had to be extremely careful, because Ron would have his head if his son had even a scratch on his body. He would have to be patient, watchful, and when Bernard left the inn, and then he could put his plan into action. Tom was stationed right behind him. He was hiding in the thick foliage by the side of the woods. He had watched Bernard come out of the inn and investigate the inside of his car. Tom knew Bernard did not know his car. No one did. He had bought it a few months before he had left to follow Bernard and it was under an assumed name. He was not worried, as he had all his equipment locked in the reinforced trunk. He was not tormented about Bernard snooping around his car.

Tom still had a few things to pick up, so he could put everything together. He had to go back to the city again to see his old army acquaintance. He needed exclusive and dangerous supplies that could not be found in a regular store, but first he called the inn. A young lady answered.

"Gabrielle's. This is Donna. How may I help you?"

"I would like to make a reservation for tomorrow evening," Tom said.

"Sure. For how many people and how many nights?"

"Just one person for two nights," Tom answered. She seemed nice.

"Your name, sir?"

"Sharp, Oliver Sharp." That was the name on his counterfeit passport. *How pleasant she was. Too bad she might not be around for much longer.*

Three days should give him enough time to execute his plan. He had to get rid of his car and purchase another one, maybe a motorcycle, depending what was available. Bernard had looked at his car, and he did not want to attract any more attention to himself that he needed. He had to be anonymous—that was the only way he would be able to escape and not be detected by the police. Tomorrow would be a busy day and he had to bring his most elaborate project yet to life. Tom had a stoic look on his face as he took one last look at the inn and drove away. This was going to be one of his finest moments. He loved his work, plus he was paid to do it—that was the best part of all. It was going to be one of his most memorable events, especially for this small country town.

CHAPTER 12

Gabrielle had a good night's sleep, but when she opened her eyes in the morning, she felt nauseous again. She could not believe it, and she did not want to move. She could feel Bernard next to her sleeping soundly. After a few minutes, a terrifying thought occurred to her. *She did not have the flu!* She began searching her mind for an answer. She had been so busy with work since she had returned from Boston with the preparations of the inn for the summer season, she had completely forgotten about it. Oh! Mon Dieu, this was not good. This could not be happening. She was over-reacting. There was no way she could have been that careless. She could not remember the last time she had her monthly period. She scanned her memory. Her last period had been before she had gone away on vacation. That was more than two months ago. She concluded she might be pregnant.

Her heart was beating so fast she could not think straight. She had to find out for sure. She quietly slipped out of bed without disturbing Bernard. She held her breath while she grabbed a blouse and a pair of capris. She tiptoed to the bathroom to get dressed as quickly as she could without making any noise. She opened the door softly and turned around for a quick glance at Bernard. He was still sleeping. *Thank God!* She hurried down the stairs as fast as she could.

She went directly to the kitchen, looking for Suzanne, and spotted her cutting some vegetables for the lunch crowd. She approached her quickly, stood next to her and as casually as she could, and touched her arm. Gabrielle spoke to her in a hushed voice.

"I need to speak to you right now," Gabrielle said, trying to drag her outside the kitchen. Suzanne was looking at her with a look of wonder.

"Okay, okay. Where's the fire? I'm coming. What's so important Gabrielle that you had to drag me out here?" Suzanne was laughing at her behavior.

"Listen. What I'm going to tell you has to stay between me and you," said Gabrielle. She could feel her legs shaking.

"Okay. What is it?"

"Promise me."

"Promise," Suzanne sighed.

"You know how I haven't been feeling well lately?" Gabrielle was looking straight at her.

"Yes, I know."

"Well, I think I may be pregnant."

Suzanne's face turned from laughter to utter shock. "Are you sure? How do you know?"

Gabrielle's head was spinning in every direction, and all of a sudden she became pale as a wave of nausea struck her. She had to sit down. Suzanne knelt next to her.

"I'm not sure, but all I know is I missed my last period. I need to go to the pharmacy to get a pregnancy test. Can you cover for me?"

"Sure, no problem," said Suzanne, stunned.

"Bernard is still sleeping upstairs. When he comes down, don't tell him where I went. Tell him I had to go to the market and that I'll be back shortly, okay?"

"I won't breathe a word to anyone. Don't worry about him. I'll take care of him until you return," Suzanne told her.

"By the way, don't forget to pick up something at the market," Suzanne reminded her. Gabrielle gave her the best smile she had, and she was on her way. Gabrielle scooted out the door nervously.

Gabrielle's first stop was the pharmacy, and she went down the aisles looking for the pregnancy tests. She finally found them, and grabbed two different kinds off the shelf. She put them in her basket, and she almost ran to the cashier to pay for them. Now, she had to go to the market to pick up spices for Suzanne, so when Bernard asked where she was, Suzanne did not have to totally lie to him. She bought fresh basil and thyme, and then she drove back home to find out the answer to this crucial question.

When she returned home, Bernard was still sleeping. Thank God! She took her two tests and went directly to the bathroom. Suzanne was trailing not far behind her. Gabrielle quickly read the instructions and urinated on the stick. It would take ten minutes before she had the results. Gabrielle and Suzanne both waited together anxiously for the results. It seemed like an eternity. It was the longest ten minutes in Gabrielle's life. She was afraid Bernard would wake up before the time was up, and then what would she do?

Finally, it was time for the answer. Both Suzanne and Gabrielle were in the tiny bathroom in the back of the kitchen looking at the test results, and neither one of them was talking. They were just staring at the sticks of the pregnancy test. Gabrielle's mouth just opened to speak, but nothing came out. Suzanne and Gabrielle stared at the sticks in disbelief, and neither one of them spoke. It was dead silent. Gabrielle kept glancing at Suzanne. Tears were forming in her eyes, and she looked astonished.

"What am I going to do? I can't be pregnant. How am I going to tell him?" Gabrielle had a thousand questions, and she did not have an answer to any of them.

"Don't worry Gabrielle. It will work out. I'll help you," Suzanne said, trying to comfort her.

"He's going to think I did this to trap him. I do not even know if he wants children. Oh! *Mon Dieu!*" Gabrielle looked petrified, and tears were beginning to fall down her cheeks. Suzanne embraced her and told her it was going to be all right.

"Don't worry. A child always brings good luck," Suzanne told her.

Gabrielle sat on the toilet seat, trying to put herself together before she saw Bernard. She finally got up, wiped her tears away and told Suzanne she was going for a walk in the park for a few minutes. Gabrielle really needed time to think this through before she decided what to do concerning this pregnancy. She could not breathe. She needed air, and she had to get outside.

As she was walking out the door, she encountered an old gentleman. He was polite, and he held the door open for her as she walked out.

She exited as fast as she could. She did not feel like seeing anyone at this moment. She walked to the park down the street, and she sat down on one of the benches away from the people under a big oak tree facing the water. She could smell the ocean in the breeze as it brushed against her face. She needed to be alone for a while so she could try to think clearly.

Gabrielle was trying to clear her head. How could she have let this happen? She analyzed her financial situation in her head. There were no money problems, but the question was, could she raise a child by herself? Did Bernard really want a child now? Should she even tell him? He was not going to stay here with her. It wasn't realistic, as his company was in Boston. She could never have an abortion, so she really did not have many choices and she could not put it up for adoption, either. She already loved this child. It was hers and Bernard's. Her career was just starting, and she had worked so hard to get where she was at this moment in her life. She was not going to tell Bernard right away ,because she did not know where she truly stood with him. She knew he loved her, but now that she was having a child, he would not stay here in Canada. She did not want him to think she wanted to ambush him for his money, either. She wanted him to stay with her, but not just because of the baby. She still had many decisions to make, but one thing was very clear: she was keeping the baby, with him or not. She was strong enough. She could raise this child by herself, and there would be lots of love to give this child.

Gabrielle felt much better and decided she was not going to cry anymore. She could handle this. This was a major decision, and she had made up her mind. She got up from her bench, and she started walking back to the inn. She could deal with the bumps in the road as they came along. She was a strong person. She was pregnant. It did not seem real, but that was the situation. For good or bad, it was done. The first thing she had to do was make an appointment with her doctor to make sure she did everything right. She would tell Bernard after her doctor's appointment.

Tom had been in the nearest city, a placed called Moncton. It was not a big city, only about two hundred thousand people, but big enough you could be anonymous if you needed to be. He had sold his gold car dirt cheap at a local dealership, no questions asked. He then bought himself a newer model of a black Honda from a guy in the newspaper. The guy selling it to him just wanted to get rid of it, so he paid him with cash. With a couple of extra hundreds, Tom had convinced him to leave the plates on the car for a few more days until he could get to the motor vehicle department. By then, he would be out of the country and back in the good old United States.

Tom had met up with his friend Michel at an abandoned warehouse that used to house machinery for the railroad. He had phoned him the night before and told him what he needed for his plan. Michel's friend Nick worked for a construction company that specialized in demolition and specialized solely in explosives. The price for what he wanted was excessive, but Tom had the funds to pay for them. He also understood the risk he was taking by selling him the explosives. Ron had made sure he had enough money to buy anything he wanted, even illegal stuff. The transaction was done in a matter of minutes, and then both men went their separate ways. Both men were happy that they had both gotten what they wanted. Tom delicately locked everything in a suitcase, and he headed back toward the inn. Now it was show time. It was only a matter of time and he was counting the minutes until he could execute his plan.

Tom drove back to Shediac as fast as he could without going over the speed limit. He stopped at the first local motel he saw and rented a room for one night. He went to the back of his car and unlocked it. He grabbed his suitcase and carried it inside with him. He placed it on the bed and opened it. He was tired, so he lay down on the bed and fell asleep within a half-hour.

The next morning, he had woken up early and was ready to start executing his master plan. He walked to the suitcase, took his things out, and placed them on the top of the bed. He lay out one gray hair wig and one silicone prosthesis of an aged man for his face. He undressed and started his work. First he applied cream on his face and then carefully put a bald cap on. He handled the hair with care, put glue on the inside of it, and placed it on his head. He took the silicone nose, applied glue, and placed it over his nose, and then he smoothed the edges out. The most delicate job was yet to come, applying the right colors of makeup and blending it properly. He worked for over two hours with sponges, colored pencils, and brushes. He finally looked in the mirror and smiled at himself. He was pleased with the final results. He put on a checkered shirt, an older cardigan with patches on the elbows, suspenders, and loose trousers. He placed a floppy hat on his head and grandfather glasses on. His last piece was a wooden cane. He walked out of his room, got in his car, and drove toward the inn.

After he registered at the front desk, Tom went to his bedroom. He had not left his room since he had arrived hours ago. He had been a busy man. On a small table in front of his bed, he had organized all of the parts that he would need to build the explosive devices. He had a timer, blowing caps, black and red wires, disposable cell phones that could not be traced, plus three pounds of C4. He had acquired all these things from his not so standup guy. All he needed to do now was assemble his bombs together. He was going to get rid of this girl. He needed to protect the Rian family from a gold digger. She was not right for the family.

Everything about these explosives was delicate and extremely tedious work. It was time-consuming and definitely not for the faint at heart. He had hung a *Do Not Disturb* sign on the doorknob outside his room and had locked the door because he did not want any unwanted surprises or discoveries while he was working on these devices. In less than a couple of days, he should be done, and he would be on his way home if all went as planned. He was in a cheerful mood; he was humming an old song as he worked. Beads of sweat were forming around his forehead, but he was a determined man. He attached each component with extreme care. His hands trembled from time to time, but he would get it right or die trying. He would protect the Rian family.

He needed to make at least three bombs. He had finished one of them by mid-afternoon. He only had two more to assemble, and then he needed to plan a strategy for his next moves. He had to analyze where he should install the bombs so they would have the maximal effect. They had to be positioned at three individual spots to create the most damage. Afterwards, he would sneak a safe distance away so he could detonate and observe the fire show with delight. Mr. Rian would be happy that Tom had taken care of her, just like the last time an unsuitable woman had come along.

The ringing of his phone awoke Bernard. He opened his eyes to see he was alone in the bed. Gabrielle must have gotten up without him noticing. He reached over to the end table where his phone was ringing, and he answered.

"Hello, this is Bernard."

It was his friend Paul, returning his call concerning the information on the old gold car.

"Hi, it's Paul. Hope I didn't wake you. I have the info you wanted."

"No, no. What do you have for me?" Bernard was still groggy, and he was trying to wake up. He sat up against the backboard of the bed and listened attentively to Paul.

"The car is registered to a Nancy Hull from Beverly. She does not have any criminal record, and she looks clean. That is all I have for now. I am going to keep looking. I will call if I find anything else," Paul said, waiting for further instructions.

"Thanks a lot Paul, but let me know if there's anything else." He hung up the phone. He was relieved that this gold car did not belong to Tom.

He got out of bed and he went to take a quick shower, hoping it would wake him up. He wished Gabrielle were here with him. He dressed, sprayed on his Chanel Blue cologne, and he went to find her. He wanted to take her into the city if she was free. He walked down to the dining room to look for Gabrielle, but she was not there. He saw Suzanne walk by and stopped her.

"Hi, Suzanne. Do you know where Gabrielle is?" he asked.

"Good morning, Bernard. She went to the market to pick up a few things," she answered.

"How long do you think she will be?"

Suzanne looked at him and hesitated a moment. "I do not know. Would you like some breakfast?" she asked.

"Well, I was hoping to have breakfast with Gabrielle."

"Why don't you have a seat? I will get you the daily paper, and I do make a mean lobster benedict," she said and smiled at him.

"I am tempted. It sounds really good."

"Great! We are all set. I will bring you a newspaper and coffee right away."

He watched her walk swiftly toward the kitchen to cook his breakfast.

Gabrielle came back through the back door, and Suzanne was pleased to see her. She seemed resolute in her decision. Gabrielle gave her thumbs up. At least she was not crying anymore, thought Suzanne. Gabrielle motioned Suzanne to follow her to her office. She wanted to talk to her in private.

"I just wanted to thank you for being so kind to me earlier. I'm fine now. Do not worry about me. I will explain everything later. Do you know where Bernard is?"

"He's in the dining room having breakfast. He asked about you, and I told him you went on an errand. Are you sure you're okay?" Suzanne asked.

"Yes, I'm fine. Don't worry. And thanks again."

Gabrielle got up, gave her friend a grateful hug, and then walked toward the dining room with her head held high. Rays of sunshine were coming through the humongous windows that surrounded the dining hall. It warmed her heart and gave her strength that she had a lot to be thankful.

"Hey there, handsome," she said cheerfully, as she hurried over to his table. She kissed him on the cheek and sat down next to him.

"You were gone when I woke. I missed you."

"What if we went for a drive in the city? We could do a little shopping and maybe we can walk around," she said, hoping he would not notice she was preoccupied.

"All right, you win. When do you want to leave?" he asked.

"Is something wrong?"

"No, I'm fine. It's just the pressure of work."

"Just give me a few minutes to make a few calls, and then we'll get going." She got up, kissed him lightly on the mouth, and walked away.

Gabrielle went to her office to call her doctor. She made an appointment for the next day at the women's center. She had to make sure she really was pregnant. It really had not completely sunk in yet. She picked up her pocketbook and walked out to find Bernard. She found him outside on the porch waiting patiently. He was leaning against one of the posts. His arms were crossed over his chest, and his bicep muscles seemed to bulge out of his tight shirt. His blue eyes were hidden behind his black sunglasses, and his pants were tight in just the right places.

Gabrielle could not resist him and she advanced toward him. She put her arms around his waist and gave him a hug. Her hand glided up to touch his hair, and she played with it for a moment. Bernard leaned his head down and kissed her on the neck. She could sense his desire. She looked up, and she placed her hand on his cheek.

"Ready?"

"Oh! Am I ever?"

Gabrielle poked him lightly in the ribs. He laughed, took her hand, and pushed her toward his truck. The city was about half an hour away. It gave Gabrielle time to try to see where she stood with him.

"Are you having a nice time?" she asked.

"I'm having a great time as long as I'm with you," he said and turned to look at her.

"I understand that you are going to go back. Do you know what your plans are yet?" She held her breath for the answer.

"Why so serious? Right now, as long as you want me, I will stay. I might have to buy a few things, but I am staying put. I am happy here, and I have no plans to return in the near future," he said.

"And what about your work? Your company?"

"I really don't need to work. I can get reports online, and the board of directors can run it. I only have to check in with them periodically."

Gabrielle was pleased to hear that. She needed answers, and it was a start.

"I am just trying to figure out ... us." She wondered if she was pushing too hard.

"Gabrielle, I love you, and I'm not going anywhere. Let's take it one day at a time, okay?"

Gabrielle felt a little better. She decided to leave it be for now. She was just going to enjoy herself. She put her hand on his thigh while he was driving, turned toward him, and said, "I love you."

Ron was getting impatient. He had not heard any news from Tom in the last few days. He hoped he was doing his job. He dialed his cell phone number. It rang twice before he answered. They jumped straight into the conversation.

"What seems to be the problem?" Ron inquired.

"No problem. I just needed to pick up supplies. Now, I'm on schedule, sir," Tom answered.

"Did you scare her off like I asked you to do?" Ron asked.

"I scared her a bit, but she went back to Bernard. I am going to really frighten her this time," Tom told his boss.

"What are you planning, Tom? I only want you to tell her to stay away from Bernard." Ron was worried Tom was going to do something he would regret later.

"Do not worry. I will protect the Rian family name. She will not know what hit her," Tom chuckled.

Ron felt a chill down his back. He had to gain control of this situation before Tom did something he would regret.

"Tom, be careful. Do not get caught, and make sure you only scare her. Do you understand?"

"Oh! I understand perfectly, Mr. Rian," Tom answered.

"Keep me in the loop with your progress. That's all." Ron was anxious to be done with this problem.

"Yes, sir," Tom said. He hung up the phone and continued his tidiest work on his devices.

Ron was afraid he was out of control. Tom had gone rogue. This man was crazy and Ron hoped he was not going to hurt anyone.

Bernard parked the truck on the street and they decided to walk down Champlain Street. This street had many tourist stores, bookstores, and several outdoor cafés. They walked leisurely stopping occasionally to do a little window-shopping. Bernard saw an outdoor café, and he told Gabrielle to find a table. He would be right back. She agreed. She gave her name to the hostess while the waiter cleaned a table so she could sit down. He gave her a menu to look at while she waited for Bernard and brought her an assortment of breads to nibble on. Gabrielle wondered where he had gone, but she occupied herself by reading the menu.

"Where did you go?" She was looking at the bag he was carrying.

"I wanted to get you this." He handed her the bag. She looked at it, then at him.

"You didn't have to ..."

He put his finger on her lips before she could finish her sentence. "Shhh! Just open it." He smiled at her. She carefully unwrapped the paper and opened the box. She gasped and touched it lightly with her finger. It was the most beautiful pendant she had ever seen. Her eyes pooled up.

"How did I deserve this?"

He took it out of the box and placed it around her neck. The pendant fell right between the valleys of her breasts.

"Do you like it? You deserve a lot more, but this is jade, my favorite good-luck stone."

"It's beautiful. Thank you," she said, leaning across the table and kissing him on the lips.

They both ordered lunch. Gabrielle had pastrami on rye and Bernard a chicken pesto with a cold draft beer. They talked, and they had a few good laughs. Gabrielle forgot all her worries for an hour. It was a perfect day to be sitting outside. They watched the shoppers go by with their purchases and enjoyed the day. By late afternoon, they decided to head back to reality, so they drove back home to the inn.

CHAPTER 13

Bernard and Gabrielle took the long way home. They wound along the back roads, the scenic routes that clung to the ocean coastline. They could see the sailboats on the water from the road, and there were lots of lobster fishing boats traveling in the deep. Small, modest homes were hugging the street all along the side the roads. These bungalows had nicely manicured lawns and all kinds of flowers in the front yards. Bernard and Gabrielle were savoring the time they had left of their perfect day. They were back just in time for the supper rush. Gabrielle told Bernard she needed to help her staff for a few hours. He told her that was fine because he had a few calls to make, and he had errands to run. He would return in a few hours, and they could go to dinner in town later. He said his good-byes, he gave her a long, slow kiss, and he was on his way.

By late afternoon, Tom was ready to put his plan in action. All the components were ready, and he was confident it would detonate as planned today. His plan was going to go through. He had worked hard these past few days, getting things together. Tom understood Ron had told him just to scare her, but he knew by observing them these past few days that Gabrielle would not stop or go away with just scare tactics. He had to act now, before it was too late. Tom was going to take care of everything. He was going to permanently take care of her. Ron would thank him when he got home for doing such a great job.

He had disguised himself as the old man and was sitting on the porch, observing the comings and goings of the people of the inn. He was waiting with anticipation for the loving couple. He finally spotted Bernard and Gabrielle as they drove up the circular driveway. Tom watched them get out of their vehicle, and he hoped Bernard would leave again so he could orchestrate his scheme. He had to make sure Bernard was nowhere around. He was elated when he noticed Bernard get back in his Rover and drive off toward the town. That was his cue to carry out his plan.

He climbed the stairs up to his room, and he carefully stashed his inventions in his carry-on bag. First he attached the timers on the bombs, which were to be activated only by dialing the phone number he had attached to them. He was being prudent in his proceedings, dropping off the bombs at specific areas of the inn. He was very shrewd; he wanted to deliver them where they would inflict the most damage on impact.

He installed one device in the men's room. He hid it under the sink in the cabinet. He made sure no one saw him, and then he walked out casually to his next destination. He dropped one in the front area of the inn near a chair in the waiting area. He noticed a rack full of magazines. It was perfect place to hide it. The third explosive was more difficult to place because he did not have access to the kitchen. He needed it in or near the kitchen, but the traffic flow of people coming and going made it too risky, so he decided to look outside. He walked around the outside perimeter toward the rear entrance. Suddenly, he saw a foolproof and ideal place to deliver his last device. He hurried so he would not be seen, and he placed it under a propane tank near the back door of the kitchen. He knew this one was going to really produce the most impact of all his bombs. He felt a sensation of triumph at the execution of his master plan.

He turned around slowly and casually walked away. He pretended he was going for a stroll down the street. When he arrived at the end of the road, he started hiking toward the wooded area. He wanted to be in the proximity of the building so he could watch as his masterpiece destroyed the inn. He expected a total elimination of the surroundings. Tom crouched down, and then lay on the ground and took his phone from his bag. He did not even hesitate; he pushed the buttons to activate the remotes. He began to count aloud, "One, two, and three. Go." A perfect execution of his plan. He heard the violent outbursts of his work. Now all he had to do was observe the unfolding events.

The first explosion came from the bathroom. He could see smoke coming out of the small side window. It had made a hole in the wall, and fire was engulfing the side of the building. The front area was next, and though he could not see the damage from the angle from where he was watching, he could hear the bomb go off and the subsequent horrified screams of the patrons. He could see people coming out on the side of the inn, all bloody and limping, trying to get safely out of the range of the explosion.

Finally, for his greatest showpiece of all, the propane tank blew up. A huge cloud of black smoke went up in the air. It covered the sky, and the fire that erupted afterwards was uncontrollable. Flames shot from every orifice and the roof was slowly giving in as the fire tried to escape. Pieces of wood and glass had flown in all directions, from the kitchen area to all over the backyard. The whole back of the building was gutted. It was destroyed, and a magnificent fire burnt forth. Tom had a smile on his face. His adrenaline was pumping hard and he was pleased that his plan had come together so successfully. He decided to stay a while to watch the commotion that was unfolding in front of his eyes. Tom was enjoying the confusion and the all drama. He could imagine how proud his boss was going to be. *Ron was going to thank him for taking care of this delicate problem.*

Gabrielle was in the front area of the inn when the first explosion occurred. She did not know what was going on. Mystified, she rushed toward the back area, and then she heard screams and saw people running toward the exits. Suddenly there was a secondary explosion. The impact of the blast threw her against the wall as wood, debris, and glass hit her in the back. She fell down on her hands and knees, and then something crashed over her. By the time she saw it coming toward her, it was too late. It was one of the ceiling beams. She tried to avert the collision, but it was so quick. It hit her hard directly on the side of the head. She tried to get up, but the side of her head was bloody and hurting badly. She was extremely dizzy and disoriented. She tried to push the piece of wood off of herself, but she didn't have enough strength. She realized she was trapped. She could smell the burning wood, and she was having a hard time seeing anything because of all the black smoke. She was having difficulty breathing. Oh! *Mon Dieu!* She told herself this could not be happening. She had to get out of here. The smoke was not good for the baby. She could lose the baby. She heard a third explosion, and her head was pounding so badly. She tried to get up again, to push the beam off, but she could not move. The room was spinning. She could not hear or see anything. *I am going to die*, she thought. Like a lightning flash, everything went black.

Suzanne watched as customers came out of the building. People were yelling and crying everywhere you looked. The scene was uncontrolled. People were bleeding and trying to seek help for their wounds. They all looked to be in shock. Most of the people were scrambling to get to safety. The majority of the building was being consumed by fire. The flames were shooting out from the holes in the building and the rooftops. The black smoke was now coming out of the inn. Debris was scattered everywhere you looked, and everything seemed to be in chaos. Broken glass had flown all over the front lawn from the blast. Neighbors had come forth to try to help in any way they could. In all the confusion, someone had called the fire department and the paramedics. You could hear all kinds of sirens coming toward the inn. The emergency trucks and personnel were all converging to the parking lot of the inn. The chief had called other small towns in the vicinity to send their brigades of fire trucks. It was a monstrous fire, with the possibility of many casualties.

Suzanne was calling Gabrielle's name. She was nowhere to be found outside. All she could see was the damaged building. Her friend was somewhere inside this inferno. The fire fighters arrived quickly, and the captain took charge of the situation as fast as he could. He first issued a safe perimeter, and he was trying to prevent people from coming too close to the building. The captain was shouting commands to his crew. Ladders were deployed, water hoses were unrolled immediately, and the fire fighters were trying to contain the blaze.

***

Bernard was in town shopping for a few personal items at Shoppers Drug Mart when he first heard all the sirens. He saw all the fire engines, and then he saw the ambulances go by him. He was wondering what the commotion was all about when he noticed they were all going toward the inn.

He got a knot in his stomach, and a bad feeling crept up inside him. He decided to go see what the entire disturbance was about.

He first saw the black smoke filling the sky. He thought it looked like it was coming from the inn. The closer he got, the more alarmed he became. He heard himself say Gabrielle's name aloud. The police department had blocked off the street, so he pulled his Range Rover on the side of the road. He jumped out and he started running toward the building. He was praying everyone was all right, especially Gabrielle. He was yelling her name and looking everywhere for her, but he could not see or find her. He became frantic, running everywhere. His heart was pounding in his ears and his breathing was irregular. He finally saw Suzanne at one side of a fire truck crying her eyes out. Her hair was a mess, and her jacket was bloody. He stopped cold in his tracks, and a feeling of doom came over him. He did not want to ask her, but he had to know the answer to his question.

"Where is she? Is Gabrielle all right?" Suzanne was sobbing uncontrollably. It was difficult to understand her. She was pointing at the building.

"I don't know—I think she's still inside. A fireman went to try to find her," she finally said in between sobs. Bernard was shocked. He started running toward the front door, but a policeman grabbed him and forcefully held him back. Bernard was struggling with him and screaming at him.

"She's still in there! Let me go!"

The policeman was holding him back, yelling back at him over the noise. "You can't go in the building, sir. They're looking for her."

Bernard's whole brain stopped functioning and he could hear himself yelling, "Oh! Dear God! Not again. Gabrielle!" he screamed. She had to be okay.

He felt someone take his arm and lead him to a safe area. He realized it was Suzanne trying to console him. She was rubbing his back lightly. His eyes were tearing up. It was as if he were watching a movie. This was not happening to him. He sat down. His hands went up to his face and he started to cry.

All he could see was this huge fire, the black smoke, and the flames coming out of the windows and the roof. He had already lost hope that Gabrielle would be found alive. Water was being thrown into the building as fast as they could deliver it. More engines were arriving to help with the fire. Bernard could not accept she was gone. He had to hope and pray they would find her. Suddenly, he saw the image of a fireman carrying a person over his shoulder through the thick, black smoke coming out of the front entrance.

It was Gabrielle. She was not moving. She was limp, her arms falling to her sides and her head just dangling backward. The fireman laid her down on the ground, and he started CPR immediately. A paramedic ran over and connected an oxygen mask over her mouth, while another started an IV in her arm. She was bleeding from a head wound. They quickly bandaged her head. Bernard rushed by her side. He reached out to her, but an officer pulled him away again as quickly as he got there. He whispered, "Be strong. I'm here, Gabrielle."

"Stay back. They need room to work!" a fireman yelled.

Bernard just stood still. He felt like a helpless child. He did not know what to do. Bernard repeatedly asked, "Is she alive? Please don't let her die."

No one answered him, as the paramedics were too busy working on Gabrielle.

Finally, one of the paramedics said, "I have a pulse. It's weak, so let's put her in the ambulance and let's roll."

Bernard felt a sense of relief pass though his body. She was alive. Alive. Suzanne was giving Gabrielle's information to an attendant—her name, address, and age. Bernard watched as they rolled her inside the ambulance and closed the doors. The vehicle took off in a rush toward the hospital with the sirens blaring loudly. Bernard kept his eyes on the ambulance until it was out of sight. He found Suzanne nearby, grabbed her arm, and they both started running toward his truck to follow the ambulance to the hospital.

***

Tom was ecstatic. After all his hard work, his plan had come together perfectly. Ron was going to be so proud of him. He had gotten rid of Gabrielle. He packed up the remainder of his stuff, and he was ready to head home. His mission was accomplished, and he was happy. He did not believe too many people could have survived this explosion. Tom decided, first thing, when he cleared away from there, he would call Ron to tell him the good news. It was easier than he thought. He slipped to the next street where his new car was waiting for him. He drove off as if he were just sightseeing in town. Several miles later, he found his cell phone, and he called his boss. Ron answered right away. He did not speak, just listened.

"Mr. Rian, I just took care of her. My plan was a success, and everything was taken care of. I blew up her inn," Tom said.

"You did what? I never told you to blow up her inn!" Ron yelled.

"I know, but I decided to take care of her. She is gone," Tom answered.

"I did not send you there to kill her, you idiot. I just wanted you to scare her away from Bernard. I am not going to have any part of this. Do not expect to get paid for something I did not agree to," Ron said.

"You will pay me, otherwise I will tell Bernard it was your idea, sir."

Tom's voice was calm, but he was confused. He could not believe that Ron did not agree with him. Ron should be thanking him, not yelling at him.

"I should be home later on tomorrow. We shall talk when I get home," Tom said.

"Fine," Ron answered.

Tom did not bother to say goodbye—he just hung up the phone. He was proud of how he had executed his project and that his business had gone down so perfectly. He was done, and he had not been caught. He considered himself a professional. Tom was driving back to Boston. His job was finished, and he felt a satisfaction akin to that of a father being proud of his child. He had no idea that he had not won.

***

Bernard and Suzanne had arrived at the emergency department at the Moncton hospital not long after the ambulance had arrived there. The paramedics had wheeled her directly into the trauma section of the hospital. Unfortunately, no one was allowed in that area but personnel, so Bernard and Suzanne had to sit in the nearest waiting room. Bernard was frantic. He wanted to see her and he kept getting up to pace. He kept walking to the nurse's station to try to get information, but it was fruitless, and the attendant kept sending him back to the waiting room. They waited impatiently.

"My God! Suzanne, what the hell happen when I was gone?" He was trying to find answers to an unbelievable situation.

"Bernard, I really don't know what happened. All of a sudden there were these explosions, one after another. My husband and I were running for the door. All I remember was that Gabrielle was taking care of the front area. It happened so fast. I tried to put it together, but I was not able to. It was unbelievable. Who would do such a thing to hurt Gabrielle?" Suzanne asked.

"I shouldn't have gone to town. Maybe I could have done something." He felt guilty and so helpless. He looked at Suzanne, and he noticed she was holding her arm. She had gotten hurt, and she was bleeding. Her whole shirt was covered in blood.

"You're hurt. Let me get you some help," he said.

"It's not bad. I'll be alright," she said softly.

Bernard returned to the nurse's station to get someone to assist her. A nurse came by to quickly look at her arm. She went back in the emergency area and retrieved a large bandage. The nurse told Suzanne that she probably needed a few stitches and that as soon as they had free room, and she would come get her.

An hour later, Bernard saw a doctor in scrubs coming toward the waiting area. He jumped up from his chair immediately, ran his fingers through his hair, and sighed impatiently.

He was staring at the doctor, waiting to hear if she was going to be all right.

"I am looking for Miss Leger's family members," said the doctor.

"She's my fiancée," said Bernard. He had to make a quick decision because he knew the doctor would only talk to family. So he blurted it out in order to be told anything. Yes, he wanted to marry her. Bernard extended his hand to him.

"I am Bernard Rian," he said, and they shook hands.

"Mr. Rian, I'm Doctor Dubois. I'm in charge of the trauma unit. Gabrielle Leger is my patient. She was brought in critical condition. We have sedated her. To put it simply, she received a bad blow to the head. She has a bad concussion. Her brain lining is swelling up with fluid, and it is pressing against her cranial bone. She is also having a slight problem with her lungs. She must have inhaled a lot carbon dioxide from the smoke, so we are giving her oxygen. We are going to put her in a coma to try to and bring the swelling down. The good thing is she does have some mobility in her legs. It's going to be a long night and we don't know if she'll survive."

"Can I see her?" Bernard asked desperately. He had tears in his eyes and he kept rubbing his hands together.

"First, I need to know if she has any major allergies or health problems we should know about before we sedate her." The doctor looked at both of them. Bernard did not know of any, but Suzanne was looking at Bernard with alarm, her eyes bulging out. Suzanne sighed, and then she nodded at the doctor.

"She's pregnant," Suzanne said in a low voice.

"What?" was all Bernard could say. His jaw opened, and he kept looking at Suzanne in shock.

"I'm the father?" he stared at Suzanne until she nodded. "Why didn't she tell me?" he asked Suzanne.

"She was not sure how you'd feel," Suzanne answered.

"How could she not know that I would be delighted?" he turned and looked at the doctor.

"I can't guarantee we can save the baby if she has more complications, but we'll do our best. How far along is she?" the doctor asked.

"She's about three months along," Suzanne bowed her head, tears trickling down her cheeks.

"She will be moved to the intensive care unit on the second floor in a few minutes. You can see her there."

Dr. Dubois thanked them, shook Bernard's hand, and walked away to attend to his patients.

Bernard was pale and speechless for ten minutes. He had to sit down in the chair. He thought he was going to faint. He kept staring into space. He was going to be a father. It was going to change his life, he thought. He had never thought of having children before. Gabrielle would be a great mother, and he would find a way to raise the baby with Gabrielle. Now, they had to survive.

"She's pregnant," he said aloud to himself.

"Bernard, I'm sorry you had to learn it this way, but I was afraid ... she was going to tell you ... Bernard, are you okay?" Suzanne took his hand in hers.

"She's pregnant," he uttered again. "Why didn't she tell me?" He was trying to make it sink in. He was looking at Suzanne for answers. "I'm going to be a father."

"She hadn't been feeling well, and she only found out this morning. She was going to tell you," Suzanne was babbling away, but Bernard was not hearing her at all. He was going to be a father.

"Let's go see her." He stood up and he ran to the elevator. He pressed the number two button. It was short ride up, but when the doors opened, he stepped out quickly. He walked with long steps to the nurse's station to ask for directions. He asked the nurse where Gabrielle was located.

They told him she was in room number three. He walked down the hallway to find her. Everywhere he looked other people were in the same situation as her. They were all in critical condition. Bernard hurried to find her, but when he saw her, his trembling hand went to his mouth and he sucked his breath in. He kept shaking his head in disbelief, and saying, "No, no, no." His eyes pooled with water, tears were falling. He stood frozen on the spot, unable to breathe. He was not prepared for what he saw. She was lying in a bed with a breathing tube going down her throat and IVs running down to her arm. She was also hooked up to multiple monitors, and her head was bandaged. Tears welled up in his eyes; he truly could not control them. He deeply loved this woman. She could possibly die, and now she was carrying his child.

"Dear God, don't let them die. She's my life," Bernard said aloud. He slowly stepped forward and cautiously took her hand. He bent down and gently kissed her forehead. He was trying to be the strong one.

"Gabrielle, I'm here. You have to fight ... I can't live without you ... I love you," he said. His voice was breaking up, even trembling. It was only a whisper.

"I'm going to be right here until you wake up, you hear me? Right here." He pulled the only chair right up to her bed.

Suzanne went to stand beside him. She did not know how to comfort him, he was so incredibly sad. She placed her hand on his shoulder to try to comfort him, but there were no words or actions that could take his sorrow away. She stayed next to Gabrielle's bedside for a few hours. Suzanne took one last look at Gabrielle and, with tears in her eyes, she turned to Bernard.

"Do you need anything before I leave? I'm going to go see what or if there is anything salvageable of the inn. I'm going to get my arm taken care of. I'll return in a few hours."

Bernard lifted his head from where it was laying on the bed. Shook and nodded his head with understanding, "I'll be right here. I'm not leaving her."

"I'll be back later on. You have my phone number. Let me know if her condition changes, okay?"

Bernard only nodded. She bid him goodbye, and she kissed Gabrielle on the cheek.

"You get better. That's all you need to do. Love you!" she told her, and then she was gone. Bernard was left alone with Gabrielle. He could not comprehend who might want to hurt his beautiful Gabrielle. She was so innocent. She would never hurt anyone. Hours passed without any changes on her condition.

"How is she doing?" Bernard asked the doctor when he came to see her.

"Her condition has not changed yet. That is a good sign because that means she might be turning the tables around soon. We are not concerned that she has not improved yet. At least she has not had any other complications," Dr. Dubois had told him.

The nurses and the doctors came and went without saying anything different. She was still under critical watch. It was nightfall when someone knocked lightly on her door. He had not been aware that somebody was there. He looked up and saw two men dressed in suits standing in the doorway. They motioned for him to come to the door. Bernard got up from his vigil near Gabrielle's bed and he went to see what they wanted.

"Good evening, sir. My name is Detective Brown," said the older of the two men. He was in his mid-fifties, short, with thinning brown hair. He seemed tired, and his suit was somewhat ruffled.

"And this is Detective Murphy," he said, indicating to the other detective.

They both showed him their badges and their identifications. Bernard just stood there and casually looked at them.

"My name is Bernard Rian. I'm Gabrielle's boyfriend. What can I do for you?"

"We just wanted to ask you a few questions concerning what happened at the inn this afternoon," the detective said.

"Sure. What would you like to know?" Bernard asked.

"Do you know of anyone who might want to hurt Miss Leger or destroy her business?"

"God! No, I really do not. "

"The bomb squad determined there were three separate explosive devices that were planted at the scene. Do you know anything about that?"

Both detectives were looking at him.

"Oh! My God! I didn't know that. She received a written threat a couple of days ago, and then she was assaulted the other night, but ... I ... Wow! That's horrible."

Bernard was taken aback by the information. The detectives were watching his every movement and every expression. He felt a chill and rubbed his arms nervously.

"One more question, if I may. Where were you this afternoon when the blasts occurred?"

"I had gone to the pharmacy to pick up personal supplies when I heard all the sirens go by. I got curious then worried, so I rushed back to the inn," he said, eyeing them curiously.

"Can anyone confirm your whereabouts this afternoon?"

Bernard suddenly felt uneasy. He shifted his weight from one leg to another. "The cashier, I suppose. I would never hurt Gabrielle. She's carrying my child ... never." He could not believe that they thought he could harm her. "Check the videos at the store. I was there."

Both detectives looked at each other and nodded.

"And where were you when she got attacked?"

"I had just dropped her at her door and left, and then she called me. I came right over to stay with her," Bernard said, becoming nervous. It did not sound too good. He really had no alibi.

"We will check everything. That's all for now. And Mr. Rian, don't unexpectedly leave town." They stared at him, and then they turned around and departed.

Bernard was in disbelief that they could even think of such a thing. He sat down near Gabrielle to reflect on what they were thinking of accusing him of doing. *And bombs? Who could assemble them, and why would anyone want to hurt her?* The detectives thought he was a suspect. What was he going to do if they arrested him? He was afraid. His hands started to tremble. He decided to call his father to tell him the circumstances. He might need an attorney for legal advice. He wanted to have a lawyer if anything else happened. He did not want to wait for them to arrest him. His father could arrange to help him with these legal matters. He dialed his father's number. It was late, but he did not care. He needed advice and an attorney fast. He hated to ask him for help, but he did not know anyone here. He knew his father had trailed him earlier in Boston, but now he wondered if he could be so monstrous as to burn down Gabrielle's inn and try to kill her. He doubted it and he had no proof he had anything to do with this.

"Father, I'm in Canada. I don't want to alarm you, but I think I might be in trouble," he said.

"I thought you were going to Maine. What's wrong? What are you doing in Canada?"

Bernard decided to tell him the truth. "I'm going to make it brief. I came to see Gabrielle. An accident happened to her and her business. There were explosions, and her inn burned down and now the cops think I had something to do with it."

"I am so sorry to hear that. What do you mean they think you are responsible? That's ridiculous. Did anyone get hurt? Are you okay?"

"I'm fine, but Gabrielle was badly hurt. I need you to find me an attorney in this area."

"I'll send someone right away to help you. Are you sure you're all right?" Ron asked. "How is she doing? How badly was she hurt?" Ron asked

"She is in a coma. She received a blow to the head. One more small detail you know how you always wanted grandchildren? Well, she's pregnant with my child." Bernard was not so sure he should have said anything after what he had just said. He bit his tongue. His father was speechless.

"Father, are you there?"

"Yes, I am," Ron whispered. "I'm going to be a grandfather."

"Yes," Bernard answered.

"Oh! God, I have something important to tell you that cannot wait," Ron said.

"What?" Bernard was hoping he did not have anything to do with Gabrielle's injuries. "Father, what is it?" There was silence at the other end. Bernard could hear his father sigh heavily.

"Bernard, you know I love you, and I would never hurt you, but Gabrielle's accident was not an accident," Ron said.

"What are you talking about?" Bernard could not believe what he was hearing. He closed his eyes and continued listening.

"I had hired a man named Tom to scare her from you, but he decided to go further and try to kill her. He is crazy. I had nothing to do with it. I swear. Please forgive me," Ron pleaded. Bernard could not speak. He had a bad headache. He dropped the phone. He could still hear his father shouting in the phone. "Bernard. I am sorry. Forgive me."

Bernard was furious. He threw his phone on the floor, and it broke into pieces. He walked outside to the front entrance of the hospital. He needed fresh air. He could not breathe from the anger raging inside him. Bernard finally sat down on a nearby bench. He placed his hands over his face and cried out of desperation. His father had betrayed him for the last time. He had gone too far.

CHAPTER 14

Bernard was exhausted. It had been three days since Gabrielle had been hurt. He had not left her side. He had not been able to sleep much and he really needed a shower, but he would not leave the hospital. The whiskers on his face needed a shave, his hair was a mess, and his clothes were disheveled. The doctors had told him the baby was doing fine and Gabrielle's vital signs were improving every day.

The swelling of the lining of her brain had begun to subside and if everything went well, in the next day or two they would take her breathing tube out. Her lungs had improved, so she should be able to breathe on her own. She still had many obstacles and the doctors could not tell how her injury had affected her mentally or physically, but time would tell. She was not out of the woods just yet, but her chances were improving each day. Her health had a much better outlook than when she had first arrived at the hospital.

Suzanne came by every day. She had told Bernard that the inn was destroyed and that no one had been seriously injured in the explosion, just some cuts and a few broken bones here and there. Gabrielle was the only one who had been seriously hurt. It had taken most of the afternoon to extinguish the fire at the inn. There was not much left that was salvageable. The building had a lot of fire and water damage. It was extensive. Most of the structure was uninhabitable. It was a total loss.

The chief of the fire department had called in the forensic arson team and a criminologist team from the police department. This was definitely a suspicious fire—it had not been an accident. The investigators interviewed many patrons. They were trying to determine who would want to start this fire. How had it had started? And why? People were saying they had heard three separate explosions. The chief and his crew investigated the areas and they decided to also call the bomb squad in on the party. With their expertise, they had a better chance of determining what they needed to collect. The bomb squad, the arson investigators, and the criminologists joined forces together to try to find answers.

They were gathering evidence from the ruins, especially fragments of the explosives from the entire building. It was an unusual crime and they determined it was definitely a professional hit. They were set on resolving this crime because they wanted to find out who could construct a bomb and why would they want to destroy her business. Their energy was concentrated on finding out who in the area had the expertise and knowledge, as well as the means to buy the explosives. They started their search with the ex-military people from the area and certain companies that were experts in demolition. There was a lot of work ahead, but they were determined to examine all possibilities. They were thankful that more people hadn't been hurt.

Suzanne had brought Bernard fresh clothes and something to eat every day that he had been by Gabrielle's side. Bernard kept hoping for things to return to normal when she woke up. Today when Suzanne came to visit Bernard, she approached him. She smiled at him, and she extended her hand to him.

"Bernard, I'm not going to take no for an answer. These are the keys to my house. Please go shower. I will stay with her until you return to the hospital. I will not leave her," she said.

"I'm okay. Thanks anyway," Bernard said. He was afraid to leave Gabrielle.

"Bernard, listen to me. If she wakes up, and she sees you like you are now, she won't be too happy. Now go. I'll be right here. I won't leave her." She extended her keys to him again, and she waited. He looked at her. He was so tired. He did not know what to do. He rubbed his eyes with his fists and exhaled.

"You promise you'll call me if there's any change?" He really needed to be reassured. A shower and a small break might do him good.

"I promise you."

He took the keys from Suzanne, and then he kissed Gabrielle on the cheek and told her he would return shortly. He carried a huge burden. He blamed himself for not being there to keep her safe. Bernard felt so much better after taking a shower and putting on a new set of clothes. It did him a world of good. Now he could face anything.

***

Ron was pacing the floor of his library. He was elated but also scared that he might get implicated in this mess. He decided to call his attorney to see where he stood with this situation.

"Hello, George. I need some advice on a delicate matter," he said and explained the situation.

"I do not think they can charge you with much. You did not know what he was going to do, but I advise you to go to Canada and tell the police what you know and try to find Tom," George said.

"Thank you George, I will consider it," Ron said. He was not sure what to do.

He was going to be a grandfather. How wonderful—an heir. Bernard had never mentioned children before now. His son was going to be a father. He had to go see his son to try to help him. He could be in Canada in a few hours. He called his pilot to prepare his plane.

***

Tom had arrived back home and had decided to take an extra day off. He was fatigued. It had been a long trip back, and it had been a stressful assign-ment. He arrived to report for work, but when he got to the big house, his boss was nowhere to be found. He wanted to be paid for his work. He decided to investigate where Ron could be. He went behind the garages of the house where all the automobiles were kept. He found Dan, Mr. Rian's chauffeur. They did not get along too well, but Tom needed information. With this in mind, Tom casually approached the man.

"Hey Dan, how are things?"

Dan looked up and saw it was Tom. "Fine, what do you want?" he said as he continued cleaning the car.

"Have you seen Mr. Rian today?" Tom was getting impatient. He was tapping his foot on the ground. He was getting nowhere with him.

"He left late last night. I drove him to the airport," he answered.

"You wouldn't happen to know where he went, would you?" He was about to lose his patience, but he knew he had to control his temper if he wanted answers.

"From what I heard, he was going to Canada to help Bernard get out of a legal jam, but you didn't hear it from me. Now go away and leave me alone. I have work to finish," Dan said.

Tom was baffled and mystified as to why Mr. Rian would go to Canada. Something must have happened since he left, but what? He searched his mind, trying to put the missing pieces of the puzzle in place, but he could not achieve it. His mission had been successful, so what had happened? *Dan had said legal matters, but what did that mean? Bernard or Mr. Rian needed legal representation?* Tom did not like it when he did not have answers. He would have to just stay put and wait patiently until he came back so he could get paid. Eventually he would find out what was going on in Canada. He just hoped it did not have something to do with him.

***

Now Bernard's only concern was Gabrielle and his child. He drove to the hospital at a slow pace. He needed time to think about everything that had happened in the past few weeks. He was the happiest he had ever been in his life, yet he was facing the biggest hardship of his life at the same time.

When Bernard reentered Gabrielle's room, he felt refreshed. He grace-fully thanked Suzanne for her hospitality and most of all her concern for both of them. Suzanne had been a good friend to both of them. She had brought Gabrielle a book from her favorite author—Jeffery Weaver. She told Bernard to read to her aloud. Gabrielle needed to hear his voice, to know he was by her side. Bernard told Suzanne he would make sure to read to her. He thanked her again, and she left him alone with Gabrielle. He had fallen asleep on his chair while reading to Gabrielle. His head was on the side of her bed. He was holding on to her hand. Ron smiled at his son when he noticed him. As he approached the room, Ron saw that Bernard was sleeping near her and holding her hand. He looked so tired and lost.

Suddenly Bernard woke up, looked up, and saw his father. What was he doing here now? After all the pain he had caused him, why would he come here? Bernard did not want to talk or see him at this moment. As he approached him, a feeling of anger and disgust began to build in his gut.

"Back away from this room," Bernard said. He stood up, his fists clenched, and walked toward his father. He watched his father take a few steps back.

"I came as soon as I could to try to help and explain." Before he had time to finish his sentence, Bernard punched him with a right hook so hard that his father fell backward. He fell down and ended up sitting on the floor. Ron was stunned. His mouth hung opened, and he could not utter a word. Ron's left eye was bleeding. He had a cut above his eyebrow. He raised his hand to touch his wound, his head throbbing from the blow. He looked at his fingers and saw that there was blood on them.

"It was you who caused all this mess," Bernard said. Bernard wanted to beat him until he could no longer breathe. He had never in his life distrusted or hated someone as he did his father at that moment.

"I did not have anything to do with it. I swear."

Ron was slowly getting up. He saw a few people looking their way. They were watching them closely, but they did not dare approach.

"I know he did this. I know you told him to destroy Gabrielle's inn and now she could die. Tom only works for you. You are responsible for this."

Bernard was having a hard time talking, he was so bent out of shape. He was so angry. His face was turning red.

"It's not what you think ... He's crazy ... I would not—"

Bernard did not let him finish. He grabbed his father off the floor by his coat lapels and collar, lifted him up, and then forcefully shoved him against the wall. He got in his face. His mouth was close to Ron's ear and he whispered to his father between his teeth.

"Don't ever come near me, Gabrielle, or our child again. Do you understand?" He let him go, and then he pushed him against the wall one more time.

"Bernard! Son! It was not my—"

Bernard clenched his fists so hard that his knuckles turned white. His face showed disgust and repugnance. He turned away from his father, and he walked away. He never turned around because if he did, he might not be able to stop himself from killing his father right there and then.

***

The days that followed were long and lonely for Bernard. He kept praying for a miracle for Gabrielle. The doctors came in with the best prognosis so far. The fluid around her brain had diminished enough that they were going to remove the breathing tube and replace it with oxygen alone. Her lungs had healed, so she should be able to breathe on her own without pain. They were hoping she might wake up by herself within a day or two and they had stopped sedating her as much as before.

Next, the doctors wanted to check on the baby more closely. The obstetrician was concentrating on the baby. They performed an ultrasound and had kept a heartbeat monitor on the baby. Fortunately, the baby and Gabrielle were still doing just fine. It seemed the baby had not been directly affected by the coma. The doctors had told Bernard they were not going to sedate her to see if she would wake up on her own. He was still worried about both of them.

Bernard was grateful that she was doing so well. Now all he desired was for her to wake up and be a great mother to their child. The next few hours turned into two lengthy days, but on the third day he heard her moan softly and stir a bit.

Bernard jumped to his feet, leaned close to her, and started calling her name.

"Gabrielle, open your eyes. It's Bernard," he said to her softly.

She gradually opened her eyes a bit, and she looked at him. She was still half comatose, and she was trying to fight the drugs and open her eyes.

Bernard had the broadest smile ever. "Hello, sunshine. Welcome back."

She was trying to say something, but he could not understand.

"Shhh! I am going to get the doctors. I will be right back. Don't say anything." He kissed her, and he ran outside the room to the nurse's station.

He was ecstatic. He told them she was awake. They came at once with Bernard leading the way. He was almost running, he was so happy. The nurse came in and checked Gabrielle's vitals and asked her if she was thirsty. She nodded slightly. The nurse said she was doing just fine, and then she went to get her ice chips. Bernard took her hand in his and kept kissing it repeatedly.

"How are you feeling? Do you hurt anywhere?"

Gabrielle could only shrug.

"You're going to be just fine. You're in the hospital. You had a nasty bump on your head," he said, but she kept closing her eyes. He could tell she was trying to open her eyes.

The nurse returned with ice chips. She took a spoonful and put it in Gabrielle's mouth. The ice chips melted and then Gabrielle swallowed and made a face.

"I know your throat hurts. That's because you had a tube down your throat. It will get better," the nurse said, trying to encourage her. "Just rest. Try to sleep now. The doctor will be in soon."

She turned to Bernard and smiled, and then she gave him the cup of ice. "Just give her a little bit at a time, and if she sleeps, don't worry. It's all right. I'll be back in a few minutes."

A day later, Gabrielle was still waking up slowly.

"Everything is fine now. All you have to do is rest," Bernard kept saying to her. He could tell she was trying to speak to him. She kept moving her lips and making sounds. Bernard put his ear real close to her mouth.

"Fire ... Inn ... Hurt..."

That was all he could understand from her. He looked at her and quietly spoke to her.

"There was an explosion at the inn. No one got hurt but you. Everything is fine now. You don't have to worry, just rest and get better." He did not dare tell her the inn was destroyed. She seemed to understand, and then she closed her eyes. She drifted asleep again.

"I'm right here. I am not leaving you. I'll be here when you wake up."

He pulled his chair closer, and he held her hand. She squeezed it lightly. That small gesture made him feel so much better. He finally could think ahead without so much pressure on his shoulders. About a half-hour later, the doctor came in and he checked on her progress. He told Bernard she should recuperate. Right now she just needed to rest and try to regain her strength, but the worst was over. If everything went as planned and she improved gradually every day, she should be able to go home.

Gabrielle was sleeping soundly when Bernard noticed the two gentlemen at the door again. He had not expected to see them so soon. He stood up, and he greeted them. It was detectives Brown and Murphy. Bernard had called them earlier in the day and had told them he wanted to meet with them. They shook hands and Bernard guided them to an empty waiting area down the hall. He did not want Gabrielle to overhear their conversation. He did not want to upset her. They sat down next to each other in an empty waiting room. Bernard was a little nervous. He was hot, and his shirt was wet under his armpits. He had to let them know what he had discovered in the last few days.

"Thank you for coming," Bernard started. They did not say anything, just nodded at him, so he continued talking, "When you were here last time, you asked me if I had any information about the incident at the inn. Well ... now I do." The detectives just looked at him and waited for him to continue.

"I will have to start from the beginning. First of all, I now believe a man named Tom Smith probably constructed and planted the explosives devices." The detectives were taking notes and listening attentively.

"And when did you receive this information?" Brown asked him.

"I found out this information a few days ago, but I can't prove Smith had anything to do with it. I've been sitting here with Gabrielle since the accident." He was not very convincing, so he continued his story.

"This man is a military guy—he knows about explosives," Bernard said, trying to make them understand. The detectives were confused.

"What makes you think he's responsible?" the younger detective asked.

"He works for my father."

There, he had said it. He might as well continue. Murphy and Brown looked at each other, and the older one raised his eyebrows. All of the sudden, they were interested.

"And ..." Brown kept on him.

"Okay, I'll tell you. My father is a very wealthy man. He always gets his way and what he wants he gets ... always. He didn't like me dating Gabrielle. He would have preferred I date someone with more, shall I say, means. I think he sent him here to destroy our relationship or to hurt Gabrielle."

He had finally said his piece.

"Where can we find this man, Smith? And we will need to talk to your father, too." Now the detectives were very curious. They had found out Bernard was a prominent wealthy man from the Boston area. He had no criminal record, and he seemed clean in their eyes. Now his father was a new angle to investigate. They were interested in the facts.

"They both live in Boston. I can write down the address down for you." Bernard wrote all the information on a piece of paper.

"Has he done this before, this Smith? Has he follow you around or caused you harm?" Brown asked as he took the paper from him.

"I know he was doing it when Gabrielle and I were in Boston. I confronted my father at that time. He promised me he wouldn't do it again, but I really don't know," Bernard finished. His testimony had taken all his strength out of him. He had implicated his father.

"Very well then. We definitely will investigate this. Oh! By the way, we checked out your alibi, and you are cleared. We saw you on the surveillance video. Sorry for the inconvenience, but we had to eliminate everyone, even you."

Brown was a calm one, thought Bernard. "I understand. Please let me know what you find."

"Yes, we will, but we might need your help later on. This evidence is useless if we can't prove any of it," Brown replied.

"That's fine. Just let me know if I can help," said Bernard. He was determined. He would give everything he had in him to convict Tom.

"We will look into it. We'll be in touch."

They shook hands and they were on their way.

Detective Brown went back to the police station. Since they were in Canada and this Smith guy was in the United States, he was having problems retrieving information, so he contacted the Royal Canadian Mounted Police—the Canadian equivalent of the United States FBI. They were a federal agency. The detectives had to work with them, but at least they would know more about these men. The RCMP had jurisdiction over matters like this one, especially when it was an international crime. The next day they were fortunate to receive the information the detectives needed for their investigation.

"I just acquired Smith's military records and his rap sheet from the United States," Brown said to Murphy.

"What does it say?"

"Well, Smith had incidents of violence when he was a juvenile, but after he joined the military, he did not have anything except ..." Brown trailed off, thinking.

"Except what?" Murphy asked.

"He had a dishonorable discharge issued to him. This one is a bad egg. The only problem is we do not have any solid evidence to corroborate what Bernard is telling us."

"I could not find or prove anything on him entering or leaving the country. Even worse, where he would have bought parts for explosives," Murphy answered.

"I do believe Bernard, but knowing the weight Ron Rian carries ... it is almost impossible to pin him down without an attorney, because the minute we approach him, we lose all access to him," said Brown. He was pondering a new direction.

"You are right. We have to find another way," Murphy said.

"I have got it. There is only one scenario we might have to get this guy and be able to convict him. We need Bernard."

"How?" Murphy asked.

"We could ask Bernard to try to convince his father to cooperate in the apprehension of Tom. He would have to try to have his father admit to his part in this plot to destroy the inn and in trying to murder Gabrielle. One alone is almost impossible. What do you think?" Brown was nodding his head at Murphy.

"It is a touchy situation because Bernard would have to not only give up Smith, but also his father's involvement."

"It's the only shot we have in closing this case. We need to plan this out, because right now we are at a dead end," Brown said and closed Smith's file.

A few days had gone by, and Ron was beside himself. He would not see or talk to anyone from his staff or, especially, work. Ron blamed himself for this disaster in his life. Ron was so depressed he could not eat or work.

He had not showered or changed his clothes since he had arrived from Canada. He had spoken to his attorney again but still had not been able to make a decision about giving up Tom. He had to try to protect himself from being charged in this mess. He thought maybe helping the cops catch Tom would help his own case and get Bernard back in his life.

He was still wearing his bloody shirt, and his eye was black and blue. He did not care. The only thing that helped was whiskey. The bottle had been his best friend ever since he had arrived home. Ron had lost his only son and now his only grandchild. He had to do something to try to rectify the situation. God help him, if he got his son back, he would never again interfere in his affairs. He still could not get the last words Bernard had said to him out of his mind, *"You caused all this mess. Stay away from us."* *What had he done?* He was ruined without Bernard. He was his only reason for living. He prayed Bernard and Gabrielle could find it in their hearts to forgive him. Otherwise, he would definitely die of sorrow. He could not live without his family. He had to find a way to be complete again and only Bernard could do that for him.

Suddenly, Ron had an idea about how he might be able to show how sorry he was and fix everything. He was going to give up Tom to the police. At least then maybe he might have a shot at forgiveness. He picked up the phone and called his attorney.

"George, I want you to set up a meeting with the police and the district attorney. I want to go to Canada and tell them what I know about the incident, but I want immunity for my testimony," Ron said.

"I advise you not to do that before we know if they will give you immunity. You might be charged in this crime."

"I really do not care. I want to talk to the lead detective in Canada. Now just arrange it," Ron said and then hung up the phone. He was going to do the right thing for once in his life.

CHAPTER 15

Gabrielle was getting stronger every single day. She had been in the hospital for almost a month now. Bernard was thankful she had no brain damage or significant physical problems. She still needed care, like physical therapy, and he had hired a private nurse who would come to help her during the day for a few weeks. The baby was healthy and growing bigger every day. She was to be dismissed from the hospital later on today. They were waiting for her to undergo her last examination by her doctor and hopefully be released. Bernard could not wait to get her home to make love to her. He was counting the minutes. He just wanted to feel her body next to his. That was the one thing he had missed the most while she had been hospitalized. He had missed being able to hold her close, touch her, and caress her. Right now, Gabrielle was his only concern. She had been devastated when she found out that her precious inn had been destroyed. A million tears had fallen, and Bernard wished that he could have taken away all that pain.

Bernard did have a huge surprise that he could not wait to tell her. He had bought her a small cottage on the ocean in which she could recover from her injuries. It was only a mile away from her inn. It was a small bungalow with only two bedrooms, but he found it quaint and so charming. An older retired couple had lived in this little house for years. He had wanted it for Gabrielle, so he had offered them a sum of money they really could not refuse, because it was enough to allow them to buy themselves two houses. It had a small backyard, there were no neighbors nearby, and the view was spectacular. He wanted to try to make amends for what his father had done to her.

The time had finally arrived when the doctors had given her the green light. She could go home. Bernard was wheeling her to the front entrance when he decided it was time to tell her she was not going to stay with Suzanne.

"I have a surprise for you. I hate to disappoint you, but you are not going to do your recovery at Suzanne's house."

"What do you mean? What are you up to now?" she asked.

"You'll see. That's all I'm telling you."

He was being secretive, and he loved to make her wonder. They finally were seated in his truck. He made sure she was comfortable. He brought a pillow for her to lean on and a light blanket if she got cool. He started the short drive to her new home. She kept asking him questions, but he would not answer her. Half an hour later, he was driving up an unpaved road that led to the ocean. He knew how much she loved the water. Bernard parked his vehicle in front of the small bungalow.

They were staring at this nice little cottage by the ocean. It sat on top of a cliff. Small birds were flying by the edge of the cliff. They had made holes in the walls of the cliff for their young. A small stairway took you to your own beach down below. On both sides of the house, fields of hay moved with the wind, and in back near the woods stood a lone barn. The cottage was painted white with a red roof and a long porch facing the ocean. There were beautiful flowers all around the property and a big oak tree with a brand new swing. She could see a trail on the lawn that led down to the beach. It was all so peaceful and alluring. You could smell the ocean in the breeze. It looked like a small villa by the water.

"Do you like it?" He was looking for a reaction, but she was just staring at it. She had a blank expression on her face.

"It's a lovely place, but why are we here?" she asked.

"I bought it last week. I want you to have it so you have a home of your own." He took out a set of keys from his pocket, and he put them in her hands. "It's all yours. I wanted you to have your own place."

She looked at the keys in her hand. She did not say anything.

"Do you like it? I know it's not that big, but until we find a bigger place ..."

He saw a tear fall from the corner of her eye. His heart broke every time she cried. He reached over and wiped the tears away.

"Come, let me show you the inside. It's very nice. You are going to like it."

"Thank you so much. I already love it."

She stepped out of the Range Rover and walked toward the front door. She turned around to make sure he was still behind her as she opened the door. A broad smile came to her face. Bernard thought her smile was worth all the money he had made over the years. Gabrielle and Bernard were looking at the water through the windows in the living room. You could see small sailboats on the water and the seagulls flying by. The sun's rays were coming through the front windows of the living room. It was magical. It really warmed her heart that he cared so much that he wanted her to have her own home.

The house was freshly painted in white and baby blue. The kitchen was small, but it had all new kitchen appliances. She started to walk around when he grabbed her by hand and led her to the first bedroom. It was a tiny one. Bernard had bought a crib and a dresser. The room was painted in yellow with baby giraffes that matched all the accessories of the room. It was adorable. He had made sure everything the baby would need was there: a rocking chair, changing table, and lots of baby clothes. He really wanted this child. He would be a good father to his child.

"What do you think? Do you like it? You can change it if—"

He did not have time to finish his sentence. She had her arms around his neck, and she was kissing him. Her fingers played with his hair. He pulled her close, and he pressed her tight against him.

"Thank you. I truly love it, I really do. It is the cutest room," she replied, still kissing him.

They embraced and made love. After an hour or so, Bernard slipped out of bed quietly. He did not want to disturb Gabrielle. He went to the bathroom and took a quick shower, and then he proceeded out the door to bring in from his Range Rover what little Gabrielle had with her. There was only a simple duffle bag. He dropped it at the door of the bedroom. He returned to the kitchen to make a sandwich for Gabrielle. As he turned to get a drink, his cell phone rang. He reached over and answered it.

"What do you want?" Bernard was not going to be manipulated by his father.

"I will do anything to have you back in my life again. Anything! I will talk to the police, tell them everything. Forgive me. I want you and Gabrielle and your child back in my life. *Please*," Ron pleaded.

"Father, I do not want you to call me again. That is all," Bernard said firmly.

"Please, I'm so sorry," Ron said.

Bernard hung the up phone. He was in an emotional turmoil. His father had never begged. He did not know what to think right now. He did not want to have anything else to do with him. He felt sorry for his father. He had lost him, but he did not think he could forgive him for what he had done. He did not wish him harm, but he did not want to see him either ... not just yet, anyway. He did not look back. He now had his family to take care of, and his father no longer was part of it.

***

"How did you know I was famished? It must be the baby," she said when he sat next to her.

"I like to think it was the sex," Bernard said.

She smiled.

"Ahhh! Nevertheless, you love the mystery of the man."

He was teasing her while they were enjoying a cool evening sitting on the porch eating their sandwiches. The stars were bright, and the light of the moon reflected on the water. She could see fireflies flying and dancing in the light breeze. It was a relaxing night.

"I have something I must talk to you about now that you are out of the hospital," Bernard said.

Gabrielle could tell he was very serious. He took her hands in his and looked her straight in the eyes.

"What is it?" she asked.

"First, I love you with all my heart ... I would never hurt you ... but my father doesn't feel the same way. He ordered a man named Smith to burn down your inn and hurt you. He claims Tom did it by himself, but ... I am very sorry it happened," he said and bowed his head.

"Why?" she asked.

He lifted his head to look at her. "Well, my father is old school and believes his son should marry someone he chooses. I didn't agree, so he ... I'm truly sorry."

"This was not your fault. I understand that," she said and tightened her grip on his hands. They sat quietly as they watched the moon and the stars sparkle high above.

"I'm exhausted, so I think I would like to go to bed early," she said.

The next week and the following, Gabrielle was up earlier and getting stronger. The nurse came by to make sure she was taking her medications and check her vitals. Everything was well, and Gabrielle would be out of the door with a list as long as her arm for things for the house or the baby. Bernard thought she was so funny, running around the house trying to get things in place as fast as possible. What she did not know was he was really looking for a much larger home for them, but why take her fun away just yet? She was happy and he loved to hear her enthusiasm about all her new findings, like baby pictures or handmade baby clothes.

One afternoon Bernard was relaxing outside watching the birds fly by and the fishing boats out on the horizon. He heard someone walking on the front porch. Bernard thought, *it's Gabrielle!*

"What did you forget now?" He was expecting to see Gabrielle, but to his surprise, it was not her at all. Standing in front of him were the two men he thought he would not have to ever see again. They were both dressed in dark suits. Bernard never heard them drive up the driveway. He was not happy to see them. It was the two detectives that he had spoken to at the hospital: Brown and Murphy.

"Good morning, Mr. Rian. Could we have a moment of your time?" the older one asked.

"What can I do for you?" Bernard was wondering what they were doing at his home.

"How did you find this place?" Then it hit him, it was a small town. Everyone knew everybody's business, and they were detectives. They did not have time to answer. He invited them in.

"Please, come in."

Bernard did not know what to expect from them. He led them in and they all sat down on the couch in their small living room.

"I'm going to get straight to the point," Brown said.

"We investigated that guy Smith that you told us about. We do believe he is capable of this crime. We have enough evidence to convict him. We talked to your father on the phone, and he decided he would give Tom up. Your father's testimony helped us a lot, but not until the district attorney and his lawyer worked out a deal that gave him full immunity for his involvement."

Bernard was listening intently. He was in shock to hear what his father had done.

"We also believe that until Tom is in custody, you should be careful. We have not been able to apprehend him yet."

Bernard was still in disbelief about his father. "What can I do?" he asked, looking at them, waiting for the answers.

"We would like you to make sure you lock your doors, and if you see anything—and I mean anything—out of the ordinary, call us right away. Do you understand?" Brown told him.

"Do you think he will come back this way again?" Bernard asked Brown, concerned for Gabrielle's safety.

"We do not know for sure. Your father said he had gone rogue and since it's an international crime, we spoke to the FBI, and they will be assisting us. We are still talking to your father. We have solid evidence for a conviction, but we really do not know where Tom is at the moment," Brown informed him.

He was the only family that his father had right now. He just wanted Smith to pay for this crime. He would never forget what his father had conspired to do, but now Ron was trying to protect him and Gabrielle from Tom. Bernard was speechless.

"Just keep your eyes open. We will contact you when we have more information," Brown said to Bernard.

Brown and Murphy got up to leave. They shook hands and walked away and left without another word. Bernard just stood at the door, watching as they got into their car and drove off.

A few minutes later, Gabrielle was pulling into the driveway. She was carrying bags of groceries. Bernard greeted her at the door and he kissed her. He took the bags from her and placed them on the small table in the kitchen.

"Was that the detectives I saw driving off?" she asked him.

"Yes, it was," Bernard said. He did not know how he was going to tell her about the new developments in the case. She was the one that had lost everything and had gotten hurt.

"So, what did they want? Did they have news about the case?" she asked looking at him, waiting for answers.

"You'd better sit down. Let me try to explain what's going on," Bernard said, hesitant to tell her, but knowing he had to do it. "They came to tell me about the man who burned down your inn and tried to murder you. They are trying to find him. My father gave him up. They have enough evidence for a conviction."

He waited for her reaction, but she did not say anything. After a few minutes, she finally she spoke up.

"Do you think he will come here?" she asked.

"We really have to be vigilant," he answered. He had to tell her the rest. He hoped she would understand. "There's one more thing. My father will receive full immunity for the testimony he gave the police. They are not going to charge him with any crime."

He let out a deep sigh. He bent his head down to look at the floor, getting ready for their first fight. She was not saying anything. A few minutes went by, and it was pure agony for him. He took a step away and then lifted his head to look at her. She seemed calm. She sat in silent. She had not said one word since he had stopped talking. She looked at him and she finally uttered only one word, then she waited for an answer.

"Why?"

He tried to find the right words to try and make her understand, but the only thing that came out of his mouth was, "Because he is trying to protect us, and he still loves me. I think he is looking for forgiveness from us."

He had said his piece. That was what he was so afraid to tell her. He waited anxiously for her to respond. Neither one spoke. It was tense and there was complete silence between them. Gabrielle just got up and she went to sit outside on the porch. He decided to give her space to think. She had not said anything and now he dreaded the answer.

The sun went down, the beach-goers went home, and the stars came out, and still Gabrielle was sitting on the porch. Bernard made her a sandwich, and he brought it to her on the porch. She still did not speak to him, but she ate some of the food. He could not stand it anymore. He went and sat next to her on the porch, and he waited for her to say something. He was hurting deep inside, and he could not take the silence anymore. He had to talk with her.

"Gabrielle, I am sorry for the outcome of this investigation, but Father is now trying to make amends." He looked at her. She turned toward him.

"I have been sitting here thinking about everything, and I love you more than anything in this world," she said as Bernard listened to her attentively. "And I know you love your father, too. I'm sure he tried to protect you from me, but I would never hurt you. I probably would have done the same. He assisted the cops to make it right. I'll stand beside you in whatever you want to do."

Bernard could not move. He was so amazed by her answer. He reached over and kissed her deeply.

CHAPTER 16

Brown and Murphy had gone to talk to their captain about their situation with Mr. Rian. The captain was not pleased either about the latest outcome, so he had, in turn, gone to talk to the district attorney, Elizabeth Roy. She was a petite woman in her mid-forties. She was a hardworking person and a very dependable woman who lived to get criminals off the streets. She was not thrilled at all about the developments of this case. The deal that the detectives wanted was the lesser of two evils.

It was not acceptable to Ms. Roy, but she really had no other choice. She had gone over all the evidence and other possibilities many times. She was trying to catch a break by finding a loophole in the law so that she could get both men. She had looked at it from every angle, but she had not been successful. The only way to maybe get both was to be patient and watch them until their next hit, to see if one of them would make a mistake. It could take years. There was no way to convict either one without Ron Rian's cooperation and granting him immunity. Ms. Roy was definitely not happy. In fact, she was furious that she had to let him go free. She would give in to the total immunity agreement for Ron Rian, but she would make sure from this day on, his every move would be scrutinized, and he would be watched to the fullest. She would call agent John White from the FBI Boston branch to arrange the extradition of Tom Smith after his capture.

Ms. Roy was going to collaborate with the warrants in the apprehension of Tom Smith as soon as she heard back from the FBI. The next day, she got the green light from all the agencies involved to serve the warrants pending the testimony of Ron Rian. She finally dialed Detective Brown's number after all resources were exhausted. She gave him the go-ahead, and she told the detectives they were to come down to her office to revise everything. She told them after that, they could pick up the immunity agreement for Mr. Ron Rian.

***

Bernard took his phone and he sat down in the living room. He was feeling extremely nervous, so he kept looking at his telephone in his hand. The clock on the wall read three o'clock. He kept looking at the ocean and then the phone. He knew his father was probably at home having an afternoon drink. He thought about what he was going to say to him beforehand, so he would not mess up the conversation. Now all he needed was enough guts to do it. He finally pushed the speed-dial button. There was no turning back now and it started to ring. He could feel his heart beating in his chest. He was thinking about how he was still afraid of his father's authority over him, but would never admit it, not to anyone, not even to Gabrielle.

Ron pick up his phone immediately when he saw Bernard was calling. His heart jumped a beat at the prospect of patching things up with Bernard. He downed the last of his scotch.

"Father, I just called to thank you for what you did, giving up Tom. It was the right thing to do."

"Bernard, I was just going to call you. I am truly sorry about how things turned out. I wanted to call and inform you. The cops can't find Tom. I am worried and afraid for you. You need protection. He must be mad and ...," Ron said while pacing the floor. Ron did not want to think about what Tom could do.

"I'm fine." He was holding back to see what his father would say.

"I truly regret hurting you. Can you ever forgive me?" Ron waited for his response. There was none.

"It is not me you should ask for forgiveness, but Gabrielle."

"I'll be there tomorrow afternoon to talk to her and help you."

"Very well."

Bernard was not sure if it was a good idea, but he gave his father his new address, and they were done. He walked outside because he was trying to calm himself and at the same time prepare himself for the confrontation that was going to occur tomorrow. He had done his part. Now it all rested on his father's shoulders. He was relieved that it was almost over.

Ever since Ron had talked to the district attorney and had gotten his immunity, he had been trying to track down Tom. No one on the compound had seen him. Tom had not answered his phone when Ron had called him. That was the worst. Tom was like a ghost. Ron was very frightened for the safety of his son and Gabrielle. He was also afraid Tom might have found out about the deal he had made with the cops. The FBI had searched Tom's home and been around Ron's grounds looking for him. Ron decided he was going to accept this woman, even if he did not like her, and keep his mouth shut. He had to return to Canada to try to protect them from Tom. Ron suspected Tom might have returned there to seek revenge and hurt them for his giving him up.

Ron called his pilot to prepare his jet for the voyage back to Canada. Ron picked up his phone on the desk and called his pilot, Jim. Jim was a trustworthy man. He had been flying Ron's jet for about eight years now. He was a family man, with two beautiful sons. He was also one of the most reliable employees Ron had. Ron had full confidence that Jim could be discreet, so he decided to call him first, as it gave him more time to prepare everything.

"Good morning, Jimmy. How are you?"

"Very well, sir."

"Could you please prepare my jet for tomorrow afternoon?"

"Yes, sir. What is your destination?"

Ron did not want anyone to know where he was going. "Destination ...?" he asked, thinking about Bernard, but he needed to tell Jimmy. He needed his flight plan, fuel, food, etc., so he decided he had to know.

"Moncton, Canada, Jimmy," Ron said. It was the airport nearest to where Bernard was located. "And Jimmy, keep it under your hat. No one is to know, understood?"

"Yes, sir. I'll be quiet about it. I'll be ready around one o'clock. Will that be satisfactory?"

"That will be perfect. Thank you." He hung up the phone, and he felt happier that he had been in weeks. He then called his chauffeur to bring the car around to the front door. Ron decided he would open a trust fund for his future grandchild. He called his attorneys to set it up. This child would not need anything as long as Ron was alive. He had the money and that was where he was going to spend it, on his grandchild. What he did not notice was the car that was following him.

***

Gabrielle came back to the cottage not long after Bernard had spoken to his father. He was sitting on one of the chairs outside facing the ocean. She approached him slowly and she sat down next to him. Bernard lifted his head, and then he looked at her. She reached over and kissed his cheek softly. He was very quiet, and she could see the concern on his face. She felt his pain, but there was nothing she could do but support his decision. Bernard and Gabrielle were very apprehensive about this meeting.

Tom had followed Ron to the airport and had concluded he was headed back to Canada. Where else would he go? Tom had arrived ahead of Ron at Bernard and Gabrielle's residence. Immediately after he had landed, he had called his ex-Army friend in the city so he could acquire a few more things. He had purchased a nine-millimeter with extra bullets, and he borrowed his friend's sniper rifle with a scope, just in case he needed it. He had found the perfect hiding place about three hundred yards away in an old abandoned barn.

The barn was set near the woods. Old farming equipment was lying around that was either broken or had rusted away. They must have used it to pick up the bales of hay, because there was a large field right next to it. Tom managed to climb up to the second level of the barn, using a broken-down wooden ladder that someone had left behind. It was still good enough to use to climb up. He laid it against the second level of the barn where it had been used to store the hay and climbed up carefully. He had a perfect view through the wooden doors that were broken and rotting away. He had been lucky to find this place, because he did not really know the terrain, and he needed a place to hold up. It was a great hiding place, and he had a direct view of Bernard's front window in the cottage. He would be fine there.

Tom had not had much time to consider the turn of events, but he was content with his position. He could now observe them. Tom watched Gabrielle walk up to the house and disappear behind the door. He pointed his rifle toward the house. He had a good view of the inside of the residence with his scope. He watched Bernard go from one room to the other, probably waiting for Ron.

He did not have to wait too long, because fifteen minutes later, he saw a Mercedes Benz drive up the road. He knew only Ron would rent a Benz in this small town. His suspicions were confirmed when he saw Ron get out of the car. Tom laughed aloud. This was a good. Let the games begin. He was going to show them he could finish his job. Ron should not be talking to them. Ron should not betray him after all the work he had done.

Ron was so excited to be reuniting with his son. He was a nervous wreck. His knees were weak, and he was sweating. It was worse that signing a major deal, but he told himself that after he got through the first awkward moments, it was going to be smooth sailing. He had put the address in his GPS, so it had not been difficult to find the cottage in this small town. He pulled up the small road to the residence. He walked what seemed like an ever-ending walkway to the front door. He gently knocked on the door, and he waited nervously for his son to come answer the door.

CHAPTER 17

For the first time in Bernard's life, he looked at his father, and he saw a man that had fear and confusion in his eyes. Bernard felt sorry for him, but at the same time he was savoring this short period. His father had caused so much pain to so many people. Ron finally looked human. Bernard noticed his hands were trembling slightly, and he had small beads of sweat on his upper lip. He looked like a lost child that was waiting for direction, and it was Bernard's turn to lead. He gently touched his father's arm and spoke to him in a soft voice, "Dad, please follow me."

It was the first time in a long time he had ever used an informal name for his father. Ron looked at his son and decided to follow him quietly. They went to the kitchen area where Gabrielle was waiting patiently. Gabrielle stood up immediately when he had entered the house. She straightened the flowered dress that she was wearing, her small belly showing. Ron entered the kitchen. Bernard went to stand beside her and wrapped his arm around her waist.

"Father, this is Gabrielle," he said and glanced at her.

"Gabrielle, it's a pleasure to finally meet you," Ron said. Ron extended his hand and shook her hand. He smiled at her.

Bernard took the lead, "Father, please have a seat."

He motioned him toward a chair. Ron walked to it and he sat down. He waited until they were all sitting. He did not know what to expect, so he decided he would listen first. Gabrielle and Bernard were sitting next to each other. Ron noticed how she discreetly touched his hand. Ron was sweating a bit. He thought it was warm and he could feel beads of perspiration on the back of his neck. *This was the hardest thing he had ever had to do in his life.*

"I came here to ask for your forgiveness and to tell you that I was only trying to protect my son."

His father was rubbing his hands together restlessly. Ron was looking straight at Gabrielle, and then he noticed two men sitting in the living room.

"They are here for a reason," Bernard said. It looked as if Brown and Murphy were going to burst in and arrest him.

"I wonder what that could be," said Ron as he shifted in his chair and looked out the window.

Bernard ignored his father's comment and continued. "They are detectives. They are the team that investigated the attempted murder and the explosion at Gabrielle's inn. They came to warn us that Tom was at large, and they wanted to protect us."

Ron was not moving an inch. He just kept staring at Bernard.

"That is why I came. I felt I needed to protect you, too," Ron said.

"They believe you know where Tom is, and you are not saying anything," Bernard said.

"That is ridiculous. I came to try to warn you. I do not know where he is."

"On the phone you said you were willing to do anything for our forgiveness," Bernard said.

Ron's eyes slanted, and his lips were shut tight. Bernard could see he was mad.

"Stop it right now, Bernard. I have to explain to you what happened. I never told Tom to hurt her or burn down her inn. He did all that on his own. He is crazy. He does not listen to me anymore. All I had asked was for him to give Gabrielle a warning to stay away from you. He is delusional. He thinks she is after your money, and he has to stop her from ruining the family. I never wanted her hurt. I am so sorry. I never thought it would go this far," he said. Ron did not even look Gabrielle's way. He was examining his hands.

"I would never ..." Gabrielle started to say then quieted down. She bowed her head as she reached for Bernard's arm.

"I brought you here so we could be a family again," Bernard said. He was trying to calm his father.

Bernard went over to his father and touched his hand. Ron looked up at him with tears in his eyes. He bowed his head so Bernard would not see the tears.

"Father, the two detectives in the living room are here because they need more information about his whereabouts. They think he might come here again because they do not think Tom knows about the agreement yet," Bernard said softly.

"We think you should help us put him away," Gabrielle said to him, then walked up to him and gave him a glass of water. She placed her hand on his shoulder for just an instant. Ron looked up at her and nodded slowly.

"I do not want you to get hurt. I know he is dangerous, and I will try," Ron said.

The detectives were introduced to Ron. He proceeded to tell the detectives the whole story again—how Tom had followed them but had decided to kill and destroy Gabrielle's inn without him knowing anything until it was too late. After a few hours of talking, the detectives said they had enough information for the moment and they would contact Ron later on. The detectives left them alone and drove off to the police station to finalize the papers.

"I'm staying at the Eagle Motel on Main Street for the weekend. If you want to call me, I'll be there," said Ron. He was looking at Bernard, but Gabrielle stepped forwarded and gave him a hug. Ron did not move. He just stared at her. She backed away from him and went to stand beside Bernard. She touched his arm lightly and said, "Thank you for helping us get that criminal."

"You are most welcome. And Bernard ... I am beginning to see why you love this woman," he said, and then extended his hand to Bernard. His son grabbed it and pulled his father to him to give him a hug. Ron smiled. He walked out the door and headed to his motel room.

Hidden away with his rifle aimed at Ron's head, Tom was watching attentively through the scope of his rifle. He watched Gabrielle. That bitch should have died in that explosion. What were the chances she would survive? *I should kill her right now,* he thought, aiming his rifle at her head. Seconds went by. Tom's finger was getting tighter on the trigger, but then Ron might get upset if he shot her now. *I wonder what would Ron do if I got rid of her now,* he chuckled.

"I could kill that bitch right now," Tom said to himself aloud.

He watched her walk away in his scope. Tom still had his finger on the trigger—all he had to do was squeeze a little tighter on the tongue of the rifle, and it would be the end of her.

Decisions, decisions. What should he do?

Suddenly, he lifted his rifle, repositioned it, and aimed it back at the cottage. He wondered what the detectives were doing there. Why was Ron there at the same time? He hoped he had not betrayed him to the cops. Those detectives were brainwashing Ron.

***

Gabrielle went for a walk. She entered the house and she saw Bernard sitting by himself in the living room. He was looking out the windows at the ocean. She went to sit by his side on the couch. She placed her hand on his knee. She could feel the warmth of his body against her knee, and she spoke to him softly.

"Are you all right?"

"Yes, I'm fine. I'm more hurt and embarrassed than anything else," he said to her, his voice breaking a bit as he spoke.

"Why? It wasn't your fault. You did the right thing."

He turned to look her way. Bernard took her hand in his. He was not angry, just disappointed with himself. "Tomorrow, I'm going to go talk to him again. He looked afraid and lost."

He tenderly kissed her on the cheek. He wrapped his arm around her shoulder, and he pulled her closer.

"Now, we're hungry!" she said, smiling and then pointed at her belly.

"We're hungry!" he repeated, and he chuckled. "Well, what would we feel like eating?"

"We would settle for a pepperoni pizza. How about you?"

Gabrielle was grinning from ear to ear—she could not help herself—and she started laughing. They both got up and decided to go out and have dinner in town.

***

Detective Brown was sitting in a beat up chair at his desk in the precinct. His desk was an old, gray metal desk with tons of paperwork on top that needed to be done or filed. An empty Chinese takeout box from last night was still sitting on the corner of his desk. The only new thing was the computer that was on the right side of his desk. Brown was facing his partner's desk, which looked pretty much the same as his. This town only had a handful of money for the detectives; the budget was not big. That was because the major crime rate was not very high, so they helped the uniformed guys on mostly domestic issues or theft. He was busy trying to track Tom down, but he had not been successful even with Ron's help. He was going to get this man behind bars, but he had to find him. His phone rang. He looked at it, uninterested, but he had to answer.

"This is Detective Brown. How may I help you?"

"Stay away from the Rian family or you will pay the consequences."

"Who is this? What do you want?"

"I'm your worst enemy. Don't fuck with me. "

Brown was now standing at his desk. He wore an expression of frustration and disbelief on his face. He was signaling to his partner to try to trace the call, but it was too late. The person at the other end of the line had already hung up. He was long gone. Brown just stood there looking at the receiver of his phone, stunned. Who would dare threaten him? He thought it over and knew there was only one possible person. *It had to be Tom Smith. Who else around here knew The Rian family?* He was positive, but proving it was going to be difficult. He had only heard his voice once. He had to warn them Tom was here.

***

Tom had spent the night reflecting on the previous day. He really did not like that detective Brown. Afterwards, he had checked it out with an acquaintance. He always said that it all came down to who you know. He had called him, and he had given him a warning. He had better listen, because he would take care of him if he came close to Mr. Rian again. His boss was a good man and it was his duty to protect him. Mr. Rian had done the same for him many times. Mr. Rian was a great boss.

"Don't worry, Mr. Rian. I'll take care of you and whoever gets in your way if necessary. I promise," he said aloud. He had become a very dangerous man with no conscience.

CHAPTER 18

Bernard was waiting impatiently at Chez Lisette for his father to arrive at the restaurant. It was a small pub situated on a wharf overlooking the marina. Bernard had found a table in the back on the top floor where he could see the comings and goings on the road up to the wharf area. He saw the Mercedes driving down toward the wharf. His father had found the place and had arrived on time. Ron was escorted to Bernard's table. He greeted him with a handshake and they both sat down. There was an awkward moment, but it passed when they started to talk.

"It's important you listen carefully to what I have to say," his father said.

"Very well then, but let's order a drink first," Bernard answered.

Bernard motioned for the waitress to come over. They both ordered a cold beer with nachos and hot chicken wings.

"Go ahead. I'm listening," said Bernard. He was anxious to find out what his father had to say.

"It was a Godsend I came yesterday, because Tom was also there. He was hiding in an abandoned barn not far from your house. He said he was protecting me. I ..." Ron said.

"What are you saying? He was there?" Bernard said, "How did he know?"

"Listen, he's evil. He overheard me when I was talking to Jim, my pilot. He has a sniper rifle. I want to help you. He will not do anything as long as I am with you. I do not think he knows anything about the immunity agreement," said Ron. He hesitated for a moment before continuing. "He had a sniper rifle aimed at us."

Bernard felt a wave of panic for Gabrielle. He was in disbelief.

"He is here somewhere. He called last night at the motel, and he told me everything. We have to tell Gabrielle and call the cops to protect her," Ron said to his son.

Bernard placed two twenties on the table. He was thrilled his father had reconsidered helping him catch Tom.

"Let's go. First, we have to get Gabrielle out of harm's way. She might still be in danger. Then, we are going to call Detective Brown, and you are going to tell him what you just told me now. The rest of the story about Tom is important," said Bernard.

Both men got up to leave when Ron touched Bernard's arm and he squeezed it lightly. Bernard knew his father was sincere, but right now he was petrified something might happen to Gabrielle if he did not get home. He needed to protect her and keep her safe.

"Come on. Leave your car. We'll go together, it's faster," Bernard told his father.

They both got in Bernard's truck and took off toward the cottage to find Gabrielle. They were not far, but traffic was at a crawl that was typical in the summer. He took as many back roads as he could to find the beach house. Bernard's mind was going crazy trying to understand all the new developments his father had just told him. They still did not know Tom's location. *What if he hurt Gabrielle?*

***

Gabrielle was making herself a tuna sandwich for lunch in the kitchen. She had been humming the tune of a lullaby all day. She was dressed in comfortable shorts and a loose shirt. When she heard the bell ring, she put down her knife and turned her head around to see who could be at her door. She looked up, and she saw it was the detectives. She must not have heard them drive up the driveway. She was surprised to see them. Detective Brown rang the bell again while he was looking everywhere. He was being vigilant about scanning the surroundings, especially the trees up the hill beside the cottage. She opened the screen door with a big smile to greet them, and without a word, both detectives stormed in passed her in a haste.

"Have a seat and do not be alarmed," Brown said, and then he went directly to the windows to close the blinds. Murphy headed toward the back door area of the cottage. Gabrielle could not stay still she kept getting up and sitting because of their behavior. Brown stayed with Gabrielle in the living room and she noticed he seemed a little nervous. And then she saw it—his firearm was in his hand. She gasped.

"What's going on? Is Bernard hurt or something?" Her heartbeat accelerated. She was trembling from fright.

Brown turned towards her, his eyes darting everywhere, but in a calm voice he answered her, "Bernard isn't here. Where is he? We just want to make sure you're okay." He gave her a weak smile.

"He went to meet his father for lunch. Why?" she asked.

She was looking directly at him, but he did not answer her. She had to know why.

"What happened to make you come into my house with guns drawn and scare me half to death? Tell me?" she asked and stood up with her hands on her hips.

As soon as she did, Brown gently took her arm and made her sit down.

"I want you to please stay away from the windows and do not be alarmed," Brown said.

"Okay, this morning we received a threat about you guys. We were warned to leave you alone. We believe it was from Tom, and we just want to make sure you are protected."

Gabrielle just froze. She knew what that man was capable of doing. He had destroyed almost everything she ever had and now the only thing left was Bernard. He wouldn't dare hurt him, she knew that much, but ...

"Could you contact Bernard?" Brown asked her. She was frantic. She ran to get the phone, grabbing it off the end table to dial his number. Her hands were trembling so much she was having a hard time punching the number. Finally, she got it. It rang, but no one answered. The detective was looking at her, waiting patiently to see if she could reach him. She shook her head.

"He's not answering his phone. It keeps going to voicemail. That's why we came over right away. We thought maybe you needed help," the detective said as calmly as possible.

"Oh! Mon Dieu!"

That was all Gabrielle could say. This cannot be happening. She started praying softly.

All of a sudden, they heard a vehicle coming down the road heading toward their house. Brown got up from his position near Gabrielle and went to the window. He pulled the blinds a couple of inches from the wall and he looked out. He could see it was Bernard and his father Ron. He went to the door the minute the Range Rover entered the driveway. Brown went outside on the porch and yelled to them. Gabrielle was right behind Brown at the entryway.

"Bernard, over here. Hurry up! Come inside quickly!" Detective Brown yelled.

They scrambled out of his truck, and they started running to the house. They went up the steps and they almost jumped inside the house. Brown was the last one behind them to come inside. As he was about to enter the doorway of the house, Gabrielle heard a familiar sound. She had not heard it in a long time, but she knew it well. She used to hunt.

It was the cocking of a rifle. Then a shot from far away. She was sure of it. A bullet hit the post of the porch, barely missing Brown's right arm. They heard more shots fired. Pieces of wood went flying in the air. He sprang into action to get inside. He dropped to the ground and rolled to the wall. Brown suddenly heard a loud scream from inside the living room. He turned to investigate. It came from Gabrielle. She was screaming. She had heard the shots. Bernard was by her side, instantly sheltering her and they were now sitting in a corner on the floor. Bernard kept rubbing her back.

"Shhh, it's going to be okay. Do not cry," Bernard kept whispering.

She was whimpering, and tears were rapidly falling down her cheeks.

"Murphy, do you see anything?" Brown was shouting across the house.

"Son of a bitch. That was our car that he shot at—it's on fire. Shit!" Brown shouted.

"No, nothing! I don't see him," Murphy answered. Gabrielle could see him across the hall. He had his back against the wall, and his gun drawn beside him.

"Keep your fucking eyes open and don't do anything stupid. I'll call for reinforcement," Brown yelled across the living room to him.

"Stay down and don't move," Brown told Ron, Bernard, and Gabrielle. They were all gathered together on the floor near the couch. Gabrielle and Bernard were holding hands.

"It is going to be all right. The detectives are going to get him," Bernard said to Gabrielle. She huddled close to him. She noticed Ron was just sitting next to them, pale as snow. His hands were on his lap and shaking.

"It's my entire fault. Oh! My God! It is my entire fault. I have to do something," Ron whispered repeatedly.

"Detective Brown, it's Tom. Did you know he was here yesterday watching us?" Bernard said.

Bernard turned to Gabrielle and said, "I love you. Do not worry. It's going to be okay. The detectives are going to get him."

Brown went to a neutral corner near the entrance, took out his radio out, and radioed the police station to get some help. He informed his captain of the new developments at the cottage.

"I called for reinforcement, but there are only a handful of other police officers in this town, and they are trying to coordinate the events. They are not equipped for a standoff, so they called the SWAT team, but they're in the city." He paused to look at all of them. They were terrified. He could see it in their eyes. He continued to tell them what was going to happen.

"It's going to be a while before they can get here. Until then, we're on our own. It's going to be at least thirty minutes, but remember, he doesn't want to hurt you guys."

Brown went to crouch by the window. He slowly pulled the blind up to look outside, but kept his head down. Gabrielle heard the sound of another a gunshot. Brown fell backward onto his butt.

"Damn! He hit the windowsill. He is definitely watching us," detective Brown said.

Brown heard movement behind him. He turned around and saw that Bernard had pushed Gabrielle down flat on the floor. She was shaking uncontrollably and could not stop. Gabrielle was getting really concerned for her and the baby. She wondered, *How could this be happening?* It was all Bernard's father fault. She was beginning to think twice about her decision to forgive him. Gabrielle saw Ron crawl to the detective in the corner and sat beside him.

"Detective, what if I called him, and I talked to him again?" Ron said, his voice calm. He was hoping he did not fail; otherwise Bernard and Gabrielle might never forgive him. He could not live with himself if he did not try.

"I'll tell him to give himself up before someone gets shot. He might listen to me. He'll answer his phone and I know him."

"You should wait for the negotiator, because we don't want to provoke him," Brown answered.

"Listen, I need to try and do something. It is my fault we are here like this. I could not live with myself if someone got hurt," Ron said looking at Brown, but he did not answer. "Do you have a better idea while we are sitting ducks here doing nothing?" Ron asked him.

"Let him try. He has known Tom for years ... he might not answer anyway, but there's no harm in trying," Bernard said, supporting his father.

"No harm in trying. Go ahead, but be careful what you say," Brown agreed.

"Here goes nothing. Wish me luck," said Ron. He took his phone out and dialed the familiar number. He put the phone to his ear. He heard it ring once, then twice.

***

Tom could feel his phone vibrate in his pocket next to his leg. He knew that there was only one person that would call him—Mr. Rian. He reached in his side pocket and he answered it.

"Good afternoon, sir," he said.

"Tom, you know how proud I am of you trying to protect us, but I need you to stop firing at us. Someone is going to get hurt. You wouldn't want that, would you?"

"No, sir, but the detectives are going to brainwash you against me. You are going to betray me, and I cannot have that. I need to get rid of the detectives and the girl. She is no good for the Rian family, sir," Tom said. He had to tell him the truth.

"Tom, listen to me. Have I ever lied to you?" Ron was about to do just that.

"No, sir."

"Okay then. I don't want you to get hurt. The SWAT team is on their way. I value your friendship too much. They are going to hurt you. Please stop!" Ron was lying through his teeth to the bastard. Brown and the others were staring at him.

"I'll be all right sir. I'm equipped and prepared for them," Tom said. He wondered if Ron was going to betray him and he should kill them all.

"Maybe you are going to betray me, too, sir," Tom said.

"Tom, I would never do that, I cherish our friendship too much. You are my top guy. I trust you. Do you trust me?" Ron asked him.

The line was silent for a moment. Tom was getting confused. Maybe he was wrong and Mr. Rian did care.

"Yes, I trust you, sir," Tom answered.

"Tom, how many missions have we had together? How many? I now have another order for you. Are you listening?"

"Yes, sir."

"I want you to leave. Go to my motel now. There is lots of money in a briefcase under the bed. Go where they can't hurt you. I care too much for you. Will you do that for me?" Ron kept his voice steady. Brown was shaking his head at Ron.

"Tom, are you there?" Tom was thinking hard. He never disobeyed Mr. Rian's orders. He loved him as a father, and he had a lot of respect for this man, but he still wondered if he had betrayed him.

"Yes, sir."

"Please, leave now. Do it for me so they won't hurt us. I'll make sure. I promise you," Ron replied.

"Very well, sir, I will leave now because you asked me, but I'll always be nearby. You know how to reach me."

"You're a good man, Tom."

Ron nodded his head to the others and gave them the thumbs up.

"Thank you, sir. I hope to serve you again soon. So long, sir," said Tom.

He was sad, but not defeated. He hung up the phone. He would have to rethink this entire conversation another time.

Bernard and Gabrielle were listening attentively. So was Brown, even when he was watching outside. Ron clicked the phone off and turned around to look at them.

"Well, he told me he was leaving—now—but I can't guarantee it."

"We'll soon find out. We still have to wait for SWAT before we can leave the house," Brown sighed.

"Make yourselves comfortable. It might be a long wait. We do not know if he left or not so until then, we stay put," Brown explained.

Gabrielle felt relived. She reached out and touched Ron's hand and squeezed it lightly. Ron nodded and smiled at her. Bernard put his arm around Gabrielle. The minutes ticked away and there had not been anymore shooting. They had not moved from the floor for almost an hour when Brown's radio began to crackle then they heard.

"This is Commander Rick Cormier from SWAT. Is everyone all right in there?"

"Yes, we are all safe—no injuries," Brown answered

"We are securing a perimeter. I'm sending a few officers with shields to help you evacuate when you are clear to go," the commander said to them.

"Understood," Brown responded.

"Detective Brown, do you know how many intruders we are dealing with here?"

"As far as we know, just one. But Commander, be very careful. He might have booby traps around the perimeter," he warned them.

"Understood," Cormier responded, and then he was gone.

It took the team a few hours to secure a perimeter of the entire hillside. They wanted to make sure there was no more danger. Whoever had been firing at them was gone. They found all his gear that he had left behind, even the C4. The bomb squad was also called in for the explosives. Whoever had been there was definitely a professional, but he had departed. The coast was clear. The outside of Gabrielle's small home was chaotic, but at least no one had gotten hurt.

The paramedics had checked her out, and Gabrielle and the baby were in good condition. The detectives had finally left in late afternoon to go back to the police station. They had to fill out reports and talk to their captain. They were now on a major international manhunt. It had been an exhausting day, not only physically, but also mentally. The afternoon had been nerve-racking, and the SWAT team was almost finished with their job. They were packing up their equipment and they were slowly disappearing one at a time. The local police and the RCMP were going to take over and keep searching the town and the surrounding cities. It was going to be an ongoing investigation.

Ron was sitting on the sofa, his eyes watching Gabrielle's every move. How she paid attention to Bernard. She made him a sandwich and made sure he ate it. Bernard smiled. She glanced Ron's way, and he finally had the chance to motion her over to him. Gabrielle slowly let go of Bernard's hand, and she went to sit beside him on the couch. Bernard approached them and sat down next to Gabrielle.

"I'm really sorry for everything—can you ever forgive me? I now see I was really wrong about you," he said quietly.

Gabrielle was not looking his way. She kept staring at the floor.

Ron reached in his pocket, and he felt the gift he wanted to give her yesterday.

"When I came here yesterday, I wanted to tell you I was happy for both of you. I want to welcome you to the Rian family, you and the baby. I'm so excited about the baby," Ron said.

"Thank you, and I do accept your apology," she said sincerely. She lifted her head and she met his gaze, then she smiled. "I am so proud of you how you talked to Tom and made him leave us alone," Gabrielle said.

"I am so humbled today to have you as a father, too. It was amazing how you talked him down. Thank you."

Bernard walked over to his father, leaned down, and kissed his father on the cheek. Ron gasped. Gabrielle came forward and she gave him a hug.

"Bernard, I have to tell you something. I have been watching her and she reminds me of your mother. She loves you, and I hope you always take care of each other," Ron said, and a tear fell from his eye. He wiped it away, and then looked at them and smiled.

The detectives and Ron sat down to discuss the events that had happened. Ron was apprehensive, but after a few hours explaining and examining everything that had happened in the past few days, Ron felt better. They had heard all they needed from Ron. The question was when and if they could find Tom. He had vanished like thin air. The police had found all his gear but not his guns. They had no trace or leads to capture him. He had disappeared. Roadblocks had been ordered, but there had not been even a sighting of him. The police had put an arrest warrant for Tom Smith across the country and in the United States. His picture was posted everywhere there was a law enforcement agency. They were hoping to catch him at one of the borders if he decided to run back to the United States. That was all they could do for the moment. All authorities had been alerted of this criminal.

Hours later, everyone had finally left, even Bernard's father. He had decided to fly back home, as there was nothing else he could do to try to mend the situation. He invited both of them to come visit him in the near future and they had both agreed they would keep in touch. Ron was happy that the relationship with his son had improved and it had all worked out. He would await the news of the baby. Hopefully, it would be a boy so he could continue the Rian legacy.

CHAPTER 19

Tom was on the run. He had barely made it out of the area. He had met the SWAT team's armored truck on the road out of town. He never stopped driving until he arrived at the motel, but when he got closer, he was surprised to see police surrounding the motel. Mr. Rian had betrayed him. He would have to make him pay. Maybe not now, but in time.

He headed toward the airport. He knew if he took an international flight, the authorities would catch him at the border or upon his arrival to his destination. Therefore, he took the first flight out of Moncton for Montreal. He only had a few hours before the police put a BOLO on him, which meant 'be on the lookout' for a certain criminal. He was now a fugitive from the law. He had to find a hiding place for some time until he could move again.

He knew he would never make it past the U.S. immigration, so he decided to stay in Canada for a while longer. He first headed west toward Montreal. If he was spotted, he might head to Toronto, instead. He needed to be in the big cities of Canada where he could get lost more easily among the general public without so much worry of being caught by the authorities. Montreal housed all kinds of ethnic groups, so it would be easier for him to blend in. He stopped at a couple stores on the way from the airport to buy dye for his hair. He would also let his beard grow.

In a few days, he would have a new look and identification that could be bought on the street for a high price among thieves. Tom had seen the news and all the nationwide alerts, but he also knew that after a while, people would forget his face, and it would die down. He would not move until then. It might be a long stretch of time, but he could wait.

He had made it to Montreal. He went to the old section of the city, and he rented a room at the Voyageur Hotel, one of the cheapest hotels in town. It was a rundown place, deplorable, but the good thing was that no one looked at you twice. People in this area were mostly drug dealers, prostitutes, and crooks just like him. He was held up in this small, dirty bedroom. He had to share a bathroom with another patron. He made sure he had an exit route if he was in danger from the law. He was close to the subway and the bus system if he needed them. Most of the customers of this hotel were travelers with little or no money that were in transit to another city. He had enough money to survive for years, so he decided to make it his home for a few months, or at least until things died down. He hated the place. It was really below his pay grade, but he could tolerate anything. He had been in worse situations, and he had adjusted according to the environment and circumstances.

The one thing that really had disappointed him was that Ron had spilled the beans about everything illegal they had ever done, directly or indirectly. He could not comprehend why, but Ron had deceived him and he would have to pay dearly. No one betrayed him. *He had hung him out to dry.* The worst was that he had trusted Ron more than any other person in his life, and Ron had been unfaithful to him. The hurt he felt was inconceivable. He would have given is life for this man. He loved this man. He had protected him several times without blinking an eye. This would be the hardest thing he had done in his whole life. Now, Ron had to die.

Over the months in Montreal, he had finally met an older gentleman named Sam who would help him get over the border. Tom had met him at a local diner one morning at breakfast. This small, inexpensive place was walking distance from his hotel. Many homeless people came here to buy a meal with little money they had. Tom was seated next to the man on a stool at the counter eating when he had struck up a conversation with him.

"Good morning. The eggs are the best buy," the old man had said.

"And how would you know that?" Tom asked, somewhat amused, but he had been watching this man.

"Every time I deliver a load in Montreal, I come here to eat. It is the best greasy food around," he laughed.

"Well then, I shall try the eggs," Tom said then extended his hand.

"My name is Tom," he smiled.

"My name is Sam."

They began meeting and talking regularly when Sam came to Canada. They soon became friends, but Tom only needed him for one purpose. This man was an international transport trucker. Tom had seen him driving a transport truck one afternoon and he had asked him where he travelled.

That day was the day, Tom had found his exit strategy out of this godforsaken place. He made Sam an offer he could not refuse with lots of money if he was willing to take him back over the U.S. border—back to where he belonged, back to where he knew people and could strike back. Sam told him he had done this several times before, and he was going to hide him with his merchandise in the back of his rig where he could not be seen from the front if the border patrol checked his cargo. He told Tom the border officers rarely checked his shipments because he was a regular traveler and he had gotten to know most of them well over the years.

Tom paid him handsomely for his troubles. Like he always said, "Everyone has a price." This crossing was dangerous, but he was still prepared for any inconvenience that would arise. He had bought a gun and ammunition from a small drug dealer. It had gone as planned just like Sam had told him it would. They were successful in passing over the border. Three long months had gone by. It had taken him a long time to get back where he belonged after the standoff at the beach house. He had thought a lot about his situation with Ron. He was ready to confront Ron. He definitely, without a doubt, would kill him for what he had done to him. It was unforgivable.

**

"Are you sure you can travel in your condition?" Bernard asked Gabrielle. He was being cautious. They were going to his father's home for Thanksgiving. He was afraid of her flying on a plane because of her pregnancy.

"What if something goes wrong with the baby?" he asked. He was always overprotecting her.

"You are being over dramatic. We'll be just fine. I am only seven months along. Plus it's your jet, your pilot. He can land the plane anywhere, remember?" she said, laughing aloud at him. "Nothing is going to happen. I still have two months to go. The doctor cleared me and the baby to fly, so do not worry. Now, please let me finish packing so I do not forget anything. I am nervous enough as it is," she answered him.

He came over to her put his arms around her, and he kissed her tenderly on the cheek. Then he bent down to his knees, and he talked to her round belly.

"Your mama thinks she knows everything," he said as he patted her belly lightly then kissed it. "But remember, Papa knows things, too."

He was talking to the baby, and Gabrielle thought it was adorable.

They were going to visit Bernard's father. It was their first time back to Boston since they had last seen him. They had spoken to him on the phone many times. Bernard was a little tense, but he was happy to go see his father again. They were going to stay on his estate. Ron had insisted, and he had more than enough room. He would have been offended and badly hurt if they had chosen to stay at a hotel. Bernard had rented his condominium to one of his Bostonian friends because he had decided to stay with Gabrielle until the baby was born in Canada. They had not decided which country they wanted make their permanent home.

They were all packed and ready to go. Bernard picked up the suitcases and put them in the trunk. He was waiting for Gabrielle to get in the Range Rover. It had been four months since he had last seen his father. They took off to go to the airport, which was only a half-hour drive away. The plane was waiting for them at a special hanger not far from the main terminal. This airport was small, but they had accommodated his plane with no problems.

His pilot was waiting for them at the bottom of the stairs, and they made themselves comfortable in the soft leather chairs. The plane ride was smooth, and there was no turbulence. They had no problems whatsoever, not even with customs or immigration. When they arrived in Boston, Ron naturally had sent his car to pick them up and bring them home. On the way home, Bernard asked the chauffeur, "How is my father was doing?"

"He's been smiling a lot lately, sir," he said looking at Bernard, who nodded.

"Is he happy?" Bernard asked.

"He is. All he talks about is the baby and both of you. He is so excited. He is like a changed man, sir," the chauffeur answered.

"I am so glad to hear that. Thank you," Bernard said.

Ron awaited their arrival with anticipation. He kept pacing back in forth to make sure his staff made their accommodations comfortable. He had ordered fresh flowers for their rooms. He had even placed pictures of Bernard when he was a child in their room for Gabrielle to see. His cook had prepared a feast fit for a king. He was very apprehensive. and he was hoping everything went uninterrupted for their first visit to his home. He had a lot riding on this weekend with his family. He was really greeting Gabrielle in his home for the first time.

He walked to the front entrance to wait for them and sat on a chair in the foyer. Finally, he heard the car coming up the driveway. He stood up and opened the door. He waved to them as they were driving up the long road. He could not wait for them to get out of the vehicle. Ron reached for the handle of the car and opened the door. His son was home.

Bernard was the first one out of the car and he went to help Gabrielle. His father came forward and shook his son's hand, and then he gave Gabrielle a welcoming hug.

"Welcome to my home. How was your flight?"

"Everything was delightful. Thank you," Gabrielle answered.

"And how is my grandson?" Ron was so anxious for this baby to be born. He pointed at her belly.

"He or she is just fine," Gabrielle responded.

"Come on in. Are you tired? Do you want to lay down before lunch?" Ron wanted to make sure Gabrielle was well taken care of. It was his first priority.

"No, no, Mr. Rian. I'm just fine, but I'm hungry. I hate to say it, but I am always hungry. My appetite is in good working order, and the baby kicks when I am hungry," she said with a smile at him. She put her hand on her small potbelly.

"We can sit in the library by the fireplace. I'll tell them to set it up, and they will serve lunch right away."

He motioned to his staff to pick up the suitcases and he told them to bring them to their bedroom. He told another one to get the food ready right away. They immediately disappeared behind closed doors to prepare the meal and the chauffeur brought their bags up to their quarters.

Ron turned his attention to Bernard and Gabrielle to offer them a drink. Gabrielle sat in a large chair by the fire. It was a beautiful day, but it was breezy and a bit chilly outside.

"Do you have tea? It would take the chill out of me," she said while rubbing her arms. He ordered one of his staff to get her tea immediately. The sous-chefs arrived with trays of food and placed them on the right side of the room, on one of the tables arranged for lunch. The staff proceeded to served lunch that consisted of salad, petit four sandwiches, pasta, and lots of desserts.

"You should not have gone to all this trouble. It sure looks amazing," Gabrielle told Ron.

They chattered about what they had been doing at the house and how things were going medically with the baby. Ron told stories about when Bernard was a small child and the adventures he had planned once the baby was born. They reminisced all throughout the meal. They all laughed. It was a pleasant and enjoyable afternoon. Gabrielle could not get enough food. Everything that she tasted was delicious.

"Okay, now, I'm really too full," Gabrielle exclaimed. Ron was pleasantly surprised and thrilled she was feeling at home. Ron then escorted them to their quarters that consisted of a king-size bed; an armoire; a sitting area with a couch, chair, and reading light; and a large bathroom with separate sinks. Gabrielle wanted to lie down for a quick, half-hour nap just to refresh her energy. The men decided to have an aperitif in the living room in the meantime. They both had a Grand Marnier straight up.

"You know, she reminds me of your mother. She is simple, she appreciates the small things, and she is always grateful," Ron said while he was pouring his drink. He turned away from Bernard for an instant so he would not see his face. It was hurtful to think about Bernard's mother.

"Really, I am so pleased you noticed. That is why I love her."

Once they were sitting down, Bernard looked at his father and said, "Father, Gabrielle and I just want you to know we both have forgiven you and hope we can move past this." Bernard looked at his father. Ron had tears in his eyes again.

"I love you, Gabrielle, and that grandchild more than my life. I was so wrong," Ron spoke softly. He bowed his head.

"Have you heard anything about Tom? Have they captured him? I did not want to mention anything in front of Gabrielle. She gets agitated when we talk about him," said Bernard.

Ron's expression became serious when Bernard asked that question. "I haven't heard anything. I don't even know if he's still in Canada or not, but I did hire extra protection around the compound just in case, especially since you are here. There are men patrolling the grounds day and night. He would not dare come near here."

Ron was getting nervous talking about Tom. He kept spinning his glass around with his hand and his leg was fidgeting.

"Gabrielle was excited to come to Boston. She plans to do some shopping, and she wants to visit her friend Sophie. Thank you for inviting us for Thanksgiving dinner, but please don't go overboard with it," Bernard said, smiling at his father.

"It's my pleasure, so don't worry. I just want you to enjoy yourselves and have a good time."

Ron was concerned for them. He still worried about what Tom was up to because he had tried to find him through connections, but had not been successful. He had even hired extra security guards to watch for Tom at the estate.

"It's nice to be home. I missed it," Bernard said, looking at his father. "I am happy to have found her. I would like your blessing, as I am going to ask her to marry me," Bernard said.

"I ... I do not know what to say. You have my blessing, and I wish you two the best."

Ron was so pleased, he got up shook his son's hand, and went to the bar to refill his glass.

"It is a surprise, so do not tell her. I plan to ask her at dinner tonight," said Bernard, glowing.

"Finally, I get a daughter-in-law and an heir. I could not be happier."

Ron was full of joy. He poured himself one last drink, a single malt whiskey on the rocks. He went to sit on his favorite chair in front of the fireplace. He looked at the family pictures on the wall. He loved this chair. His wife used to sit on his knees when they were first married and whisper

189

how much she loved him. How he missed her. He was thinking how lucky and fortunate he was. His son had forgiven him and Gabrielle was now pregnant with his grandchild. What would have happened if Tom had succeeded? He never would have gotten over it. He had been really wrong. He was a proud father. His son was getting married, and he was going to be a grandfather. He finished his drink and he headed up the stairs to bed, a peaceful and content man.

***

Gabrielle could not believe where she was. It was such a magnificent home compared to hers. It truly was grand. The rooms they were staying in had a beautiful terrace off the bedroom that had gorgeous manicured trees and fall flowers. It had a four-post bed with a red satin comforter that matched the curtains, and the bathroom had a huge Jacuzzi with his and her sinks. A small living room with a flat screen television was attached to the bedroom. All the rooms had marble floors with rugs.

You could spend all day just looking at the rooms of this house, she thought. She had never stayed in such a grand home. Even Sophie's house looked like a dollhouse compared to this estate. She had been told it had 54 rooms in all. An hour later, she was well-rested, so she decided to go for a walk around the property. She really needed the exercise to digest the big meal she had just eaten.

Gabrielle walked slowly down one of the paths. She admired the well-groomed landscapes that led to the stables. Along the way to the stables, there was a huge pool and a tennis court. Bernard had told her his father had riding horses and he had told her about how he used to ride every day when he was a child. Ron had kept the horses for his grandchildren. He was hoping one day his grandchildren could learn how to ride like their father. She could see the huge red barn and the white fences where the stables were located. It was not far, so she decided to visit them. She loved horses.

They were standing in the main barn next to the stables and Dom, one of the horse trainers, explained different riding saddles to Gabrielle. She was absorbed in their conversation. Bernard came up behind her and put his arms around her waist and said to them, "Absolutely no riding for her, Dominique. Don't give her any ideas." He teased her, and they started laughing.

"I don't think so either, but it's very interesting to know all this. Dominique was nice enough to educate me a little bit," said Gabrielle. She smiled at the old man and thanked him. He just nodded, and he left them alone in the stables.

They walked back up to the main house together and admired the appearance of the terrain. Bernard told her he had made reservations for dinner at L'Espalier, a chic restaurant in the Back Bay of Boston.

"You are going to love this place. The chef makes amazing combinations that are absolutely delicious."

"I can't wait to taste it," Gabrielle answered. As far as food was concerned, she was always ready to try something new.

They returned to the main house so they could start getting ready. Gabrielle put on her best maternity dress, but when she looked in the mirror, tears came to her eyes. She no longer thought she looked sexy. She thought she looked fat. She was seven and a half months pregnant. Bernard was standing near the bathroom when he saw her expression. He laid his jacket on the bed, walked up behind her, and whispered in her ear, "You look absolutely gorgeous tonight, even good enough to eat."

She smiled at him. He always knew what to say at the right moment. Her tears disappeared.

She opened the door of the bedroom for him. She was laughing as she pointed at him to go out the door. He grabbed his suit jacket, put it on, and they went downstairs.

"So you guys all set? You are going to be late if you don't hurry," Ron said.

The chauffeur was holding the car door open, waiting for them to get in. Gabrielle looked at Bernard and blushed. It was their little secret why they had been late. After she was seated, she gently nudged him.

They enjoyed the drive. The view of the skyscrapers was spectacular. All the lights on each floor of the building were lit up. It was only a short ride in town. They were a little late for their reservations, but they did not have to wait because Bernard was regular at this restaurant. The maître d' seated them at one of the best tables by the window where they could watch the pedestrians walking by on the street. It was a nice touch. The decor was very contemporary. All the tables had glass tops, and the chairs were all black leather. The oil paintings on the wall were all abstract and on the back wall there was a large aquarium with exotic fish that took up most of the wall. Gabrielle looked around, amazed. The waiters running around were serving the customers so efficiently. They were all dressed in black jacket with black pants. The patrons looked very prestigious and influential, and you could tell by their behavior and their rich attire. Each of the patrons noticed who came in and with whom.

The menu always consisted of the chef inventions and flavors of the day. The restaurant's specialty was the haute table menu, a combination of an appetizer, an entrée, and a desert. It was called the chef's plate and everything else was a la carte. Gabrielle liked it. She thought it was over the top in the way the menu was set up. She ordered escargots, rotisserie chicken, and a crème brûlée for dessert. She told herself she could get used to this fine dining any day. She was mesmerized by the way the dishes were so beautifully presented.

They were sitting at the end of their meal, sipping on coffee and enjoying the conversation. She was waiting for her dessert to arrive when Bernard put his hand in his suit jacket pocket. He took out a small black box, slowly opened it, and showed it to his darling. Gabrielle looked puzzled and then looked at what was inside. She was shocked. She gasped!

"My dearest Gabrielle, mother to be of my child and the love of my life, will you have me as your husband and marry me?" he asked, staring at her eyes, waiting for an answer.

She kept glancing at the engagement ring, then at Bernard. Her mouth opened to speak, but nothing was coming out. Tears welled up in her eyes. She still was not answering.

Bernard kept his blue eyes on her and asked, "Gabrielle?" He reached for her hand, and when he touched it, he brought her out of her trance, and she responded.

"Yes. Yes, I will marry you!"

She was overjoyed. He took the ring out of the box, and he slipped it on the third finger of her left hand.

"Thank you. I love you so much," she whispered to him. Bernard leaned over and kissed her softly on the lips. "Sorry, I didn't answer right away. I wasn't expecting it," she said, looking at her ring.

"Do you like it?" Bernard asked.

"Oh! Yes! It is beautiful! Thank you!"

It was a three-carat diamond ring with two smaller one-carat diamonds on both sides. She leaned over and kissed her future husband.

"This calls for a celebration! Champagne!"

Bernard flagged down their waiter, and he ordered a bottle of Don Perignon to toast the big event.

They had a glass of champagne, even Gabrielle, as it was a special occasion. The evening flew by so fast that the next thing Gabrielle knew it was midnight. They had a fabulous time, and they were on their way home. Gabrielle was half listening to the conversation when she leaned her head on Bernard's shoulder, and she unexpectedly dozed off. Bernard stopped talking. She was exhausted from everything that had transpired today. They pulled up to the house. Bernard wrapped his arms around her and picked her up. He carried her to their bedroom. He laid her down on the bed gently, and he just covered her with the duvet. The alcohol must have hit her, because not even a minute later, she was sound asleep.

"I am happy about my decision to have you as my wife," he whispered to her and fell asleep as fast as his future wife had.

The next morning, Gabrielle woke up early. It was before dawn. She was feeling jubilant, because it was Thanksgiving Day, and she was engaged to great man. She opened her eyes and she turned her head to peak at Bernard, who was sleeping soundly. She noiselessly slipped out of bed without disturbing him. She still had last night's dress on, so she went to the bathroom to undress and threw on her robe. She left the bedroom as quietly as a mouse.

The first thing she did was telephone Sophie to give her the great news of her engagement. She had planned to tell her last night, but she had been too tired to call her. They chatted for a while, and they made plans to go to lunch before she returned to Canada. Then, she called Suzanne to tell her about her engagement. She received many congratulations from everyone she called. She had never thought she would marry and have a child all at the same time, but she did not regret anything. She had never been so happy.

Today was Thanksgiving and she was thankful for many things—Bernard, the baby, and her home. She walked down the stairs and she entered the kitchen area. She wanted to bring Bernard a special breakfast in bed, but the minute she stepped inside the kitchen, the staff looked at her, stunned. The woman in charge of the kitchen staff came forward.

"Can I help you, Miss Leger?"

"Oh! Yes, I wanted to make breakfast for Bernard, so ..." She noticed that they all had stopped working, and they were all looking at her standing there in her robe in the doorway of the kitchen.

"Miss, let me help you. Just tell me what you would like, and we will prepare it for you," the lady gracefully replied.

"I'm sorry. I didn't know I couldn't cook it myself," she said. She felt a little stupid and embarrassed, but then the woman came forward to speak to her.

"If you want to make it, there's no problem. I shall help you, okay? You're more than welcome. It's just no one ever comes to the kitchen to cook. They usually just tell us what they need, and we make it. Please, follow me. I'll show you where things are."

They started to walk deeper into the kitchen.

"Thank you very much. I just wanted to make something special for Bernard," Gabrielle said.

"No problem, no problem. My name is Diane. I am one of the cooks. This refrigerator should have everything you need. Let me know if you need anything else," she said and smiled at Gabrielle.

"I just need a tray, eggs, toast, bacon, and fruit, if you have them."

"I shall assist you, miss," Diane replied. They prepared a nice breakfast, and Gabrielle put it on a tray so she could take it upstairs to Bernard. She thanked Diane and left.

She was going up the stairs when she noticed a dark shadow duck behind a wall outside. She stopped, turned, glanced over to the French doors, but did not see anyone. A frightened chill passed through her. She dismissed it, because whomever it was had disappeared. She concluded it was probably a security guard doing his rounds. They were all over the property anyway. She continued going up the stairs to surprise her fiancée with the breakfast she had made. She opened the door as Bernard was just waking up. He was sitting up in bed. He saw the tray and smiled at her.

"Good morning, sleepyhead. I brought you breakfast."

She walked to the bed and she kissed him.

"Wow! Is this what I can expect every morning from now on?" he joked.

194

"Don't count on it, mister," she said laughing. She sat on the bed next to him, and she started eating with him.

"Is that all I get for breakfast?" he teased. He started cleaning her fingers by licking them, one at a time.

"Well, now it depends," she murmured in his ear. She took the tray from the bed and laid it next to the bed. He just sat there and he watched her.

"How would you like to pay for your breakfast, sir?"

Bernard grabbed her softly and he pushed her down on the bed. "Let me pay my bill, " he said kissing her neck. She started giggling.

***

Downstairs near the mansion, Tom had gotten around the guards unde-tected; it was a holiday, so he knew there would only be a third of the rota-tion of the security staff on the property. It was customary at this estate because most of the guys had families and celebrated the holiday at home. That was what Tom was counting on and he was right.

He knew the outline of the estate like the back of his hand. He had been in charge of the security detail for a long time before he was replaced, so *why would they change it now?* He snuck along the perimeter of the house, hiding behind whatever he could find—sometimes it was a shrub and sometimes it was a car. He did what he had to do to get close to the house. He still had the master key of the estate. *What a fool his ex-boss was to not change the locks.* He finally entered by through one of the French doors. His key still worked perfectly. He slipped inside the house undetected. It was so easy. He hid in the corners of the rooms and he snuck down to the old cellar like he had planned. No one had even bothered to ask him who he was, because he dressed like the other security men on the grounds.

Not many people went down the basement unless there was a problem with the heating or electrical system. Since it was cooler down there, it was more of a storage area for the wine and the champagne bottles than anything else. It was a perfect place to hole up until he was ready to act upon his plan. There were a lot of dark corners and small unused rooms. Sometimes you could hear people talking or walking upstairs, depending on where you were downstairs. If the air vent was close by and if you stood near it, you could hear their whole conversation, and he had done this many times over the years when he really needed information. He had not brought anything but his gun with him. *What else did you need when you were planning a murder?* Tom had the ultimate plan. It would work, and he would have his revenge.

CHAPTER 20

The maids were setting the table, the florist was delivering bouquets, the cooks were preparing the last of the dinner, and the bartenders were prepping the bars. Ron had invited a few other guests for the Thanksgiving dinner. Gabrielle was feeling a bit overwhelmed with all the affluent entourage. She was under the impression that the ladies were judging her because she was an unwed mother. They kept staring at her and whispering to each other, and then they would turn their backs to her. She would hear her name being mentioned, and the women would narrow their eyes at her.

"Gabrielle, do not let these people offend you. They are a bunch of snobbish women that only care about what achievements their husbands make or what they have acquired from it," Bernard said to her in a low voice while pulling her away.

"I know, but they are talking about me. I heard one woman say I should not eat so much, and another does not like my dress. Don't they know I hear them?" She was trying to ignore them, but it was hard.

"These women like to gossip and guess what? You are the new girl. Do not let them intimidate you, because you are better than them," Bernard whispered in her ear then enveloped her in his arms.

"I will do my best," she answered. He stayed near Gabrielle most of the time, as he did not want them to hurt her with their selfish comments.

Gabrielle was amazingly holding her own. She would smile and walk away. She was doing great until the staff started mixing drinks and passing appetizers in the grand salon. As usual, Gabrielle was famished. She tasted all the small bites of appetizers that the waiters were serving. She was hungry, so she just ignored the other women's attitudes. These women kept talking in a low tone to each other every time Gabrielle would come near food.

Sylvia, a very slim lady with too many jewels, who she had met earlier, was condescending about Gabrielle's situation. She was married to a wealthy banker from Boston. She was always very particular about with whom she associated herself. She looked at Gabrielle and said, "You might not know this, but it's very hard to get the extra pounds off after you have the baby. You shouldn't eat so much."

Gabrielle turned to face her, swallowed her bite, and said, "That's all right. I wouldn't want to be as skinny as you anyway."

Sylvia was stunned. Her mouth opened and then she marched off in the opposite direction. She was utterly offended by her remark. She snubbed Gabrielle, and then she went to stand by her husband. Gabrielle just stood, still shocked at what had come out of her mouth, and watched the woman walk away.

Gabrielle searched for Bernard. She did not know what to do. She stood alone among the guests. Bernard had overheard the whole conversation between the two women. Gabrielle bowed her head. She thought, *I should have kept quiet and my mouth shut.* Suddenly she felt Bernard touch her hand and he squeezed it gently. He then whispered in her ear, "Great comeback. She is too skinny anyway. She needs a little more meat on her." He glanced at her and gave her a big smile. She felt better, but she stayed next to Bernard the rest of the evening. She did not want to insult anybody else.

Dinner was served in the dining room promptly at seven. The servers were all lined up at the entryway of the dining room, greeting the guests and helping them find their seats. This room was a spectacular sight, with a long oak table that sat twenty-four people. The walls were wallpapered in red and gold velvet. Two majestic chandeliers hung overhead. They had been specially made for this room in red and pink crystals. The china was white with a red border and the crystal glasses shone a red glow to match the dining red velvet chairs. The room looked like it was a photograph out of a magazine.

When the guests were all seated in the dining room, the staff brought two large turkeys with all the trimmings. There were three kinds of stuffing, vegetables, and mashed potatoes with gravy. The staff served bottles of sparkling white wine with the meal, but Ron told one of the servers to retrieve a few bottle of Don Perignon champagne from the cellar. The young server headed down to the basement to recover the champagne bottles. He left the room and walked to the cellar door.

The door to the cellar creaked opened, and someone had put the lights on. Tom moved swiftly to the darkness at the back of the room and he hid behind a huge crate of imported wines. Someone was coming. Tom took his nine-millimeter gun out and screwed his silencer on quickly. If he was detected, the server would be a casualty of battle. The young waiter walked to the wall and began searching in the champagne area for the right bottles. He was against the far wall of the cellar searching the racks. He had picked out four large bottles, and he was trying to figure out how to hold them against himself. Tom poked his head to see what was going on, but he accidentally dropped his portable flashlight. It had slipped from his pocket while he had crouched down.

The server turned his head abruptly.

"Hello? Anyone there?" he said. He went to peak around the corner, but he did not see anything. He had not even come close to where Tom was hiding. Tom froze. He was barely breathing. He did not want to have to hurt this guy. He watched him, hoping he would return upstairs. The young man picked up the bottles once again, and he headed back up the stairs. Tom saw the light go out and he heard the door close. He breathed a sigh of relief. That was close. He had better be more careful from now on.

Tom could hear all the people talking upstairs. He could hear them walking from one room to another. He knew when they were sitting down to eat or had changed rooms to have desert. He knew the routine of a dinner party at the Rians'. It had never changed in ten years. It was like a ritual when Ron had company. He was being patient, waiting for the staff to clean up and go home. Once it was quiet upstairs and he heard only a few footsteps, he would make his grand entrance. He knew from experience

Ron always had an extra drink after the guests had all left. He toasted a drink to himself for a great gathering and a successful dinner party.

That would be his cue to confront Ron, and he would make him pay for betraying him. It would be his personal revenge, but for now, he was waiting with anticipation for his meeting. He would kill Bernard and Gabrielle, too, and then he would vanish. He was getting antsy down in the cellar. He kept checking his watch every five minutes. They had better finish soon, otherwise they were all going to be in for a hell of a surprise ending to a Thanksgiving party.

***

Gabrielle was glad the last of the company was leaving, as it had been a long, exhausting day. Ron, Bernard, and Gabrielle stood in the doorway of the front entrance, shaking hands and saying their last good-byes. The employees had almost finished clearing the last traces of the evening. All the dishes were cleaned and packed away for the next event. The leftovers were stored away in the kitchen, and the servers and the chefs had left for the evening. Bernard and Gabrielle were walking hand-in-hand, with Ron trailing behind, to the library for one last nightcap before retiring for the night.

On their way, the head of the staff came to talk to Ron. He told him his team was almost finished with the cleanup, and they would be leaving within a few minutes. He also wanted to know if Mr. Rian needed them for anything else, otherwise they would finish cleaning and make sure that everything was in order. Ron thanked them, and then he dismissed the crew and said they could return to their homes.

There was only the three of them left in the house. They were sitting in the library by the bar area, taking in the last of the evening.

"What would you like to have for a nightcap?" Ron asked his son. Bernard looked at Gabrielle.

"Go ahead. Have a nightcap with your father. I am going to go upstairs and change. I am tired, so I think I will call it a night. If I feel better after I change, I'll come back down, okay?"

"Are you sure you don't mind? I can ..." He did not have time to finish, as she was on her feet and by his side. Gabrielle touched his arm lightly. She leaned forward and she kissed him on the cheek.

"I'm positive. Take your time. I'll be fine. Thank you for a pleasant evening, Ron. Now I'll say good night to both of you." She nodded to Ron, turned around, and headed up the beautiful wood carved staircase to their quarters. She was climbing the stairs when she heard the creek of a door opening. She stopped, slowly turned around, and looked down from the top of landing. She did not see anyone, so she continued on her way to the bedroom.

***

Tom slowly crept up the stairs one at a time so no one would hear him. He stopped at the door to listen for any noise. It was absolutely silent, except for Ron and Bernard talking casually in the library. He turned the knob, and he pushed the door just enough so he could look around. The coast looked clear. He stopped. He wanted to laugh aloud because he could see the alarm system of the house had been activated. He continued hugging the wall in case he encountered someone, like an employee, so he could hide quickly, but he knew that the guards did not usually stay inside the house. He knew that they had their own barracks at the back of the house. He was confident the morning staff only came inside at six in the morning. The security personnel were protecting the perimeter outside the mansion from intruders like him. With this in mind, he continued around the corner near the dining room. Everything was clean, and you could not even tell a dinner had just taken place a few hours ago. He had seen Gabrielle going up the stairs. He stopped, and he hid behind a door. She had not seen him, but he waited a minute before he continued forward.

He figured she was probably going to bed. She must be tired after the long day of festivities. Too bad she was not going to be around when he took care of Ron. Tom could hear their voices nearby. Tom would know that voice anywhere. It was Mr. Rian. The other voice sounded like his son, Bernard. He knew they were in the next room, the library. His adrenaline started pumping and he felt invincible. He slowly approached the doors, one step at a time. One of the doors was closed and the other was still open.

He felt his gun in his hand and he tightened his grip. He was ready. He deliberately stepped into the doorway, ready for his grand entrance. He was ready to kill Ron, Bernard, and Gabrielle. He would kill them all.

***

Gabrielle got to her room, sat down on the bed, and took her shoes off. She was relieved the day was over. She went to the closet and took out her red robe with the matching nightgown. She laid it neatly on the bed and went to the bathroom, washed her face, and then changed into her sleepwear. She opened the covers of the bed and she lay under the duvet, exhausted. She closed her eyes, but she kept turning and tossing in bed. She was so overtired and, for one reason or another, she was having a hard time falling asleep. Gabrielle sat up in her bed again. She was thirsty. She pushed the covers off and got up again to go to the bathroom to have a glass of water. She walked to the sink, but there was no cup in the bathroom.

Did she really want to go all the way downstairs for a glass of water? Maybe she would ask Bernard to warm her some milk, but he was still downstairs in the library with his father. She thought about her options for a moment. She figured a warm beverage might help her sleep better. Therefore, she slipped her robe and her slippers on and started slowly walking down.

Bernard was listening to his father talk about the difficulties of the stock market when he heard the floor creek slightly behind him. He thought Gabrielle had changed her mind and she had come to join them. He turned to greet her, but to his horror he saw Tom standing in the doorway. His glass crashed to the floor—it fell out of his hand when he saw him. It shattered to a thousand pieces. Ron stopped speaking, and he looked at Bernard. He had not seen Tom yet, but when he saw his son's expression of surprise and disgust, he turned around to see what he was repulsed by. It was the sight of Tom.

A feeling of rage went through Bernard, and Ron put his hand on his arm immediately to restrain him back. You could see the rage in Tom's eyes. He was beside himself.

"Don't, Bernard. He has a gun. He will shoot you. He will not hesitate," Ron said in a low voice. Tom raised his gun, and he aimed it at Ron.

Bernard had not seen the gun when he first saw him, but now it was clear. He had raised the gun and was pointing it at them. Bernard held back. He was afraid for his father's well-being at the moment.

"What do you want?" Bernard asked as clearly as he could utter the words.

"Get out of my house before I call the police, do you hear me? You will never get away," Ron was shouting. But Tom did not care. He just stood there, and he leered at Ron.

"You are no longer in charge here, Mr. Rian. I am. So shut the fuck up and listen." It was his turn to talk. He had thought about what he was going to tell him for a very long time. He had thought about it every single night that he had stayed in that deplorable hotel in Montreal.

"What do you want? Money? I'll give you money," Ron said. He was becoming nervous, and his hands were shaking slightly. He was more petrified for Bernard than himself. On the other hand, if he could keep him busy talking, maybe Bernard might find a way out of this mess, but it had not occurred to him yet.

"I don't want your money. Do you have any idea why I am here?" Tom spoke very calmly.

"What exactly do you want?" Bernard tried again.

"I want my freedom. Do you think I can have that back? What do you think?" Tom said very peacefully. He was staring at Ron. Neither Ron nor Bernard answered him. Fear was starting to build in Ron's eyes.

"You betrayed me after all I did for you. I never refused you anything you asked. I trusted you, and you have no idea how much you hurt me. I tried to do the right thing and get rid of that girl, then...."

Tom was no longer calm. He was no longer in control. His voice was quivering. He took a step forward. The two other men were becoming extremely afraid.

"You ... you gave evidence against me ... to have me prosecuted for crimes you ordered," Tom said in a loud voice.

Bernard noticed Tom's hand was starting to shake.

"Tom, let's talk about this. I was wrong. I ... ," Ron tried to continue, but stopped speaking as Tom approached him, still pointing the weapon at him. He was now ten feet away from them.

"I'm sorry, Tom. I had no choice. I helped you as much as I could in Canada."

"Shut the fuck up. You only thought about yourself, and," Tom raised his voice. "Do you know what I went through these past months? Do you?" He was yelling at them and waving the gun.

***

Gabrielle was in the kitchen heating up the milk when the sound of someone yelling interrupted her. At first she thought it came from the library. She was correct, but she did not recognize the voice. It was not Bernard or Ron that was shouting. She decided to go investigate cautiously and when she got near the library door, she stopped cold. She hid behind the large baby grand piano near the outside of the library. Gabrielle was listening to the screaming and suddenly she realized who was having this outburst. It was none other than that cruel man Tom Smith. Chills ran down her spine. She was horrified. *What was he doing here? Oh! Mon Dieu, he has a gun, and he is going to kill them!* She had to help them.

She carefully advanced toward the door. She did not know exactly what was going on, but she knew one thing: he was a fugitive. He was the one who had destroyed her inn and tried to murder her. He had tried to ruin her life. She became angry. She clenched her fists until they were white. She became fearless, even in her condition. She slowly moved closer, and then she realized he had a gun. It had finally sunk in.

"Oh! Mon Dieu," she screamed under her breath. He had a gun. Her hand went over her mouth to muffle her scream. She had to do something, but what?

Tom had not seen her or heard her yet, so she scanned the area to see what she could use as a weapon. She needed to help Bernard and his father. Gabrielle knew she did not have the strength to jump him, and she did not have time to go back to the kitchen to call the police or alert the guards. He could shoot them any minute. Even if she did go back to call, it would take too long for them to arrive anyway.

The only thing she could see was a crystal vase on an end table near her. It looked like it was a heavy one. She tiptoed over to it, reached over, and picked it up as carefully as she could without making a sound. She did not want to make any noise that would alert him. Gabrielle placed her hands on both sides of the vase, and she held it high above her head. She started walking quietly towards this mad man. She did not care anymore if she got hurt, but he was not going to allow any harm to come to anyone else if she could help it. She planned to hit him over the head with it. It surely would disorient him, maybe even knock him out. Gabrielle approached slowly. She could see Bernard had seen her. He took a step forward.

Tom started to turn around to see what was going on behind him, but it was too late. Gabrielle hit him with all her strength on the back of the head with the vase. She took a step backward and fell down. The vase shattered into a hundred pieces. There was glass everywhere. Tom lost his balance, and he had to reach out with one hand to steady himself on the arm of a chair. Tom became disoriented for an instant, and he tripped over his feet. His face was in a painful grimace. His mouth twisted, and his forehead frowned. Gabrielle saw Bernard lunge forward to belt him one. He swung as hard as he could and hit him with his fist. Tom stumbled backward, and he fell against the wall. Gabrielle could tell Bernard was enraged. His face was red and his eyes were slanted. She watched in horror as Bernard punched Tom in the face with his fist repeatedly.

Tom pulled the trigger. The bullet went wild. Bernard was on top of Tom like a flash, and they both fell down on the floor. Bernard grabbed his wrist and pounded the gun from his hand so he could not shoot anyone. Bernard was hitting him with his other hand. Tom was still struggling, but the hand that held the gun was pinned down.

Tom was trying to fight back with his other hand, but the blow to his head and Bernard's hard hit had weakened him a lot. Tom did not have the strength to fight. Bernard was finally winning the battle. Tom had not even swung one punch. Bernard lifted his arm up high again, and his fist came down hard like a brick on Tom's face. Bernard punched him so hard in the face that Gabrielle heard a crack from Tom's jaw. Bernard shook his hand and looked at it. He stared down and saw Tom lying on the floor unconscious. He was not moving anymore. Bernard bent down and took the gun from him with disgust. Tom was not going anywhere this time around. He would not hurt them anymore.

"Are you all right? Are you hurt?" Bernard asked running to Gabrielle. "I'm fine, but ..."

She noticed the blood on Ron's jacket and his shirt. Horrified, she and Bernard both rushed to his side to try to help him and see how badly he was injured.

"Father!" Bernard said, alarmed. He carefully was trying to take his father's jacket off to look at the wound and saw that his shirt was all bloody. Oh! God! His father had been shot. Bernard started to apply pressure to the gunshot wound.

"Call 911, hurry! My father's been shot," he said. She hurried to the phone on Ron's desk and dialed the emergency number. She kept her sight on her future father-in-law. She prayed silently he would not die. In a shaky voice, she told the operator what had happened and to send the paramedics and the police. She gave them the address, and they were on their way. Ron's security team that was protecting the perimeter of the outside was stomping into the house. She could hear them shouting orders to disperse and protect Mr. Rian. They had heard the sound of the gunshot from outside the house.

"How badly hurt is he?" asked Gabrielle, alarmed. Her whole body was trembling, and her hands were shaking. She kept looking at Ron and then at Bernard.

"What do you think?" Gabrielle said. "How bad is it?" She kept asking. Tears were falling down her cheeks.

"I don't know," Bernard replied, shaking his head from left to right. His hand was on Ron's chest, applying pressure to the wound. He was trying to stop the bleeding. Ron was slumped on the floor, not moving much. Ron kept looking at them with hooded eyes. His breathing was shallow. His color had changed, and he was very pale, almost white. He was having difficulty breathing. Gabrielle could hear a raspy sound when he inhaled, and his contorted face indicated that he was in excruciating pain. Bernard laid him down flat on the floor as gently as he could. The minutes were long and slowly ticking by since Gabrielle had called the emergency people. All she and Bernard could do was wait and hope he would survive.

"I love ... you ... I'm so ... sorry," said Ron, struggling to speak. He would open his mouth, but only incoherent sounds gurgled out.

"Hang on, Father. Help is on the way," Bernard told him. "Don't even think of leaving us now, do you hear me, Father?"

"It's going to be all right. Stay with us," Gabrielle said, trying to encourage him.

All of sudden, Gabrielle heard the sirens coming from afar. Gabrielle looked over and saw that the guards had handcuffed Tom, and two men were watching him very closely as he finally came to. She heard him moaning from pain, but the security people really did not give a damn about his cries of pain. Tom was now struggling to get free from the guards. He was trying to untie himself, but the guards were on top of him, holding him securely until the police officers arrived to take him to jail.

"Let me go this instant. I'll kill you. I swear, I'll kill you all," Tom said to the guards while they dragged him away to another room.

They heard a voice in the hallway say, "This way! Follow me." One of the security guys was leading the way for the paramedics. They rushed to where Ron was laying on the ground. They dropped boxes of their equipment near the patient. The woman spoke to Bernard in a soft voice. She seemed to be the one in control.

"Sir, please move to the side. I need access to him and room to work."

Bernard backed away a bit. "He's been shot," he told them. He stood by and he watched them work in total disbelief. He looked at his bloody hands and was trying to wipe them clean on his pants, but was largely unsuccessful.

The lady cut open Ron's shirt quickly. She told the man to start an IV on his arm and to give him oxygen. She checked his pulse. It was weak, but at least he still had one. She put a collar around his neck, and then she examined the wound. She knew from the location of the bullet hole that it was a serious injury. It had stopped bleeding, so she just put a bandage on it. She rechecked his pulse. It was still very weak, but he was still alive. They turned Ron on his side to see if there had been an exit wound, but there was none. The bullet was still lodged inside somewhere. The man took a wooden board, and he slid it under Ron's back and strapped it to him. They lifted him up, transferred him on the gurney, and then wheeled him out to the ambulance.

The detectives of the Boston Police Department had arrived to investigate. They were interviewing Gabrielle and Bernard about the incident, but they were having a hard time because both wanted to leave to go to the hospital. They let them go after some questions were answered. The detectives would need more details about what had happened, but for now they knew where to find them. Bernard also referred them to detective Brown in Canada for further information. He gave the investigators his number and told them that Brown could fill in all the loose ends about the man they had in custody.

Gabrielle had gone to change her clothes quickly. She and Bernard were in his truck and on their way to the trauma unit in Boston as soon as they were given permission to leave the house. He gazed at her. Gabrielle's heart broke. She was powerless to take his sorrow away.

"You were so brave tonight. You never hesitated to save us. Thank you. I'll never be able repay you," he said. She took his hand in hers, and she kissed it lightly.

"It's going to be alright. You'll see. The worst is over; your father is a strong man. He'll pull through this." She was praying he would not die, but she did not want to say it aloud.

"I hope you're right. Are you sure you're okay? I was so scared for you."

He had been frightened for her and his child she was carrying inside her when they fell. His heart had stopped beating for an instant.

"We're just fine. The paramedics checked us out—nothing to be concerned about. Let's concentrate on getting your father the best care and back home again," she said, trying to encourage him. They drove the rest of the way to the hospital in silence, each of them consumed with their own dreaded thoughts.

CHAPTER 21

Bernard's father was still in the trauma unit when they arrived at the hospital. The doctors were working strenuously to keep Ron alive. Bernard rushed to the nurse's desk for information on his father's condition and to fill out admission forms. They told him the doctor would come out as soon as the patient was stable and they knew more about what was going on. The nurse led him and Gabrielle to a waiting area and told them to wait. Bernard's mind was spinning. Feelings of déjà vu overwhelmed him.

Bernard had all these unanswered questions concerning the events of the night. First, how had Tom made it through all the security at the estate? Where had he been before he decided to attack them? Eventually, the authorities would deliver the answers.

Bernard kept pacing back and forth in the small waiting area. Gabrielle was sitting quietly, waiting for some word on his father's condition. Bernard kept looking down the corridor every minute or so, hoping for a glimpse of some news.

An hour came and went. The second hour passed even more slowly than the first. Bernard was out of his mind with worry. He wanted answers, but he had no choice but to wait. Finally, he saw a doctor coming toward them. He was wearing blue scrubs with matching hat and booties and looked to be in his mid-fifties. He looked very preoccupied with his work. Bernard stood up immediately.

"Mr. Rian?" He looked directly at them, and he extended his hand to shake Bernard's hand.

"My name is Dr. Steward. I'm in charge of the trauma unit. Your father was brought in with a bullet wound. Right now he's in critical condition, but stable."

Bernard was speechless. He just listened to him speak. His eyes were tearing up again, and he rubbed his neck to try to relieve the stress that was pounding in his head.

"The bullet is lodged on his spinal cord. We just sent him for an x-rays so we can determine if we can operate on him or not. I can tell you now, he doesn't have any sensation or movements in his limbs from the waist down."

Gabrielle interrupted him to ask a question. Bernard was just staring at the floor with his mouth open.

"Will he be able to regain any movements after the surgery?" Gabrielle asked.

"We won't know until we operate. If we can remove the bullet, there is a slight chance, but we can't determine that at this moment. The neurologist has been called in, and we will know more after he reads the films. So, sit tight, and I'll update as soon as I know something," Dr. Steward said. He got up to leave the room.

"Can we see him?" Bernard asked, his voice quivering.

"Not at the present time. He's heavily sedated because of the pain—maybe later," Dr. Steward answered.

"If he wakes up, could you tell him we're here and we're unhurt? He was wounded during a home invasion," Gabrielle told the doctor.

"I will do that." The doctor shook both their hands, and he disappeared down the hallway.

Bernard and Gabrielle just sat there, numb from the news. Tears quietly fell from her eyes. Bernard put his arms around her and held her tight.

"He's alive. That's what counts. He's a tough son of a bitch. He'll make it. You'll see. He'll make it."

"It's all my fault. I should have done something differently. Maybe then he wouldn't have gotten shot. I'm really sorry."

"It's not your fault. You saved us," Bernard said. He did not know if he was trying to comfort her or convince himself. His father was going to pull through. Both of them were traumatized from the developments, and Gabrielle was exhausted. It was close to midnight now and she could not keep her eyes open. She laid her head on Bernard's knees, closed her eyes to rest, and prayed for a good outcome.

An hour passed before another doctor appeared in the small waiting area.

"I have news. We are taking your father to surgery. We need to operate right away to minimize further complications," Dr. Kirk said.

Bernard just nodded at him.

"We need to stabilize the spinal cord and try to remove fragments of the bullet right away. It is going to be a very delicate operation, as he was shot in the thoracic area. We administered a high dose of antibiotics to prevent infection that is common among spinal cord injuries."

"Is he in pain?" Bernard asked

"He was given pain medication to try to relieve his discomfort," the doctor answered. "We want to try and relieve some of the pressure that the bullet is causing on your father's spinal cord so that with therapy, he may be able to regain partial sensation in his legs, but that's all that could be determined with time. The risks are great, but without the surgery, he might never have a chance of walking again."

"Do whatever is necessary to save his life," said Bernard.

The doctor told them he would be back after surgery and then walked away. Bernard brought his hands to his face and rubbed it. He would wait at the hospital until his father was out of surgery. The nurses and hospital staff were very kind and accommodating. They had brought them blankets and they gave them directions to where they could get coffee or something to eat. The surgery was going to take several hours, depending on Ron's vitals. If there were any complications, it would take longer.

Bernard sat on a couch. He was troubled, and he was not speaking. He could not accept his father might never walk again.

"Is there anything I can get you?" Gabrielle asked, but he just shook his head. She laid her head on his knees, and she closed her eyes. He covered her with the light blanket, and he told her to sleep. He would wake her up when the surgery was done, and the doctor came to give them news. It was going to be a long wait. All they could do was wait and pray. Ron's life depended on the outcome of this surgery.

At dawn, Dr. Kirk came to tell them the surgery had gone well and that Ron was in the Intensive Care Unit. He was stable but still in critical condition. Bernard could visit him for a few minutes, but Ron needed to rest. Bernard had insisted Gabrielle go home so she could rest properly, and he had told her he would call her to give her news when Ron was out of danger. She did not want to go, but in the end decided it was for the good of the baby. She said she would return later in the day with a change of clothes for him.

Bernard entered his father's room, and he pulled a chair next to him. He gently touched his father's hand to let him know he was not alone. While keeping a vigil on him, Bernard thought about all of the good times he'd had with his father. He could not die now. Bernard thought the best years of his life were yet to come. He held his father's hand, and he prayed. The doctors had told him Ron still had no sensation in his legs. They had said it could take a few days and not to worry about it until then.

The hours went by slowly. It was the third day, and Bernard had not left his father's side.

His head was resting on the side of the bed when he heard a moan coming from his father. Bernard lifted his head, and he could see Ron was trying to open his eyes, so Bernard stood up and spoke to him softly.

"Father. Father, can you hear me? It's Bernard. Everything is fine. You're in the hospital." Ron was trying hard to open his eyes, but Bernard could tell he was still groggy from all the medication.

"Gabrielle ... how's ... baby?" said Ron, trying to speak.

"She is just fine, and the baby is, too."

Ron kept his eyes closed, but a frail smile appeared on his face. He was happy everyone was safe.

"Tom ..." he barely whispered.

"The police arrested him, it's over. It's all over. Now please rest. I will be right here if you need anything. We'll talk later."

Ron made a small nod with his head, and a few moments later, he was sound asleep.

Over the next few days, it was imperative that Ron get some kind of sensation in his legs, even if it was just a tiny of feeling of some sort so he could have hope. Bernard consulted with other physicians, but to no avail. They all had the same conclusion: nothing could be done at this time. Ron was feeling stronger. He had been so grateful to Gabrielle for coming down at the time that she had, otherwise she might have found both of them dead.

Alas, the next few weeks went by without any good or significant changes in Ron's condition. The reality of it all was hitting Ron hard. He would never walk again. He was a paraplegic. It was going to be an ongoing medical battle for the rest of his life. Bernard hoped he would adjust. Eventually he would lead a semi-normal life, but Ron was not looking forward to it.

There were days he would not even talk. He would just stare at the wall he was so depressed. Some days he would throw anything he could get his hands on at the nurses. Physically, there was not much they could do. Many of his problems were mental. He was under the care of a psychiatrist who was helping him cope with his traumatic situation. He had started physical therapy, but it was slow. The doctor had told Bernard that with regular medication and therapy, it would get better in time. Bernard was providing as much time and encouragement as he could. A month had gone by so fast. It was going to be a difficult and a very bumpy road for Ron. He would adapt in time. He was fortunate: he had the means to get all the medical help he needed. That was a great relief for Bernard and Gabrielle.

***

The lovebirds were having lunch at home for the first time in weeks. They were enjoying their time together. It had been a very hard reality to face, and now Bernard faced his most difficult decision ever. He needed to discuss their future together. Gabrielle was relaxing. She hadn't been able to go to the hospital as much because she was getting closer to her due date. She only had a few more weeks to go before the birth. She had not been feeling her best, and she got tired easily. Bernard was dividing his time between her and his father.

"Gabrielle, you know I love you more than life, and you are carrying my child. I have a crucial question to ask you. I do not want you to give me an answer today. You need to really weigh this out."

Bernard was torn, but he had to plan for their future before his father returned home from the hospital. He was looking at her intensely.

"As you know, my father's condition requires a lot of care. I want to be with you, but I cannot do both if I return to Canada with you. Therefore, I am asking if you would consider living with me here in Boston. We could keep the cottage, too. If you want me to open another inn around here for you, I would be happy to do so. I mean, it's up to you."

He felt as though he had finally taken a huge load off his shoulders. The only problem was, would she stay? It would break his heart if they were living in separate countries. He did not know if he would be able to choose between his father and his life with her. His guilt might be his downfall.

"I don't know what to say," said Gabrielle. "I need time to think this over. I'll let you know later today, okay?"

Then she turned and walked away, leaving him alone at the table. She went up to their bedroom to try to figure out what she would do. Tears were trickling down her cheeks. She was thinking about all the friends she would have to leave behind, but Bernard was her life, and now there was the baby.

Bernard was sitting at the table by himself. He already knew that she would have to juggle things in her mind before she answered him. He hoped when he got home tonight, she would give him the right answer. That night when all was quiet, Bernard snuggled against Gabrielle. She responded by putting her leg over his, as she usually did when they curled up together.

His question had been on his mind, and now he needed an answer.

"Gabrielle, are you happy here?" he asked her. He was looking straight into her brown eyes. She was so beautiful, with her long hair framing her face.

"Yes, I am."

"I know I asked you before, but will you stay here with me here after we are married?" He held his breath for the answer he longed to hear.

"I will stay anywhere as long as you are with me."

Bernard was delighted.

***

After many struggles, Ron was still depressed with his outcome. He would not speak to Bernard or anyone for days on end. He would sit in his chair and would not participate in his therapy.

As the days went by, the medication and the impeding birth of his grandchild helped him to adapt. He began to familiarize himself with his condition, especially his chair. He was in an electric wheelchair and he was alive. He was doing quite well under the circumstances. His low spirits were starting get better. He was trying to accept his paralysis and move on. Bernard had hired medical personnel to help him adjust to his infirmity and disability. They would take care of all his needs around the clock. Even his therapist and his nurses would live at the house. Money was not an issue, so he could buy comfort, and that was exactly what he did.

***

A week later Gabrielle was laying down on her bed. Her head was pounding; she had a headache from hell. It must be from all the stress of the past few weeks. She wanted to take a nap because she had been feeling small contractions in her belly all day, and it had been uncomfortable. The pain was moderate and it would come and go, but she did not want to alarm Bernard just yet. Gabrielle woke up in pain and with wave of fear. She was having bad contractions in her belly and her back. They were not like the regular contractions she had felt before—these were intense.

She grabbed the side of the bed and tried to get up, but it took her a minute to be able to move, to stand in between the sharp pains.

The baby was coming—she could feel it. She had to get to Bernard. She screamed as loudly as she could for him. It echoed throughout the house. It was a big home, but Bernard heard it as if she were standing next to him. He jumped up from his chair where he was working, and he ran up the stairs two at a time. He opened the door of the bedroom and saw Gabrielle holding the bedpost, unable to move. She looked at him, and he could see instant relief in her face, even though she was still scared. The pain was unbearable, and the expression on her face changed. She shut her eyes and tried to breathe through the contractions as they came.

"I think the baby is coming," Gabrielle said, a look of terror on her face.

"It's going to be all right. I'm here. Can you walk?" he asked.

She shook her head, and then nodded. He put his arms around her waist, and he escorted her out of the house and to his truck as quickly as he could, as fast as she could. Her overnight bag had been stored in the trunk for the past week.

"Do you think we'll make it to the hospital before the baby comes?" he asked.

"Yes, we'll make it. It usually takes many hours before a baby is born." She was starting to breathe harder. Her hands were on her belly, and it was as if she was telling the baby to wait. "The contractions are about eight minutes apart. We'll make it," she said, watching the contractions and timing them as best she could.

Bernard was trying to keep his eyes on the road, but every time Gabrielle had contractions, she would cry out, and he would look at her. They finally arrived at the hospital, and he jumped out and ran to get a wheelchair for Gabrielle to sit in. The maternity ward was on the second floor, so Bernard wheeled her into the elevator, which they took to the second floor. Bernard ran out of the elevator to the nurse's desk.

"She's having the baby. We need help," Bernard said to the lady at the desk.

"Where is she?"

"Oh! My God!" He realized he had left her on the elevator. He ran back down the hall to get her. He wheeled her down the corridor to the nurse's station.

"Sorry, Gabrielle. I'm kind of nervous."

The nurse directed Gabrielle and Bernard to a labor and delivery room, which was outside an adjoining operating room, so that if complications occurred, they would not have to go. It was a bright room, and the sunlight was coming in through the large window. Gabrielle looked around. There was a hospital bed and a small sitting area. They went in, and Bernard helped Gabrielle take her clothes off. The nurse gave her a gown to put on, and she lay down on the bed. The nurse hooked up monitors to her belly so they could keep track of the baby's heartbeat and the intensity of her contractions.

"Do not worry. First labors take forever. It will be a while," the nurse told them.

Bernard stayed by her side hour after hour. Dr. Carter, the obstetrician on-call, came by to check on her periodically. The position of the baby was correct. Now, all they needed was time. Gabrielle was tired and hot from the exertion of the labor pain. She saw Bernard pacing the floor and sighing. Occasionally he rubbed her back. He breathed and counted with her. He would give her ice chips when her mouth was dry. The doctor had offered her an epidural to help with the discomforts of labor. She knew Bernard was anxious. Gabrielle wanted her pain to vanish, but she also knew the end results would be life-changing for them. It was three o'clock in the morning when Dr. Carter came in, examined her, and said, "I do not believe this, but the baby is coming now."

The doctor was in positioned at Gabrielle feet. She was exhausted, but she kept on persevering. Bernard was beside himself. The doctor told her to push as hard as she could to try to deliver this baby. She started pushing. It was excruciating. One hour, then two hours went by. It was a slow process, but she knew in time there would be an end to this agony.

One push, two, three, and all of a sudden, a tiny person appeared. Bernard almost fainted. He turned very pale, but he jumped up and down, kissing Gabrielle on the forehead. Bernard was happier that he had ever been in his life.

"We have a son. You did it. We have a healthy son," Bernard told Gabrielle. She could hear the baby's small cries. She was so relieved that the ordeal was over and that both she and the baby were fine.

"I am so glad you and the baby are all right. He is beautiful," Bernard said and held her hand. The nurse placed the baby on her chest. He was wrapped in a blanket.

"He looks like his father. Look at the dark hair. He is perfect," she said, then looked at Bernard, who had the biggest smile ever. They were both admiring the little man in his mother's arms.

"Now, what are we going to name him? Have you decided on a name?" Bernard asked, staring attentively at the little bundle she was holding in her arms.

"I'm not sure yet. Did you have one in mind?" Gabrielle replied. She had a name, but she was not sure if he would approve.

"I really do not have one in particular," he said and shrugged. So, since he did not answer, she went ahead with her thought.

"I have a name," she said quietly.

He was surprised, because they really had not discussed it a lot. They were going to wait to see if the baby was a boy or a girl. He was excited to hear her response.

"What is it? Tell me?"

Gabrielle paused for a second. *Here it goes,* she thought. "Well, what about Ron Junior?" she glanced at him, hoping he would agree.

"Are you serious? Why?" he asked.

"Well, over time I came to love your father, and I know how much he wants an heir for your family, so I thought he would be honored if we named him Ron Junior or just Junior. It might lift his spirits, but if you do not like it, I understand, and we can find another name."

"You are so amazing. I love the name. Ron Junior it is. My father will be so pleased. I can't wait to tell him and see his face." He smiled at her, and then he got up. He kissed her on the lips. He was going to go tell his father. Ron was going to love it.

"I love you so much," he said.

"I love you, too," said Gabrielle.

The birth of a grandchild who would carry his name had given Ron hope for a regular life. He planned to spend lots of time with him. A few days later, Ron was at the front door waiting for Gabrielle and Bernard to arrive from the hospital with Ron Junior. He saw the car pulling up the driveway, and he smiled. The car door opened, and Gabrielle got out. She went to the back seat to unbuckle the baby, picked him up in her arms, and walked the short distance to the entryway. Bernard was standing beside her. She placed Ron Junior on his grandfather's lap.

"Ron, I would like you to meet your grandson. This is Ron Junior," Gabrielle said. Ron's eyes filled with tears. He gently touched the baby's small fingers.

"He is absolutely the most beautiful child in the world," Ron replied. He would make sure this child has whatever he needed for the rest of his life. He was happy. He finally had his heir.

ABOUT THE AUTHOR

As a world traveler, Ann El-Nemr is trilingual in French, English, and Lebanese, and she is culturally connected to this story. Her love of reading inspired her to write this novel. She currently lives in the Boston area with her husband and three children, where they are all avid fans of the New England Patriots. Over the years, she has worn many hats, and being an author is her newest one. She can be reached at www.annelnemr.com.

THE STORY OF *BETRAYED* CONTINUES IN *FORGIVEN*—

Although it was a long time ago, Tom's anger still burned brightly—but he was not the only one who remembered and who craved revenge. Tom wanted to meet this guest of the family, this woman called Chantal. His plans were set, but she could ruin everything he had planned during the past ten years in prison. Will Tom take a chance with Chantal—take a chance on love—or will he continue to pursue the revenge that he has craved for so long? Will Chantal's love erode his resolve to fight the Rian family? How will Tom explain the lies and defend himself to Chantal?